Murder at the Murder Mystery Weekend

A Sanford 3rd Age Club Mystery
David W Robinson

Based on an idea by
Maureen Vincent-Northam

Printed for Crooked Cat by Createspace

First Black Line Edition, Crooked Cat Publishing Ltd. 2012

Discover us online:
www.crookedcatbooks.com

Join us on facebook:
www.facebook.com/crookedcatpublishing

The Author

A Yorkshireman by birth, David Robinson is a retired hypnotherapist and former adult education teacher, now living on the outskirts of Manchester with his wife and crazy Jack Russell called Joe (because he looks like a Joe).

A freelance writer for almost 30 years, he is extensively published, mainly on the web and in small press magazines. His first two novels were published in 2002 and are no longer available. His third novel, The Haunting at Melmerby Manor was published by Virtual Tales (USA) in 2007. He writes in a number of genres, including crime, sci-fi, horror and humour, and all his work has an element of mystery. His alter-ego, Flatcap, looks at the modern world from a cynical, 3rd age perspective, employing various levels of humour from subtle to sledgehammer.

A devout follower of Manchester United, when he is not writing, he enjoys photography, cryptic crosswords, and putting together slideshow trailers and podcast readings from his works.

David's online blog is at: **http://www.dwrob.com**

By the same author

The STAC Mystery series:

The Filey Connection

The I-Spy Murders

A Halloween Homicide

A Murder for Christmas

Murder at the Murder Mystery Weekend

My Deadly Valentine

Other work:

Voices

Murder at the Murder Mystery Weekend

Prologue

"I want more."

She shook her head, lips pursed pensively. "You were paid for the work you did as you asked. It was a one-off payment, and the understanding at the time was that you signed away all rights. I don't see how you can come back now demanding more of the spoils."

"You tricked me. You made me believe that it was worthless."

She laughed. "We tricked you? I think if you search your memory, you'll find that it was you who were only too eager to take what you could and be out of here." She raised her folded hands and let them flop into her lap. "No, I'm sorry, but according to our best legal advice, you have no call on the company. It's as simple as that."

"You bitch, I'll…"

"I wouldn't do that if I were you." The man's voice remained calm, collected, but all the more ominous for its lack of threat.

"You think you're big enough?"

The second man retained his aplomb. "I don't think. I know."

She signalled for calm. "This is getting silly. There is no place for these macho, playground threats and counter threats." She rounded on the complainant. "The legal position is quite clear. You have no claim, and even if you had, how much of it do you imagine would be left by the time the lawyers had taken their fill?"

"My ideas. My concepts. This is theft."

"We bought them fair and square," she argued. "And you were happy to take my money and run when times were tough, weren't you? You signed everything over to us. Our lawyers have assured us that your claim is not valid. As far as we're concerned, that is the end of the matter."

The angry complainant made for the door. "I'll make you pay for this. Both of you. You'll regret the day you crossed me."

He turned and stormed from the room.

The other man wiped imaginary beads of sweat from his brow. "I thought you handled it pretty well."

She was not so sanguine. "We had a contract. It was that simple. "

Chapter One

As always, Reginald Grimshaw, known to everyone who worked for him as Reggie, was last to board the minibus outside the company's Sheffield factory. And as always, he did not rush. Whether the sun was shining or, as now, rain poured from leaden skies, Reggie took his time.

"Morning all," he said, taking a seat beside his wife Wendy. "I hope Robbie's sorted out some real fun for this weekend."

Across the aisle from him, Robbie Kendrew, the sales manager for the Eastern Region grinned slyly. "Actually, it was your good lady wife's idea, but I've done my homework, Reggie, and if anyone gets it right, I'll wear one of Fliss' dresses to next month's sales meeting." He pointed with his thumb at his wife sat beside him.

While Fliss scowled and the driver pulled out of the factory gates, turning right towards the distant motorway, Grimshaw laughed aloud at Kendrew's joke. "Careful, me ducks, or I may hold you to that."

Through rain streaked windows, the 64-year-old looked fondly on his factory as the bus passed along the front. Set in the heart of a large industrial estate, it was a sprawling unit, producing tailored kitchens for the modern house and home, and Reggie felt a certain pride and even smugness that he could have come so far in life.

"I started out as a joiner and cabinet maker in Nottingham; a chippy," he had once told a reporter from *Down to Business* magazine. "That was in the sixties. By the mid-seventies I was working for myself, and ten years after that, I was renting a shed in Brightside, Sheffield, and employing a dozen men to make and install the kitchens. Now look at me."

Look at him, indeed. Grimshaw Kitchens were renowned all over the eastern side of England from Grantham in the south to Darlington in the north, from The Wash to the Tees estuary. Through Lincolnshire, the three Yorkshires, Humberside, Cleveland, and into County Durham, Grimshaw Kitchens were an integral part of modern living.

The bus ran along the broad dual carriageway of the Catcliffe spur, Sheffields major link with the M1, the light, morning traffic of the motorway visible a mile away. To the left was a huge advertising hoarding, with his face smiling back at him above the slogan, *Grimshaw Kitchens: the dream of every housewife.* Reggie smiled back at it. How often had that slogan got him into hot water?

So it was sexist in these politically correct times. Did he care? Did he hell as like. That slogan summed up the attitudes of his youth when the man was the breadwinner and the little woman stayed home to cook, clean and bring up the kids. And when these bloody women's libbers climbed on their soapbox to rail against him, Reggie rubbed his hands with glee. It was tantamount to free publicity. Despite their occasional demands for a boycott of Grimshaw Kitchens, the company had weathered a number of recessions.

Anyway, no matter what they said about him, he wasn't so chauvinistic that he didn't recognise talent in women. Sat behind him was Naomi Barton, Northern Sales Manager, and her returns spoke for themselves; she was every bit as forceful as young Kendrew.

He had said as much in that same interview for *Down to Business.* "When it comes to employing people, I don't care if a person stands up or sits down to pee, as long as they can do the job."

The reporter had reworded it in the final draft, but the gist of his argument came across. In this game men and women were paid the same flat salary and the same bonuses for hitting their targets. Sex, whether it meant gender or recreation, did not come into it.

Selling kitchens, he had learned a long time ago, was hard work. It was also a specialised art. Unlike selling to businesses, who usually had to go somewhere for their requirements, the householder had complete freedom of choice. They could go to ABC, XYZ, the Man in the Moon, or they could decide not to bother. Getting them to sign on the dotted line, there and then (the only way to ensure the sale) was a delicate balance between persuasion and persistence. For a salesperson to leave the house on an assurance that the customer would ring back when they had made up their mind, was a cast-iron guarantee that the customer would *not* ring back. The sale had to be closed on the night, after the presentation, and that was where people like Robbie Kendrew and Naomi Barton proved their worth. For all his force of personality, Reggie had never been particularly good at it; Kendrew and Barton were world class.

Not only first rate at selling but also training others to sell, *and* keeping those others on their toes, reminding them there were targets to be met.

This was a different world, Reggie reflected as the bus dropped onto the motorway and climbed the hill towards the long, lazy junction with the M18, where they would filter off to the left, making for the A1 and Lincolnshire. When he was an apprentice working on the council estates of Nottingham, back in the early sixties, there was no choice between stick and carrot. The stick was all. He learned his trade at the hands of skilled craftsmen who would not hesitate to physically kick him up the backside when he got it wrong.

These days, the carrot mattered just as much as the stick. Of course he screamed at them the way the joiners had screamed at him. Of course, he threatened them with the sack if they didn't get their finger out. It was his way of establishing his top-dog status. But his salespeople also earned good bonuses on their deals, and every quarter, the top people from each of the two regions, were treated to a weekend's entertainment in a classy hotel.

The managers, Kendrew and Naomi, took it in turns to organise the events, and Reggie noted that there was a good deal of one-upmanship between them. Every three months, the appropriate manager was determined to outdo the previous shindig. This month Kendrew, desperate to outclass Naomi's September weekend of glider training in North Yorkshire, had booked them for a New Year Murder Mystery Weekend at one of Lincoln's top hotels. All good fun, naturally, but as a sign of the keen competition between the two managers, they had laid a private bet between themselves; £500 to the one who came nearest to solving the mystery correctly. They'd even asked Reggie to adjudicate in the matter.

He didn't mind. It wasn't really his place to mind. That kind of rivalry was good for the sales teams and anything that was good for them, was good the company. The awesome cost of the weekend – all up it would run to close on three thousand pounds – would be borne by Grimshaw Kitchens, but the loser of the bet would pay the £500 out of his or her pocket.

Competition, Reggie thought. It was good for business, good for morale, more than good for the balance sheet and by default, his private bank account.

Alongside him, Wendy, his wife of almost 30 years, stared through the windows at the heavy, Friday morning traffic. Eleven years his junior, she'd been a fine looking woman when he first met her. Not that she was bad looking even now, but the years had begun to take their toll. A former actress, the daughter of a Sheffield foundry worker, Reggie often wondered how much of her middle-aged attraction she could have maintained without the business to finance it.

"You deserve it, ducks," he said, and she turned her head to face him, a thin smile on her lips.

"Deserve what, Reggie?"

"Everything. If it wasn't for you we wouldn't be where we are."

It wasn't flattery. Reggie Grimshaw didn't do flattery, and by his logic there were no such things as delicate ears between a man and his wife. If he had strayed from the marital bed over the years, he had always returned to it full of remorse, and Wendy had always accepted his apologies. Reggie Grimshaw knew which side his bread was buttered.

So he did not flatter her. Instead, he told the simple truth. Wendy had urged him to expand all those years ago. Wendy, it was, who had spoken to the banks, securing those first loans against their humble terraced house, to get the new factory up and running, Wendy was the one who managed the company finances in the early years, and saw off the predators. Without Wendy, Grimshaw Kitchens would not exist.

She smiled more fully. In years gone by the smile would have been filled with love, adoration, even hero-worship. Nowadays it was pleasure; the simple pleasure of being together.

"Your skills, Reggie. That was the foundation. It was all you, not me." She took his hand. "Now switch off and let's enjoy the weekend. I don't want to hear another mention of Grimshaw Kitchens."

***

A worried frown creasing her brow, Melanie Markham stepped into the Scampton Room, the fancifully named lounge bar of the Lincoln's Twin Spires Hotel, and crossed the richly carpeted floor to the corner by the podium, where her troupe were sat.

"Trouble, Melanie?" Gerry Carlin asked.

A little older than Melanie's 48 years, and having worked for Markham Murder Mysteries for almost 20 years, Gerry was one of the longest serving members of the cast. Solid, unflappable, completely dependable, willing to pitch in wherever it was necessary, whether carrying props, updating scripts, or learning a new part on short notice.

But Melanie doubted that even Gerry had come across a problem like this before.

"You look like we've been cancelled," he said as Melanie joined the 10-strong group.

Gerry pushed a cup of espresso across the table to her. She took a generous mouthful and put the cup down. "I think I'll need something a little stronger."

The faces, four men, five women, looked expectantly at her. The younger, newer members of the cast were easy to spot. Fresh faced, filled with enthusiasm, they were setting out on the unstable journey that was acting, hoping it would lead to bigger, better things: the RSC, prime time TV, even Hollywood. Some of the fire had been extinguished in the more mature men and women. They'd already been around the block a couple of times and they knew the value of steady, if unspectacular work like Murder Mystery Weekends. They earned slightly above scale (the minimum an actor could be paid) but slightly above scale was better than delivering pizzas or claiming unemployment benefit.

"So come on, Melanie. What's wrong?"

She might have been able to fool some of the younger players, by telling them that the hotel had cut them short on Saturday night, New Year's Eve. But Gerry was too old a hand to be duped. The timings were spot on, and it would take days, maybe weeks, to rearrange everything.

Besides, the problem was more curious than serious.

"There's a snag," she said eventually.

"They want us to lead the crowd in a couple of choruses of Auld Lang Syne?" Emma Pemberley suggested.

"We'll be joining in on Auld Lang Syne anyway," Melanie retorted. Emma had been with them five years. A capable actress who rode on her reputation established in a long-running sci-fi TV series back in the 1990s, she was not one of Melanie's favourites.

"The hotel is busy over the weekend," Melanie announced, bringing her mind back to the problem at hand.

"I'm relieved to hear it," said Gerry. "Nothing worse than playing to a half empty house."

"Yes, well, I've just been informed that one of the parties is the Sanford 3rd Age Club. About seventy of them."

Lee Sissons, one of the younger men, laughed. "A shed load of geriatrics. Wassup, Melanie? You worried they've all got Alzheimer's?"

Melanie frowned her disapproval. "The Sanford 3rd Age Club is one of Accomplus's biggest customers, and I'm assured that they are not a mob of geriatrics. They're more like a bunch of third age rockers. Anyway, it's not the club I'm worried about. It's their Chairman; Joe Murray."

Puzzlement greeted the announcement.

"Joe who?"

Melanie took another mouthful of coffee. "Really, Gerry, I expect better of you. Here we are, preparing and presenting our own murder mysteries, yet none of you can be bothered with any research. Remember I-Spy, the reality TV series, at Gibraltar Hall during the summer? One of the Housies was murdered."

"Oh, yes. Ursula, er, Kennedy," Gerry said.

"Kenney. Ursula Kenney," Melanie corrected. "Joe Murray was the detective who solved it. He worked out who did it and how, and why if I recall correctly."

"He's a cop?" asked Danielle McMahon, one of the younger women.

"No. He's a private investigator of sorts. The police were sure Ursula's death was suicide. They didn't believe anyone could get to her with all those cameras running day and night. It was Joe Murray who demonstrated that it couldn't have

11

been suicide, and he then proceeded to show the police how it was done and eventually showed them who did it."

"A wizard?" Lee said.

Melanie nodded and finished her coffee. "He solved the murder of an MP at another of Accomplus's hotels near York, he also solved the killing of an academic at a five star place in Leeds last Christmas. He is a master. You can't fool him."

Gerry swilled the remains of his tea around his cup and swallowed it in one gulp. "And he's coming here to see us? Wonder what he'll make of our little mystery?"

"Mincemeat." Melanie finished her drink and slid the cup and saucer across the table. "Someone get another load of coffee. Ask them to charge it to the company account." While Lee Sissons leapt to obey, she concentrated on Gerry. "Murray will see through us like we're invisible. He'll spot every clue and have it solved by tonight."

Gerry laughed. "That's not possible, and you know it."

"He'll still have it all wrapped up by lunchtime tomorrow."

Her sidekick shrugged easily. "Want me to have a word with him when he and his people get here?"

Melanie did not answer right away. She considered what she knew about Joe Murray. Eventually, she said, "No. I don't think so. I think it would be better if I spoke to him."

"Persuade him with your charms?" Gerry asked.

She stared him firmly in the eye. "I don't know a lot about him, Gerry, but I do know that he's more likely to be impressed by my stocking tops than yours."

***

"What do I have to do to get you to switch off and just enjoy the weekend, Joe?" Brenda Jump asked. "Show you my stocking tops?"

"All I said was in this weather we should have stayed at the Lazy Luncheonette," Joe Murray protested.

12

December 30th had dawned with heavy rain oppressing the town of Sanford, and suppressing the fortunes of the Lazy Luncheonette.

The week between Christmas and New Year was always poor. The dray men from the Sanford Brewery called as usual, and there were the occasional passing lorry drivers to feed, but the factories of Doncaster Road Industrial Estate were mostly closed. Ingleton Engineering, whose daily sandwich order provided a large slice of the takings, was also closed, and of course, the kids were still off school, so the income from their purchases of cans and snacks was also missing. The shoppers of the Sanford Retail Park, behind the Lazy Luncheonette, would usually call in, but the persistent cold and rain of the last few days, had kept them away too.

All in all, it was a good time to be going away for the weekend.

Sanford 3rd Age Club outings always began from the same place; the car park of the Miner's Arms, the club's putative home, and normally, Joe could be found standing on the car park, ticking off the names of the members as they arrived, but with the rain threatening to wash away the ink on his printed sheet, he chose, instead, to wait just inside the bus close to the driver's seat. Keith Lowry, the long-suffering driver usually appointed to their excursions, had to be outside, anyway, to stow the members' luggage.

"I don't see any reason why we should both get wet," Joe had told his closest companions, Brenda and Sheila Riley. "Keith has no choice so I'll pinch his seat until we're all here."

Sheila and Brenda had agreed, but Joe's constant stream of complaints, mostly about the weather, had begun to grate on them, and his mention of the Lazy Luncheonette, the workman's café which he owned and where the two women worked for him, was the last straw.

"I don't wanna hear another word about the Lazy Luncheonette until Tuesday morning," Brenda warned him.

With the time coming up to 9:30, there were still a few people to come, and Keith, like Joe, was not slow to complain. Standing on the platform by the coach's open door, shaking the rain from the hood of his company issued cagoule, he said, "We should be rocking and rolling by now. The boss'll play hell if I'm late back this afternoon."

"You're not staying in Lincoln with us, Keith?" Sheila asked.

He shook his head. "The old man won't wear it. You've no excursions planned. You're staying at the Twin Spires for this silly bloody murder mystery thing, and he reckons there's no point me being there, idling about for the weekend. Besides, there's a match at Elland Road tomorrow, and I get in for nowt."

"How come?" Joe asked as a taxi pulled onto the car park.

"I'm ferrying the Sanford branch of the Leeds United Supporters Club to the game and back," Keith told him. "I always get a free ticket."

"Instead of a whip round?" Joe pressed.

"As well as a whip round," Keith returned and stepped out into the rain again as Captain Les Tanner and his lady love, Sylvia Goodson climbed out of the taxi.

Joe ticked the new arrivals off his list when they climbed on the bus a few moments later. "Morning, Sylvia, morning, Les. You're late."

"The weather, Murray," Tanner reported. "Especially bad this morning or hadn't you noticed?"

"Couldn't see for the rain," Joe quipped. "Still, as long as you weren't at it until the early hours explaining the Allies push through the Ardennes."

Tanner glared. "Were you born obnoxious, Murray, or have you had training?"

"It comes quite naturally when I'm dealing with you, Les."

Les followed Sylvia along the bus to their seats, and Keith, having stowed their luggage, came back to the platform.

"Who's still to come?"

Joe checked his crib sheet. "Raving Mavis. She'll have been on the sauce last night and overslept."

"On some bloke's nightshirt," Brenda said, taking her usual seat next to Sheila. The two women always occupied the front left hand seat, and Joe took the jump seat, in front of them, to the left of the driver. "How long will it take to Lincoln, Keith?"

"Normally, an hour and a half, tops," the driver replied. "But it's Friday, the day before New Year's Eve, and in this lot…" he held out a hand to the rain. "Anybody's guess."

From midway down the bus, George Robson, a gardener with Sanford Borough Council, and one of the longest-serving members of the Sanford 3rd Age Club, shouted, "Hey up, Joe, we're taking bets on you solving this murder mystery before anyone else. Ten to one that you'll crack it tonight, eight to one on tomorrow night and even money that you'll be the first to solve it on Sunday afternoon."

His announcement was greeted with laughter from the seventy or so bodies on the coach.

Joe took the jibes in good part. "Save your money, George. If I crack it tonight, I ain't gonna tell you. I'll come to a private agreement with the organisers and that bottle of shampoo and the hotel vouchers will be all mine."

It had been expensive, Joe ruminated while they waited for Mavis Barker to arrive. Accomplus hotels were never cheap, but the combination of New Year's Eve and a murder mystery as entertainment, had hiked the price to the extent that many of their members had cried off. Joe, Sheila and Brenda, the management trio of the club, could not.

"And we don't even get a discount for all the admin we do," Joe had complained to his two friends.

"We're a social club, Joe," Sheila had reminded him. "You do it from the goodness of your heart."

Brenda had laughed. "He keeps all his goodness in his

wallet. Although, I have heard rumours that his Y-fronts –"

Joe had cut her off at that point. Brenda's merry widowhood was almost as legendary as Joe's parsimony.

If pushed, he had to admit that he enjoyed the club outings, and he was particularly looking forward to this one: a great weekend away with a murder mystery to tax his intellect.

Another taxi pulled into the car park. Mavis Barker climbed out, dragging her small suitcase behind her, waddling hurriedly to the coach. With a muttered grumble, Keith climbed off again to stow her luggage, and Joe ticked off her name.

When Keith climbed back onto the bus and took the wheel, Joe lowered the jump seat in front of his companions, and sat down.

"Is that it?" Keith asked. "Can we get rolling?"

"Burn it," Joe invited.

The coach rolled off the car park, onto Doncaster Road, turning right, away from Sanford and towards the motorway. Half a mile on, they passed the Lazy Luncheonette where Lee, Joe's nephew and head cook, and his wife Cheryl, were idling away the interim between the morning rush and the lunchtime crowd.

"Not that there'll be a lunchtime crowd," Joe muttered.

Five minutes later, when the bus turned east on the M62, making for the A1, safe from sudden turns or swerves, Joe stood, turned and reached for the PA microphone above Sheila's head. Switching it on, tapping the head to ensure it worked, he began his announcement.

"Okay, folks, and good morning. Keith reckons we're about an hour and a half from Lincoln but it may take longer. It depends on traffic conditions and the weather. So we'll likely be checking into the Twin Spires hotel by lunchtime. Now don't forget, this is a Murder Mystery Weekend. There'll be a lot going on in the hotel. That doesn't mean you have to stick to the Twin Spires. You're free to do as you please, and all the clues will be there for you to look over when you get back from your expeditions."

"Expeditions, Joe?" Alec Staines called out. "Are you climbing the west tower of the Minster or something?"

"No, I'm climbing the walls. But anyone would when dealing with you lot." Joe paused a moment to let the subdued laughter fade. "Can I also remind you that the hotel evenings are themed, and the theme tonight is the early fifties? Apparently, the murder mystery is set in the fifties, so we're all supposed to be in part."

"Got a zoot suit have you, Joe?" George Robson shouted from the rear of the bus.

"They were 1940s, you idiot," Joe retorted. "And, no I haven't got a zoot suit. I have drapes, drains and bike chain. Mess with me and the Sanford Teds will sort you out. All right everyone. I'll leave you to it. Enjoy the journey." He glanced through the windows. "Or as much of the journey as you can see through this lot."

He handed the microphone back to Sheila, sat down and half turned in his seat so he could speak with his companions.

"You're very good at that kind of announcement, Joe," Sheila congratulated him.

"You should do it professionally," Brenda agreed. "I've heard they need a new caller at the bingo hall."

Joe frowned. "Are you well insured, Brenda? Cos one of these days, you're gonna need it." He clapped his hands together like a market trader about to offer the deal of the century. "Right, so this murder mystery thing doesn't start until dinner this evening. What do you want to do with the afternoon?"

"I'd like to take a tour round the cathedral," Sheila said, "but that will wait until tomorrow."

"There's a smashing shopping mall by the river," Brenda assured them.

Joe grinned. "Lincoln has a river? Great. I can drop you in

there, Brenda, and solve all my troubles."

She smiled. "Your trouble is repression, Joe. Give me your wallet, let me get at your Y-fronts and I'll solve your problems in less than an hour."

Chapter Two

The Scampton Room was named after RAF Scampton, the airfield, six miles north of the city, from where Guy Gibson had led 617 Squadron on their daring Dambusters raid in 1943. The walls of the room were decked with wartime photographs from the bomber base, pride of place going to a large oil on canvas of a Lancaster in flight, the bulbous projection of Barnes-Wallis' bouncing bomb hanging from its underbelly.

Joe stepped into the place, nodding to George Robson, Owen Frickley, and a few other club members, and made his way to the bar.

They had arrived at 11:15, and Joe had promised to meet Brenda and Sheila in the bar before setting off to Lincoln centre for a little Friday afternoon shopping.

A functional rather than aesthetically pleasing building, the modern façade of the four-storey, Twin Spires Hotel looked out directly on the twin towers of Lincoln Cathedral, just a few hundred yards away.

"That must be where the hotel gets its name," Mavis Barker had commented as Joe helped her off the bus.

"I would never have thought of that, Mavis," Joe replied.

An older wing was attached to the east end of the hotel. Built of redbrick, housing the 617 Restaurant, its windows were smaller, the rooms more compact but no less luxurious. Pleasant gardens lay out front and along the side of the main block, with picnic tables dotted around the lawns.

"Not gonna get much use out of them," Joe muttered as he

entered through twin, automatic glass doors.

After the usual chaos of signing in seventy people, he took his single, small suitcase to room 404, washed, changed his shirt and, carrying his topcoat, made his way down to the Scampton Room to meet with the women. He was not surprised to learn they were not there.

"I spend half my life waiting for women," he muttered as he leaned on the bar and signalled for service.

"Lock you away for that, you know," said the tall, portly man next to him.

Joe ordered a glass of lager, before responding. "Talking to yourself you mean? My old man used to say it was the only way to get sensible answers." He held out his hand. "Joe Murray. Chair of the Sanford 3rd Age Club."

"Reggie Grimshaw. Managing Director, Grimshaw Kitchens. Sheffield." He shook Joe's offered hand. "You'll have heard of us. Grimshaw Kitchens: the dream of every housewife." Reggie nodded to a small clutch of people by the windows. "That's my lot, there. Two sales managers, the two top salespeople, and my missus, Wendy. That's her with the blonde hair. And those salesmen and women are the best in the business. If they called on your good lady, you'd have a Grimshaw Kitchen fitted before Easter."

"Very unlikely," Joe said, his natural resistance to salespeople coming to the fore. He paid for his drink and took a sip.

Reggie laughed. "You don't know how persuasive they can be."

"They'd have to persuade my missus to come back from Tenerife, first," Joe countered, and looked further around the room.

In the corner, by the podium, was another clutch of about ten people, even split between the sexes. A black-haired, middle-aged woman, sat on the fringe of the group, was eyeing him with undisguised curiosity.

"Are they not with you?" Joe asked.

"No," replied Reggie. "They're the turn; the act. You know. The entertainment."

"Ah. The murder mystery weekenders, huh?" He placed his glass on the bar. "So, Reggie, what brings you and your salespeople here? Conference, is it?"

Reggie laughed. "My eye. It's a New Year treat, me ducks. Four times a year I take the managers and the top salespeople from my teams, and treat them to a weekend away. I don't organise it. The sales managers take it in turns. It's a reward for hard graft, but you look like a man who understands that."

"When it comes to the stick and the carrot, I use both," Joe admitted. "I beat my staff with the stick and feed the carrots to my customers." He grinned. "I run a café on Doncaster Road in Sanford."

Reggie frowned. "I thought you were chairman of some club."

"The Sanford 3rd Age Club. I'm also their resident DJ, but that's recreation. Like everyone else, I have a living to earn. I'm too young to retire, too old for an affair, and the state the country's in, I can't afford a nervous breakdown."

Wendy Grimshaw left her table and came towards them.

"Looks like you're wanted." Joe picked up his glass. "Nice talking to you, Reggie. See you around over the weekend."

He crossed the room, pausing at a table on which was a stack of glossy leaflets, spelling out the timetable for the weekend. Joe took one, and found a seat close to the entrance.

Haliwell's Heroes declared the leaflet; the front showed a photograph of ten people seated at a dinner table with a large map on an easel to one side. Joe could not see the dark-haired woman who had been studying him, and for a moment he wondered if Reggie Grimshaw had got it wrong.

A shadow fell over the table. "Excuse me. It's Mr Murray, isn't it?"

Engrossed in the leaflet, Joe was surprised to hear his name.

He had never stayed at this hotel, and he knew instantly it wasn't one of his members. They would have called him Joe.

He found the dark-haired woman hovering over him. Around 50 years of age, perhaps slightly younger, Joe found her instantly attractive, slender, smartly dressed in a loose-fitting blouse and dark trousers, her black hair was tied back in a ponytail, her slim face and lively eyes highlighted by a pair of black-framed spectacles perched on her nose.

"I'm Melanie Markham. I'm the producer and director of *Haliwell's Heroes*."

It took Joe a moment to realise what she was talking about and only then because he still had the leaflet in his hand. "Oh. The murder mystery thing?" He put down the leaflet and waved at the chair opposite and she sat down. "So what can I do for you, Mrs Markham?"

"Ms Markham," she stressed, "and most people call me Melanie."

Joe nodded. "All right, Melanie. What can I do for you?"

"A lot," she said, leaving him all at sea.

There was a lot which a fine looking woman like Melanie Markham could do for him, but he was not stupid enough to imagine that she was hinting at his prowess as a lover.

"I'm sorry?"

"Your reputation precedes you, Mr Murray."

"Please call me Joe." He laughed. "It is my name and it's a lot more polite than some of the things people call me."

Melanie returned a wan smile. "Very well, Joe. Even in this neck of the woods, the name Joe Murray, coupled with Sanford, means something. You're one of the smartest private detectives in the North and Midlands."

In an effort to display some modesty, Joe said, "I wouldn't say that."

"No?"

"The country, maybe, but not the North and Midlands." He grinned to show he was only joking.

Melanie returned his smile. "Very funny."

"All right, Melanie, so I have a reputation as a private detective. I'll tell you now, I don't take cases on, as such. In other words, I wouldn't agree to investigate the outcome of your Aunt Jemima's will, but if you need help I'll see what I can do."

"No, no. It's nothing like that. I'm not sure how to, er…"

While she trailed off, Joe took a sip of lager, giving her time to get her thoughts together. When she still did not speak, he put her out of her misery.

"Where I come from, Melanie, we don't stop to worry about how people will react to what we have to say. We just say it. Why don't you do that now? I promise I won't be offended."

"Well, frankly, Joe, you're a well-known detective, and you're likely to see through our little mystery long before anyone else."

"And you're worried that I'll walk off with a voucher for a couple of free nights in an Accomplus hotel and bottle of cheap champagne, meaning no one else will get a look in?"

Melanie smiled, shyly. "You see. That's a measure of your perceptiveness. It's not so much that, but you may crack this thing before we're even a third of the way through. Tell me, have you ever been to a murder mystery dinner or weekend?"

"No," he confessed. "But I've read up on them and I understand the principle. We all sit down to dinner and halfway through, someone gets murdered. It could even be the person sitting next to you. Then everyone starts to ask questions of everyone else until the cops arrive on Sunday morning and explain it all to us."

Melanie's slender fingers played around her glass, wiping off the condensation. "Most companies work like that, but Markham Murder Mysteries is different. The way you describe it is great fun, but it can be haphazard and for a hotel like the Twin Spires, it can be annoying for those guests who didn't come along for the murder mystery. You understand?"

"Perfectly. It's a bit like coming to my place and ordering a steak entrecote, and a bottle of house red, then finding yourself sitting with a bunch of truckers working their way through greasy full English breakfasts."

"I, er, yes, well, I suppose so."

"Relax, Melanie. I'm only teasing." Joe began to roll a cigarette. "The Lazy Luncheonette doesn't have a drinks licence." Spreading a thin line of tobacco along the innards of his little rolling machine, he asked, "So if Markham Murder Mysteries doesn't work like that, how do they do it?"

"We're a small company of professional actors. I'm the writer, director and producer." Her words brimmed with pride as she delivered them. "To begin with, we sit apart from the diners, at the front of the dining room, so no one is in any doubt who are the actors and who are the guests. We perform a series of little scenes, vignettes, each carrying the story that bit further forward. Each scene will give you clues as to the killer and the motive. Characters are there to be questioned after the scenes, and in some circumstances, particularly those involving our fictitious police officer, we have a formal question and answer session. We pride ourselves on the difficulty of solving our mysteries, which is why we offer prizes rather than souvenir certificates."

Joe hung on her every word, as if she were one of Reggie Grimshaw's super salespeople. "This sounds like a good weekend's entertainment, but you're obviously worried that I could throw a spanner in the works."

"I'd ask you to consider that we're not real criminals, but a bunch of actors." Melanie picked up the leaflet Joe had been reading, and held it up. "We put this production together ourselves and for someone with your powers of observation, our plot probably has holes in it large enough to drive a bus through. The guests, those who are here for the murder mystery drama, and that includes you, have paid a lot of

24

money for the weekend and I wouldn't like it to be, er, spoiled by someone cracking the case too early, if you understand what I mean."

"Perfectly," Joe replied. "Are you married, Melanie?"

She shook her head. "Only to my work."

"In that case, let's you and I make a bet. If I get to within five percent of your solution before breakfast on Sunday, you let me buy you dinner on Sunday evening before we set off back to Sanford. If I don't, you hold me up to ridicule in front of everyone. Here's how Haliwell's Heroes beat Joe Murray." He grinned. "How does that sound?"

Her eyes widened but Joe could see the pleasure in them. "I, er, I'm not sure. You'll be going home to Sanford on Sunday afternoon, won't you? If your bus leaves and you have to buy me dinner, how will you get back to Sanford?"

"That's not a problem," Joe told her. "We actually don't go home until Monday morning. Come on, Melanie. This is a win, win situation for you. If I solve your little play, I keep my mouth shut and I treat you to dinner at any restaurant in Lincoln. Do we have a deal?"

Melanie smiled broadly. "Very well."

They shook hands on it.

"Good. Now I'll tell you that the offer probably won't cost me a bean. See, when people like you write these things, you're a damn sight more devious than real criminals are. They may not leave clues lying around the likes of which you think up. Instead they leave tons of scientific evidence for the law to find." It was obvious from Melanie's face that he was not winning the argument. "Tell you what, though. I will distance myself from the prize. How's that? And even if I work it out tonight, I promise I'll still keep my mouth shut until Sunday."

"And you won't be helping any of your friends to the answer?" Melanie asked.

"You have my word on that." A thought occurred to Joe. "Here's a thing. How do you know that some members of the

25

audience haven't seen this before? I meanersay, if they've seen it before, they'll have all the answers, won't they?"

"We do get return visitors," Melanie admitted. She put down the leaflet and fiddled with her spectacles. "For most performances, we have more than one winner, so we put the names in a hat and ask a member of the cast to draw the winner. If we get someone whose answer is almost perfect, we guess that they've seen it before, and that person's name doesn't go into the hat."

The door swung open and Sheila and Brenda stepped in. Brenda looked over Joe and Melanie, and her face split into a broad grin. "Hey up, you're not letting the grass grow under your feet, Joe."

Joe grimaced at her. "Melanie, may I introduce my two friends, Sheila Riley and Brenda Jump. I say friends, they're actually my employees and at least one of them can be a proper pain in the posterior when she tries. Girls, this is Melanie Markham, director and producer of this weekend's entertainment."

The three women shook hands.

"I shouldn't take too much notice of Joe," Sheila said. "When he says we're his employees, what he really means is he couldn't run his business without us."

"I'm sure you're all the very best of friends. If you'll excuse me, I must get back to my people. We're agreed then, Joe?"

He nodded and Melanie drifted off, leaving Brenda to stare at Joe in amused amazement. "I'm sorry, Joe. I didn't realise you'd scored."

He tutted. "Must you persist in behaving like a teenager?"

Brenda chuckled. "Someone told me if you haven't grown up by the time you're fifty, you don't have to."

"And you never bothered?"

"I'll let you know when I turn fifty."

Sheila raised amused eyes to the ceiling. "I'll get some drinks." She ambled across to the bar and Brenda sat alongside

Joe.

"If anyone did that to me, Joe, I'd be furious."

Joe had one eye on the bar where Reggie Grimshaw and his wife were talking to Melanie and one of her older actors. Brenda's announcement brought a grimace of irritability. "What the hell are you talking about?"

"You and the Oscar nominee, just now. If I was coming on to some bloke and someone interrupted, I'd slice them into strips and serve them as dog meat."

"I was not coming on to her."

"I know you weren't," Brenda replied, "but she was certainly coming on to you."

The announcement forced Joe to call on his memory of the exchange with Melanie. He dug into his gilet, took out his tobacco tin and extracted his recently rolled cigarette.

A passing member of the staff spotted him. "Excuse me, sir, but you can't smoke that in here."

"I know, I know."

"Only it's against the law, you see."

Joe eyed his nametag. "Cliff Denshaw?"

"I'm the duty manager, sir."

"Right, Mr Denshaw, let me ask you a question. You see all these people?" Joe waved at the room. "Do you think any of them will be carrying cigarettes?"

"Probably."

"Then what's the difference between others carrying packs of cigarettes and me carrying a hand-rolled one? I know I can't smoke it in here, and I wasn't going to."

Brenda smiled up at Denshaw. "You'll have to excuse him. He was on a promise and I butted in."

The manager gave them a bleak smile and left.

Joe tucked the cigarette in his shirt pocket. "She was not coming on to me. She was just concerned that I might blow the entire weekend by cracking her little murder mystery."

Brenda took his hand. "What am I going to do with you,

Joe? You never were the brightest spark when it came to dealing with women. One of these days, I'll have to do more than hold your hand. You need lessons in the ways of the world."

"Not until I've locked my wallet in the safe." He downed the rest of his lager as Sheila made her way back to them with fresh drinks.

Looking beyond her, he noticed the actor next to Wendy Grimshaw slide his hand from her shoulder down to waist level. He waited to see how Wendy Grimshaw would react and when she did not even pull away, he said, "Now there's a come on, or I've never seen one."

Brenda was momentarily distracted taking glasses from Sheila's tray. By the time she had put a glass of lager in front of Joe, a small sherry for Sheila, and taken possession of a Campari and soda, then looked to the bar, there was nothing to see.

"What's a come on?" Brenda asked.

Joe checked the couple again. They were now a respectable eighteen inches apart. "Never mind." He drank from his fresh glass. "Quarter past twelve. So what do you want to do with the rest of the day? And don't tell me shopping."

Brenda appeared to give the matter some thought. "Hmm... I think... shopping."

Sheila laughed. "I shop, therefore I am." She, too, sipped from a small sherry. "What would you like to do, Joe?"

"I dunno. Just have a wander round the city."

"And shop," suggested Brenda.

Putting down her glass, digging into her bag, Sheila took out a street plan of Lincoln. Perching reading glasses on her nose, she pored over it. "How about a museum first, and then moving on to the shopping centres?"

"What's in the museum?" Brenda asked.

"Old things," Joe replied.

"You'd fit in well, then."

Never one to let an opportunity pass, Joe asked, "You know how you said you'd let me know when you get to fifty, were you talking retrospectively?"

"Ha, ha, very funny."

Cutting in on the repartee, Sheila announced, "There's the Usher Gallery and the collection not far from here. Just down the hill from the Minster. We can walk it in about ten minutes. It has exhibits on the history and prehistory of Lincoln. And after we're done there, it's only about another few hundred yards to the High Street."

"Sounds good to me," Joe agreed.

"And me. Bottoms up." Brenda downed her Campari in one gulp and let out a satisfied "Aaah. That hit the spot."

***

Joe could never understand why women always had to visit the toilet before setting out anywhere.

Standing outside, under the shelter of the main entrance, smoking his cigarette, he was eager to be moving on, away from the watchful eye of Cliff Denshaw spying on him from behind the reception counter, but both Brenda and Sheila had insisted upon visiting the Ladies to effect makeup repairs… "And other, essentials," Brenda had concluded.

Rain continued to fall from the grey skies, fogging out the upper spires of the cathedral, cladding the city in a depressing air of damp and cold, but when he asked himself whether he would be happier back home in Sanford, the answer was an unequivocal, 'no'. All he had back there were business worries, exacerbated by the extended Christmas holidays, and a self-imposed solitary confinement broken only by the days of running the Lazy Luncheonette, and the couple of evenings a week he spent in the company of the Sanford 3rd Age Club.

The automatic doors swished open. Joe turned to greet his companions, but it was not them. Instead, it was a couple in their thirties, he tall, dark haired, athletic looking, but too smart in his dark suit and pristine collar and tie, his brunette partner dressed in a dark skirt and white top, augmented by a navy blue coat which she buttoned up against the weather. Joe figured them for lawyers, or similar professionals.

"I can't stand that man, and I don't like the way you suck up to him," she grumbled.

He put up an umbrella. "Reggie Grimshaw won't always be there, Fliss," her man said.

Not lawyers, Joe thought. Subjects of the Grimshaw empire.

"And when he calls it a day, Wendy will need someone to run the sales division," the man went on.

"And you've no chance, Robbie. It will be Naomi Barton."

Robbie growled as they stepped out into the rain. "No way. Reggie is screwing her and I'm sure Wendy knows. If she doesn't know it now, she will when I tell her."

Joe considered again the tiny incident in the bar where one of the actors had put an arm around Wendy Grimshaw. His agile mind worked through many angles and caused him to wonder what it was about men and women that made them so fickle.

"Not a problem you have, Joe," Sheila reminded him when he told the tale. "Nor me." She eyed Brenda. "Nor Brenda, really."

"That was very diplomatic, Sheila," Brenda commented.

Joe reminded himself that the two women were the very best of friends, but they could not be more different. Both were widowed but where Sheila steered clear of relationships, Brenda wandered from one to another transient affair, thumbing her nose at the rest of the world and what it thought of her.

Matters were different for Joe. His ex-wife had moved to the Canary Islands and he had no regrets on the marriage or the divorce, sublimating his need for company in work and the Sanford 3rd Age Club. Only at this time of year, traditionally geared to the family, did he feel any pangs of self-pity, and the club outings usually took care of it.

Walking down the steep hill past the cathedral, and through narrow backstreets of aged, stone-built houses, he said as much.

"Work has always got in the way of relationships, and relationships get in the way of work."

"I dunno, Joe," said Brenda. "Some of these big money men seem to do all right on both fronts."

"No, see, when I talk about work, I mean real work. Graft. Not like that couple back there. Sitting on their backsides high-pressuring housewives into buying kitchens they don't need and can't afford. I mean proper work."

"Like getting Lee to take the pies off the top rack of the ovens?" Sheila asked. "Is that what you mean, dear?"

"Correct," Joe agreed, "and whipping you two into shape when the orders need delivering."

Brenda smacked her lips. "Don't talk about whips, Joe. If you gave me half a chance…"

Joe cut her off. "So where's this museum, Sheila?"

She consulted her map. "At the bottom of this street… I think."

***

"One of these days, you'll bully them once too often, Reggie," Wendy said, kicking off her shoes and lying on the bed.

Reggie sat at the escritoire and stared through the first floor window at the twin towers of Lincoln Minster. "When I was their age, me ducks, I was knocking cabinets together on building sites. No bloody company cars, no expense accounts, no collar and tie. A pair of overalls and bag of tools. I learned how to work before I could take it easy. Robbie Kendrew is a

31

smug little bugger. Never done a hard day's work in his life."

"Naomi Barton is no better. She started by selling cosmetics in a department store."

"Good enough," Reggie countered. "I don't expect women to work with their hands."

"Oh, grow up and move into the twenty-first century, will you. They're professional salespeople. They probably left school and mopped the floors in a burger bar for the first two years of their working lives."

It was as if Wendy had not said a word. "That little chap, the trucker's caterer; Murray. He knows what I'm talking about. Solid graft. And I'll bet you won't find him sat behind a desk at his caff. He'll be out there, working with his crew."

"Which is more than can be said for you," Wendy retorted. "You spend all day every day sat on your fat backside doing nothing but scream at your staff to bring in more business." Wendy glowered at him. "When you're not kneeling between Naomi's legs."

Reggie glared back. "Shut it. Right? Just shut it or I might be tempted to look at my will again."

***

The museum was not at the bottom of the hill, as they discovered when they came out on the broad, dual carriageway of the A15 where it became the eastern ring road, at which point, Joe took charge of the map while they all sheltered under Sheila's umbrella.

Wandering a hundred yards down, towards the city centre, the fumes of Friday afternoon traffic subdued by the downpour, they found the Usher Gallery, the redbrick pillars supporting open gates, spacious lawns reminding them of summer in Sanford. Following Joe's map reading, they ambled along a curving, tarmac path, past the imposing main building, and out through a side gate, onto a narrow, cobbled street opposite the museum.

"It doesn't look a bit like I expected," Joe said.

Instead of a fusty, old building of brick and stone, it was a spanking new, low-level construction, gleaming white even in the dull daylight, with an array of anti-glare windows along one side.

Admission was free. "My kinda price," Joe commented as they passed into the cool interior.

Once inside, they spent an hour and a half going through the various rooms and exhibits. Sheila and Brenda were enthralled by the displays of Roman, Viking and Saxon coins and other treasures, Joe was more impressed by the natural history section, although he puzzled at the plesiosaur on display near the main entrance.

"It looks like a crocodile," he said, studying the fossilised bones. He pointed at a drawing of the creature as it would have looked; its fins spread, elongated neck craning. "It certainly doesn't look like that."

"Appearances can be deceptive, Joe," Sheila told him. "I'm not so well up on dinosaurs, but perhaps they didn't find it all."

"Like the search for Joe's wallet," Brenda said.

From the museum, they ambled through more narrow streets lined with houses, many converted to small business premises, until they reached the shopping quarter. After a light lunch in a Tudor building near to Marks & Spencer, where Joe, as usual, complained over the price of toasted teacakes, they crossed the street and down a flight of steps to the riverside, and walked along under a giant, metal statue of what looked like gymnasts.

"It's called Empowerment, Joe," Sheila lectured him, reading from her guide book. "Two people reaching to each other across the water."

Joe studied the steel structure, and looked across the narrow river to the other side where it was also anchored. "Yes,

33

but it's only thirty yards, isn't it? It's not like they're reaching across the Atlantic."

"Yes, Joe," Sheila said, unwilling to pick up the debate.

"Hey, when you two have done discussing contemporary art, there's shopping here." Brenda jerked her thumb sideways to the entrance of the Waterside Shopping Mall.

"Perfect," said Sheila, and with a sad shake of his head, Joe followed them into the place.

Chapter Three

Known as the Gibson Suite, the dining room of the Twin Spires was dedicated to Wing Commander Guy Gibson, the man who led 617 Squadron on their most famous World War Two raid. All but the east wall of the room, which was blank, was bedecked not only with photographs of the man, but also of actor Richard Todd who had played Gibson in the 1954 film, *The Dambusters*.

Tables for four were laid out in neat rows across the hall, with generous aisles between them, and Joe calculated that there was seating for well over 100 people. Against each place setting was a springbound notebook and a souvenir Markham Murder Mysteries pen.

Several large screen TVs stood on large frames around the room.

"I wonder what they're for," Joe muttered as he and his companions took their places at table four, at the front of the dining room.

"Don't you read the literature, Joe?" Sheila asked, brandishing a copy of the Markham Murder Mysteries leaflet. "The scenes are all recorded and they're rerun during the day to allow people to get out of the hotel and catch up with the action later." She pointed to the blank wall on the right, where a professional video camera, the kind used in TV outside broadcasts, stood on a tripod, its lens concentrated on the front, left side corner of the dining room where two larger, oblong tables had been put together to create seating for nine or ten diners. The area was unlit, dimming it from the view of the restaurant, but behind the table stood a tall easel with a map of southern England and Northern France pinned to it.

Brenda, a pair of thin-framed, fashionable reading glasses perched on her nose, was also studying the leaflet. "The scenes are also shown on screen while the actors are playing," she reported. "It ensures that those people sat right at the back don't miss any of the action."

"And," Sheila took up the narrative, "guests can ask for any particular scene to be replayed."

"I wish I'd never asked," Joe grumbled. "So where does the action take place?"

Sheila and Brenda pointed to an unoccupied area at the front.

As the patrons began to fill the room, most, he noticed, had got into the spirit of the 1950s theme. He, himself, had forsaken his sensible, casual trousers and short sleeved shirts, in favour of drainpipe jeans, complete with large turn-ups, and a leather jacket he had borrowed from a fellow shopkeeper who was into the 50s. Many of the other Sanford 3rd Age Club members had entered the spirit of the evening. Captain Les Tanner had turned out in post-World War Two khaki battle dress (ensuring his three pips were in place on the shoulders) George Robson and Owen Frickley were dressed as teddy boys, while Alec Staines and his wife Julia had come out in formal evening dress, he in a tuxedo complete with bowtie, she in a spreading dress with plunging neckline lending her the appearance of Alma Cogan. For their part, Sheila had put on a pencil skirt and cropped jacket business suit, with a pillbox hat, and Brenda turned up as a teddy girl.

"You look very James Dean, Joe," Brenda commented as Joe removed his leather jacket to reveal his favoured and modern gilet beneath. "Or you did."

"And you look very, er, six-five special."

"Ooh, Joe," Sheila cried, "I wouldn't have thought you'd remember the Six-Five Special."

"I don't," he confessed. "Well, I do, but only just."

"Josephine Douglas and Pete Murray, your namesake."

"Don Lang & His Frantic Five," Sheila echoed.

"How the hell do you two remember it?" Joe demanded. "You were only toddlers, like me."

"Older siblings, Joe," Sheila explained. "My eldest brother was almost ten years older than me."

"And my sister is a good seven or eight years older than me," Brenda echoed.

"Whereas your Arthur is only two years older then you," Sheila went on, "so he wouldn't remember it, either."

Many people had opted for demob suits, and styles which were more forties than fifties.

"Difficult to pin down the early years of the 1950s," Joe commented as the waiter delivered consommé for starters. "It's only after Bill Hayley and Elvis showed up that young people began to define themselves."

Brenda tucked her napkin down her neckline and spread it to cover her white cotton top. "I wonder why this crowd chose the fifties."

"I think the map says it all, dear," Sheila said. "It's Southern England and Normandy: the D-Day landings."

Joe placed his napkin on his knee. "It also tells you in the guide if you read it."

"So you did read some of it," Brenda commented, putting out her tongue at him.

Joe was not listening. He was watching Melanie's troupe take their table in the dimmed corner of the room.

He had not been taking much notice earlier in the day, and the only one he recognised was the man who had been so familiar with Wendy Grimshaw. He was now dressed in a tuxedo and sporting a row of medal ribbons across the breast pocket. Despite their makeup and theatrical disguises, Joe could not see Melanie amongst them. He was not surprised when she appeared carrying a radio mike, and stood alongside

37

the map.

"Ladies and gentlemen, please continue with your meal," she announced, her voice booming around the room. "My name is Melanie Markham, the producer and director of this weekend's entertainment, and I'd like to give you some of the basic information you will need. Tonight is Colonel Gregory Haliwell's 60th birthday, and he has invited a few guests to join him in the celebration."

Melanie gestured at the table, and the actor playing Haliwell stood up and took a bow.

"With him are his wife and daughter, his daughter's fiancé, two business acquaintances and the wife of one of those men, his biographer and a Romanian countess, also a business acquaintance. Over the course of the weekend, at least one of them will be murdered. The clues will appear as we work our way through the weekend. Can you unmask the killer? I leave you now, ladies and gentlemen, with Haliwell's Heroes."

To a round of polite applause, Melanie ducked off to one side, and started up the video camera, and while a waiter dropped a plate of steamed fish before Joe, the lights came up over the party at the front. The actors began their work, their voices clearly audible through microphone pickups, and their actions visible on the multiple-screens.

***

Swilling brandy round a large balloon, Colonel Gregory Haliwell tossed his newspaper onto the table. "Interesting item in The Times," he said with a throwaway gesture at the newspaper. "Exactly a year today since Lydia Beauchamp was found murdered. Naturally, it remains unsolved. One wonders what the devil the police do with our taxes, eh?"

Alongside him, a dowdily dressed young brunette asked, "Lydia Beauchamp, Colonel? I don't think you've mentioned her."

The colonel beamed benignly upon her. "You may be my biographer, Miss Dolman, but that doesn't mean I have to tell you everything."

"Well, you can tell us, Daddy," said his daughter Theresa from her end of the table, on the colonel's right. "Who was she?"

"British liaison officer with the French Resistance in Normandy," Haliwell replied, and stretched across the table to pull the ashtray his way. "I never met the lady, but she had a fearsome reputation. Deadly with the garrotte. It was she and her team who gathered all the intelligence for our assault on Chateau Armand. You remember her, Wilson."

From the opposite end of the table, Captain Christopher Wilson, his regimental blazer bedecked with ribbons, shook his head. "I was never at Chateau Armand, sir. I was further North; with the 50th at Bayeux."

From Theresa's vicinity, former Lieutenant Michael Crenshaw asked, "Chateau Armand, sir?"

"Small place, a few miles south of Caen." The colonel gazed longingly at the map. "Our finest hour. You're probably not familiar with the tale, Countess Lucescu."

To the right of the table, beyond Wilson and his wife, a slender woman, her tight fitting, floor-length, spangled dress, clashing with her garish, red hair, spoke in an unconvincing middle European accent. "If it is D-Day, I know nothink of it. It was not until after the war that I had to flee my beloved Varna. When the communists took over the country, my fellow Romanians were not forgivink of the aristocracy."

"A hellish battle, Crenshaw," Haliwell declared. "But you wouldn't know, would you? I believe you were second echelon. Supply Corps."

"We came ashore on Sword, sir, and made our way inland from there. We took our fair share of flak." Crenshaw replied. "Particularly from the Luftwaffe."

"Course you did, old man. Course you did, but I'm not

39

just talking about fighters strafing us, you know. Chateau Armand was a Jerry stronghold, you know. Sits south of Caen, well hidden in the local country, and just off a major supply route for the Nazis. Well defended, too, and don't listen to any of that tommyrot about the Bosch being ready to lay down their arms and surrender. They fought like demons. We had the superior numbers. Four hundred men to their one hundred and fifty, and we had some support from the RAF, but we'd been ordered to take the place intact, so the boys in blue couldn't bomb the place. Three days. Three damned days before Jerry finally ran for it. And then we learned the swine had wired it with explosives. Brought the whole, bloody building down." Lighting a cigar, pushing his brandy glass to one side, and drawing the large glass ashtray even closer towards himself, Haliwell turned to Wilson. "You sure you weren't there, Wilson?"

"I think if you cast your mind back, sir, you'll recall that I was never at Chateau Armand," Wilson replied, stretching across the table to flick cigarette ash into the ashtray. "Saw some pretty heavy fighting, of course, but none of the close quarter combat you chaps had. Tell you what, though, I did meet Lydia Beauchamp. Very briefly. Striking looking woman. Dark-haired siren, looked like a gypsy girl. Odd thing, though. She had no sense of smell. An accident or something, with explosives. Stopped off to pick up supplies, and then she was on her way to Caen."

The elderly woman at Crenshaw's side clucked. "I do wish you would stop talking about the war, Gregory."

"Let me remind you, Sadie, if it were not for men like me and Captain Wilson, and Theresa's young fella…" Haliwell gestured at Crenshaw, "you'd be grovelling up under the heel of the jackboot. We had to fight, woman, fight." The colonel cast a sour eye on the man the other side of Theresa. "We were not sat on our bottoms shuffling money around."

"I'd have given anything to be there with you, sir," said the man.

"I'm sure you would, McLintock, I'm sure you would." Haliwell's tone was demeaning, barely the right side of scathing. "What was your problem again?"

"Heart murmur," McLintock replied diffidently. "Unfit for military service." Like Wilson, he too, stretched to drop cigarette ash into the ashtray.

"And Patrick's job with the Treasury was as vital as yours in France," Theresa defended him.

"Nonsense," Crenshaw retorted. He half stood, reached across the table, and stubbed out his cigarette.

The colonel, oblivious to the problems he was causing for everyone, relit his cigar and drew the ashtray even nearer. "Now, Crenshaw…"

Cutting him off, McLintock's response was equally critical and aimed at Crenshaw. "Where do you think the money came from to pay for the supplies you shipped to the front line forces?" McLintock left a pause filled with meaning. "Or sold on at a profit."

Crenshaw let loose his rage. "What the hell are you suggesting? For your information, McLintock, I could account for every item that passed through our stores." He, too, paused, before going on with unmistakable venom. "Which is more than may be said about the fivers passing through your books."

"Are you accusing me of embezzlement?"

"Well, no one's yet worked out where you came by the money to start up after the war."

"It was a loan from my father," McLintock argued.

"And if the rumours are to be believed, that's not the only favour your father did you. Heart murmur indeed."

"I'll show you how weak my heart is."

McLintock half rose, Crenshaw followed suit, Wilson leapt to his feet, and came half way round the table. During the furore, Countess Lucescu swapped her glass with Wilson's. It

41

was an act carried out so surreptitiously that none of the tablemates noticed.

"Gentlemen, gentlemen," shouted Wilson. "Remember where we are. We're here to celebrate the colonel's birthday and whatever our personal differences, this kind of behaviour is uncalled for."

The two men sat down, glowering, simmering at each other. Colonel Haliwell tapped his hands together applauding Wilson.

The captain reached across his superior's shoulders, and over his glass of brandy to get at the ashtray. "Excuse me, sir." He crushed out his cigarette and returned to his seat.

With the intention of pouring oil on troubled waters, Countess Lucescu asked, "Did I hear a rumour that there was a large amount of Nazi gold hidden at Chateau Armand?"

To her surprise, the colonel rounded angrily upon her. "It's utter balderdash, young lady. You hear me. Complete tosh. I know. I was there." He pointed an accusing finger at her. "You would do well to learn some British manners, madam."

"Hear, hear," said Wilson, making no attempt to hide his irritation with Zara Lucescu. "There never was any gold at Chateau Armand. You have my word upon that."

"But…"

Wilson rounded on her with a glare that plainly said, 'shut up.'

Alongside the colonel, his plump wife sipped at her brandy. "I heard a rumour, too, Zara. One that says you were not entirely unsympathetic to the Nazi cause."

"Iss not true," said the countess. "The whole of Romania was on the side of the Allies, but we were hoping they would help save the Soviets and the Bolsheviks from coming to power." She dabbed at a tear in her eye. "You should see what they do to my beloved Varna, those German bombers. A city destroyed. But I am not responsible for the actions of my government," she cried. "I am just one person. What can I do?"

"Course not, m'dear," agreed Haliwell. "You got out while the going was good. Chances are, the Reds would have had you shot or shipped off to some gulag in Siberia."

Captain Wilson clapped his hands together. "Enough of this bickering, ladies and gentlemen. We're here tonight to celebrate the birthday of our good friend and benefactor, Colonel Gregory Haliwell. I give you a toast. Colonel Haliwell."

They raised their glasses. "Colonel Haliwell," they called in unison.

Basking in their generosity, Haliwell drank from his balloon. He gasped, gagged, clutched at his throat, dropped the glass and fell, face forward onto the table.

"Do stop being so melodramatic, Gregory," insisted his wife as she shook him.

The colonel did not move. Concern etched itself into the faces around the table. Wilson's wife, Valerie pushed back her chair, rounded her husband, and pressed a hand to his neck.

"Oh my god. He's dead."

Facing the colonel, Theresa screamed and flopped to the floor in a faint. McLintock and Crenshaw hurried to be first to her. Zara put a hand over her shocked mouth, Mrs Haliwell sat stunned, Captain Wilson and Miss Dolman gawped.

"Are you sure, Val?" Wilson asked.

"I am a doctor, Christopher. Of course I'm sure." Valerie looked around the table at the brandy glasses. Picking up the colonel's, she sniffed cautiously at it. She put the glass down with a grimace. "Sweet almonds. Prussic acid." She took in their shocked faces. "Potassium cyanide."

"But he drank from the glass earlier," McLintock protested.

"Correct, Mr McLintock," agreed Val Wilson. "And cyanide works practically instantaneously, which means it cannot have been in the glass earlier. And you all know what that means. One of us put it in the glass. One of us is a

43

murderer."

***

The lights at the front of the dining room dimmed and a spontaneous round of applause broke out.

Abandoning her camera, Melanie appeared again. "There you have it ladies and gentlemen. Discord amongst Haliwell's Heroes, and one of them is a murderer. But which one? There are clues already, but I will not give you any hints." She smiled secretively at them. "You'll find maps and an encyclopaedia here on the table, which may or may not help you in your search for the truth. The dinner guests will now leave the table. The police will not arrive until breakfast tomorrow morning when a mannequin will be placed in the colonel's seat. The cast may be found about the hotel during the evening, and you are free to question them. Please don't crowd them. If you see others questioning a member of the cast, don't force your way in. Please bide your time. You'll all have the opportunity. One last thing. The colonel, played by our wonderful leading man, Gerry Carlin, will be about the hotel this evening, but he will not answer any of your questions. He is, after all, dead. He will, however, answer your questions tomorrow, when he returns as Inspector O'Keefe of Scotland Yard." Melanie paused a moment. "Thank you, ladies and gentlemen, enjoy your evening."

With an extravagant wave, she left the dining room to further applause. As it died down, conversation burst through the room, filling the void.

"I think I've got it already," said Brenda, and showed her notebook to Sheila, who by return showed Brenda hers. "We agree. What about you, Joe?"

They turned their attention to the man who was writing furiously. Brenda noticed that while she and Sheila had written down one or two lines, and the identity of the killer (according to them) Joe's spidery handwriting covered the page and, judging by his notebook, several more besides.

"What are you doing, Joe?" Sheila asked.

"He's penning the novel," Brenda grinned. "No wonder he took so long to finish his dinner."

"Memory is a fickle friend," Joe told them, without taking his eyes from the page upon which he continued to write. "I'm making notes so that I don't forget anything."

"I thought you weren't taking part?" she reminded him.

"I'm not entering into the competition." Hammering the pen to paper in the final full stop, he closed the notebook, and dropped it into the large pocket of his gilet. "But I see no reason why I shouldn't test my wits. As long as I don't tell you or anyone what I've learned."

"We've got it anyway," Brenda assured him. "Look."

They both put forward their notebooks. Joe looked them over, and declared, "You're wrong. Both of you." He drank from a cup of cooling coffee. "How could Zara Lucescu get anywhere near enough to drop cyanide in his glass? She never moved from her half of the table."

"Oh."

"Oh."

"There's something odd about her," Sheila said. "She doesn't know the geography or the history of her own country. Romania originally sided with the Nazis in World War Two."

"I know," Joe agreed. "She's obviously a wrong'un, but it doesn't make her a killer."

Brenda's gaze challenged him. "I suppose you know who did it?"

"Yep. I don't know why, but I'm sure that will become apparent as we go through the weekend."

"Go on then, Joe."

He tapped the side of his nose. "Oh no. I promised Melanie I wouldn't disclose anything to anyone, and I'm sorry, but that includes you two."

Brenda edged closer to him, and gently rubbed his thigh. "Joe. My love. You know you're the kind of man I always wanted to…"

"Bribery won't get you anywhere, either," Joe cut her off. "Not your kind of bribery, anyway."

"I was going to say you're the kind of man I always wanted to solve my murder mysteries."

"Stop teasing him, Brenda," Sheila ordered. "Joe admires so much more about women than their bodies." She laughed. "Like their ability to make perfect gravy for the steak and kidney pies."

"And doing the washing up," Joe said. "Come on. Come with me." He led them across to the table where the Haliwell Heroes had been sat, but Joe concentrated on a small section of the map centred on France inland from the landing beaches. "Notice anything?" he asked.

"Yes," said Sheila. "It's been quite badly drawn and printed, leaving out a lot of detail."

"I'll go with that," Joe agreed, "but there's enough detail there to give you a clue to the main suspect. You have to think about that map in the context of what you were told over dinner."

The women studied the map for long minutes. "It doesn't even identify Chateau Armand," Brenda complained.

"It doesn't have to," Joe said. "Chateau Armand is not germane to the issue right now. It may be later, but for the moment it is irrelevant."

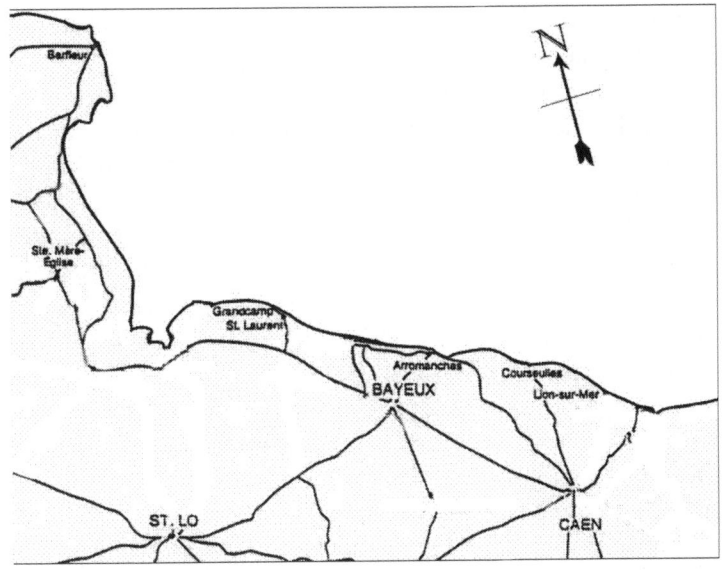

A young man, who Joe recognised as one of Reggie Grimshaw's salespeople was thumbing through the encyclopaedia. Joe waited patiently for him to finish checking his facts, and hand the book over.

"Loada rubbish," he said.

"Is it?" Joe asked.

The youngster nodded. "I'm Den Ellerby."

"Joe Murray." The pair shook hands. "So why is it rubbish?"

"There's a bookmarked page on Chateau Armand, yet I know for a fact it doesn't exist."

Joe nodded. "You've been to Normandy. Right?"

"I've travelled all over Normandy and trust me, there's no such place."

Joe began to flick through the book. "You'll be telling me next that Colonel Haliwell isn't really dead because he's a figment of someone's imagination."

Ellerby gave him a curious stare and wandered off.

"What was that about?" Brenda asked, dragging her eyes away from the map.

"He hasn't worked out this is fiction," Joe told her, and opened the encyclopaedia at the Chateau Armand page.

"Yes, well, we haven't worked out what this map is telling us," Sheila grumbled. "Come on, Joe. Give us a clue."

He tutted. "If you can't see what it's telling you, it's not because you can't see it, but because you weren't listening when Haliwell's Heroes were talking. That's as much as you get out of me."

He returned to his reading.

Although the encyclopaedia was genuine, the article concerning Chateau Armand had been printed and inserted to lend it some verisimilitude. There were convincing photographs of a ruined chateau which could have come from anywhere in northern France or southern Germany during World War Two, and a detailed account of Colonel Haliwell's three-day assault on the German forces occupying the place.

The battle of Chateau Armand took place on the outskirts of Caen between June 8th and 11th, 1944. Four hundred men of the 13th Battalion the Royal Marine Commandos, under the command of Colonel G. D. Haliwell, MC, DSO, laid siege to the chateau, defended by approximately 150 men of the Wehrmacht 3rd Infantry Division.

Haliwell's orders were to take the chateau intact, yet it was never explained why the Allies wanted it so. Set away from the main routes into Caen, although close to the main supply route, Chateau Armand was of little strategic value, and had been used by the Germans as a radio centre, monitoring Allied broadcasts from across the English channel.

Accounts of the assault vary, but what is clear is that Haliwell lost 93 men during the three day battle. Of the five officers under Haliwell's command (two captains, three lieutenants) three were killed during the engagement, but the fourth was killed in a 'friendly fire' incident when the fifth officer, who has never been identified, thought he was a German infiltrator. No German prisoners were taken and it is not known how many were killed or escaped during the battle.

The end of the battle has been the subject of some debate. According to Haliwell, the remaining German forces in the chateau detonated explosives and razed the building to the ground. An NCO under Haliwell's command, later insisted that the British forces had entered the building intact, found the explosive charges and while they were attempting to defuse them, they detonated. Colonel Haliwell has strenuously denied the report, insisting that the sergeant in question was mistaken, probably due to battle fatigue.

Allied forces later excavated large areas of the ruined building and grounds, but HM Government has never publicly admitted what it was looking for, or why Chateau Armand was so important. Colonel Haliwell and a number of his men were decorated for bravery after the battle, and no public recrimination was ever recorded against the colonel for his failure to take the building intact.

Early in 1949, The Daily Herald claimed that the chateau had been used to melt down stolen gold which the Nazis had been accumulating, turning it into bullion bars. The Herald claimed they got the story from Helmut Bruner, a citizen of Dusseldorf, a former soldier in the Wehrmacht, who had been stationed at Chateau Armand, and who had escaped during the battle. The claim was vigorously denied by Colonel Haliwell and the survivors of his battalion, and the War Office has so far refused to comment upon the matter.

Experts on the Third Reich are divided in their opinion. Some maintain that it is possible, but without evidence of bullion at the chateau, it can never be proven. It would, say some, explain why the Germans fought such a fierce rearguard for a building so strategically unimportant. These same authorities maintain that the Germans could have been trucking the gold out while holding off Haliwell's forces.

Other historians insist it is probably untrue. Whilst agreeing that there was something about Chateau Armand that was of interest to both the Allies and the Third Reich, if the Germans had been smelting gold, and, moreover, shipping it out under cover of battle, routine reconnaissance flights would have detected the trucks, and the War Office has released no aerial photographs of the area with such evidence.

At the time of going to press, the matter is unresolved.

Joe made copious notes while reading the piece, and then, when he was through, he passed the encyclopaedia to Les Tanner.

"Solved it, Murray?"

Joe nodded. "I think so."

"Well, man, spit it out."

"I think that after the war, Haliwell took a job at the town hall, and one of the council tax payers got so cheesed off with his glaring inefficiency, that he or she decided to take matters into his own hands." Joe grinned. Getting under Les Tanner's skin always gave him great pleasure. "Catch you later, Les."

Joe moved around the table, checked the glass the Countess Lucescu had switched, made a few notes, then picked up the newspaper Haliwell had been reading at the opening of the play.

Murder Remains Unsolved, read the headline of a small item half way down the home news page.

A year ago today, the body of a blonde-haired woman was dredged from the Thames near Mortlake. She had been beaten so badly that her features were unrecognizable, but personal items in her handbag identified her as Lydia Beauchamp, one of Britain's most famous undercover saboteurs who worked with the French Resistance in Normandy during the build up to D-Day.

Inspector Jonathan O'Keefe of Scotland Yard yesterday

reiterated appeals for the public's help in tracing Miss Beauchamp's last movements. "It's been a year since her murder, and we have received no information regarding her final hours. We would appeal to anyone who may have seen this lady in the Mortlake or Richmond area to come forward."

Sheila took the newspaper from him and read the item. "Rather brief, isn't it?"

"It tells you all you need to know," Joe said, and dropping his notebook in his pocket, made for the exit.

"Hey, where are you going?" Brenda demanded.

"Next door," he replied. "I'll get the drinks in while you're trying to crack the case."

Chapter Four

Joe found the Scampton Room quite crowded. In the far corner, by the windows which looked out onto the floodlit front of the hotel, a DJ was busy setting up his equipment. Melanie and her team were dotted around the room, some talking amongst themselves, others harangued by patrons, and despite her request to give the actors some breathing space, Zara Lucescu was the centre of attention, with a dozen people, mainly men, crowding around her.

Melanie herself was seated by the windows with the young man who had played the part of McLintock, while Gerry Carlin was at the bar talking to Reggie Grimshaw and a dark-haired woman, one of Reggie's party. Wendy Grimshaw sat nearer the far wall, close to the bar, talking to Robbie and Fliss, the young couple Joe had encountered earlier in the day.

There was an inevitable party atmosphere about the room, enhanced by the glittering Christmas decorations, the glimmer of the lights on the large Christmas tree and further augmented by the flickering lights of the DJ's disco display.

There were several members of the Sanford 3rd Age Club seated around the room, which hardly surprised Joe. His members may have been aged between 50 and 85, but never let it be said that they didn't know how to party.

He found George Robson and Owen Frickley at the bar and tucked himself in alongside them.

"You're not doing the disco, Joe?" George asked.

Signalling for service, Joe shook his head. "They wouldn't let me. Said they had a professional, stress, *professional* on for the weekend." Gesturing at the DJ, he turned back to the barman. "A glass of lager, Campari and soda, gin and it, please."

Turning back to his two members, he looked them up and down, both dressed in ridiculous, three-quarter length drapes, George with yellow lapels, Owen with mauve. Neither man had enough hair to comb properly, and neither had used any gel on what they had, but both had completed the ensemble with black shirts and Bolo, bootlace ties, George's sporting a buffalo skull, Owen's a Confederate flag.

"I must say, you look a complete pair of prats."

"That's what we love about you, Joe. Your tact," Owen said. "And look who's talking. You're only short of a hecky-thump cap and you'd look like Marlon Brando in that fillum."

"*The Godfather?*"

"Not that. The other one."

"*Superman?*" Joe suggested and George laughed.

Joe's drinks arrived. He paid for them and took the two to task again. "Not investigating the mysterious murder?"

"You know us, Joe. We're only here for the beer and the totty. Who gives a toss over some stupid play?" George asked. He drank from a pint of bitter, casting his eyes to one side at the dark-haired woman with Grimshaw. "I fancy giving a toss over that, when the old git with her clears off."

Joe followed his gaze. "You may have a long wait. I think she works for the old git."

"On her back?"

"Maybe. I dunno, but I'd hope not. The old git's wife is sat at the back of the room."

George and Owen wandered off, and Joe took to people watching again, mainly studying Melanie and the young man at her side. They were deep in discussion and judging by the frowns on both foreheads, it was serious.

"Good evening viewers."

Joe glanced to his left where Reggie Grimshaw and his

dark-haired employee were tittering over Gerry Carlin's impression of the late Benny Hill. Not a good impression, but the awkward salute Benny Hill had given in character as Fred Scuttle, compensating for the too high elbow with a twist of the wrist, was accurate.

Joe guessed Carlin's age at about 50, a few years younger than himself, but where years spent in the hectic environment of the Lazy Luncheonette had ensured Joe burned off most of his fat, leaving him lean and wiry, the opposite was true of Carlin, who showed a distinct middle-aged spread under his dinner jacket, white shirt and deep red cummerbund.

"The lazy life of an actor," Joe muttered to himself.

"I beg your pardon?"

He spun his head the other way and looked into the pale blue eyes of Valerie Wilson… or the actress who had played her in the dining room.

"I was talking to myself," Joe replied. "Joe Murray. Caterer."

"Tanya Richmond." Introducing herself, Tanya did not appear overtly friendly. "I thought I heard you say the lazy life of an actor."

"You did," Joe agreed. "I was just thinking about the colonel, there. He must be about the same age as me, but he weighs more. I figured it was the lazy life of an actor."

"You have my assurance, Mr Murray, acting is not a lazy life."

Joe tutted. "A touchy one, though."

"Not particularly."

"Then why so het up? It was a passing comment, and I made it to myself, no one else."

"I've had a trying day," she insisted.

"Well, finding the colonel poisoned like that can't have helped." Joe smiled at her, but he was worried it came out as more of a leer.

"Now you're taking the mickey."

"I wouldn't like to wake up next to you when you're

54

reading the critics in the Sundays."

"I wouldn't like to wake up next to you. Full stop."

Seeing Melanie making her way across the floor, Joe dismissed Tanya with a scowl, and edged further along the bar.

"Hello, Joe." Melanie greeted him with a warm smile. "How did you find our little play?"

"Intriguing," he replied, "but not difficult to work out."

Melanie's face fell slightly. "Oh dear."

"Not to worry," he assured her. "I'll say nothing to anyone else, and anyway, I haven't ironed out all the wrinkles." He took out his tobacco tin. "Can I buy you a drink?"

She accepted a cup of coffee from the barman. "That's kind of you, but I'm in the middle of some fairly important debates with the cast, so I need to keep a clear head. I'll take you up on it later, if I may, because I'd like a word with you."

He smiled benignly. "As long as I don't owe you money."

With Melanie gone, Joe relaxed against the bar, his ear cocked to the conversation between Reggie Grimshaw, Gerry Carlin and the dark-haired woman.

"It's that easy-going ability to put people at their ease which we're always looking for, me ducks. Isn't it, Naomi?" Reggie said.

"And the determination to see it through," the dark-haired woman, now identified as Naomi, added. "See, Gerry, the customer doesn't always know what she wants. It's my job to tell them that."

"Frankly," Carlin said, "I've never heard so much twaddle in my life."

Listening in, Joe couldn't help agreeing with Carlin.

"But it's true," Reggie blustered. "Once they have it, they know it's what they wanted."

"And forget this business about selling to people who don't want to buy," Naomi insisted. "That's not possible. Ask Robbie Kendrew, my opposite number in the Eastern Region if you don't believe me. Our job is about selling to someone who does want to buy but doesn't realise it."

"So when you're sick of play-acting to crowds like this, give us a ring," Reggie said, gesturing at the crowded room.

"Thanks, Reggie, but I'll stick to entertaining folks like these. I may not make the same money as your whizz kids, but I'm much happier."

"The offer's there if you change your mind, ducks." Reggie slipped a familiar arm around Naomi's shoulder. "Excuse us while we circulate." With a nod of recognition at Joe, he and his sales manager wandered off.

Carlin turned to the bar, picked up his drink and shook his head.

"He was offering you a job?" Joe asked.

"What? Oh. Yes." It was as if Carlin had just registered Joe's presence. "I knew his wife, Wendy, years ago. He seems to think my acting ability would make me a good salesman."

Joe sipped his lager. "I overheard. Joe Murray. Sanford 3rd Age Club."

"Eh? Oh. Gerry Carlin. Male lead, Markham Murder Mysteries." As they shook hands, light dawned in Carlin's eyes. "You're the fella Melanie was so worried about, aren't you?"

Joe laughed. "She was a bit concerned, yes."

"And have you rumbled it yet?"

"Oh yes." He laughed again at Carlin's surprise. "It's not that difficult. But don't worry. I won't say a word." He drank more lager. "So how come you ended up in this game?"

"Always been an actor, old son." Carlin's pride glowed through his words. "Nothing big. Rep, mainly. I've had a couple of speaking parts on TV, too. Ever see Inspector Hucknall?"

Joe shook his head. "I don't watch much TV."

"Pity. I played a serial killer in one episode."

Ignoring the obviously ribald comment, Joe felt obliged to explain. "I run a café in Sanford. I have to be up at five thirty every morning, so I feel like a serial killer most of the time. It doesn't leave me much time for any kind of entertainment, except when we get away on one of our weekend jaunts." He sipped his lager again. "So is this all you do, now?"

"Occasional commercial, odd bit parts on TV, and last summer, I had to drop out of the Markham Murder Mysteries. I was cast as Davies, the old man in The Caretaker. Three week run in Leicester. Course, with rehearsals and what not, I was missing for a good deal longer than three weeks."

"How does your wife deal with it?" Joe wanted to know. "I mean, actors are famous for, how do you say it, resting, aren't they?"

"Not a problem, old son," Carlin admitted. "Mrs Carlin is no longer an issue. Ran off with a kitchen salesman ten years ago." He grinned.

Slow to realise that Carlin was taking a rise, Joe eventually smiled. "Yes, very funny. My missus cleared off to Tenerife ten years ago, too."

"Same here. Norwich rather than Tenerife, but same principle. Mercifully, she didn't leave with a kitchen salesman."

From the corner of his eye, Joe caught sight of Sheila and Brenda as they came into the bar. He signalled to them. "My friends," he explained.

"Two of them." Carlin was impressed. "Lucky man."

"Not as lucky as you think," Joe said, and passed drinks from the bar to the women. "Ladies, meet Gerry Carlin, the late Colonel Haliwell. Gerry, this is Sheila Riley and Brenda Jump."

"Ooh, a real actor," Sheila said as she shook hands.

"Yes, but you're dead, aren't you?" Brenda complained. "We can't ask you anything about the killing and Joe won't tell us."

Carlin half bowed and kissed the back of her hand. "Were it at all possible, my lady, I would return to the land of the living to aid you in your quest."

Brenda giggled. "What play's that from, then?"

Carlin frowned. "None as far as I know. It was a spot of

improvisation."

"It was very good, though," Sheila commented, her face spelling out her admiration for Carlin. "I do appreciate thespians. I think the ability to cloak your own identity in that of other characters is a wonderful talent, and it must give you deeper insight into the human condition."

"Er, yes," Carlin replied. "Sadly, my dear lady, the condition of this human is starving. You'll forgive me if I disappear to feed my face."

"What a charming man," Sheila commented as Carlin left them.

"You think so?" Joe asked. "I think he's full of…"

"Joe," Brenda warned.

"I was gonna say, hot air." He turned to the bar, quickly rolled a cigarette, and said, "Right, girls, I'm off for a smoke. If anyone wants me, I'll be outside at the front door."

"Anyone in particular?" Brenda called after him? "The Secretary General of the United Nations?"

Ignoring her, Joe walked out into the night air and lit his cigarette.

The rain had stopped, but the sky remained cloudy. Several hundred yards away, the twin towers of the cathedral were lit up, glowing across the dull sky like a beacon. Light traffic passed the front of the hotel, and from further along the street came the sound of revellers from a pub or disco.

Joe felt a sudden sense of peace. He spent most of his life in a state of semi-permanent irritation, caused mostly by the pressures of long hours and maintaining a viable business. It was an attitude that could have done so much to leave him friendless, but he was not. The members of the Sanford 3rd Age Club were his friends; even the antagonists like Les Tanner, would be there if he needed support, and that gave him the feeling of calm and belonging so often denied others, particularly single men and women over the Christmas and New Year period.

The click of heels on the tiles distracted his attention. He turned to find Robbie lighting a cigarette.

"All right, son?" Joe asked.

Robbie scowled. "If you must know, no, I'm not all right."

Joe blew a thin cloud of smoke out into the night. "Curious. Listening to your boss, I thought everything in the Grimshaw Kitchens garden was coming up roses."

"For him, yes. And for that bitch Naomi Barton."

"She's the good looking, dark-haired woman who was with him at the bar?"

Robbie nodded. "The good looking, dark-haired woman who's opening her legs for him."

"Ah. I see."

Robbie drew on his cigarette. "I hear you run your own business. Do you favour your employees for sleeping with you?"

Joe laughed. "If Sheila Riley heard you say that, she'd cut off your wedding tackle. And Brenda Jump... well, never mind. No, son, I don't favour employees who sleep with me, for the simple reason that my employees don't sleep with me. We're very old fashioned about such things in Sanford. Besides, I run a café, not a kitchen company." Joe turned and stubbed out his cigarette, dropping it in the wall-mounted receptacle. Taking in Rob's angry features, he guessed the younger man was in a mood to get it off his chest. "So, what's the problem? Is Naomi leap-frogging you by offering her favours to Reggie?"

"He's ready for retiring, old Reggie," Robbie explained. "Wendy keeps pestering him to pack it in. That means one of us, either me or Naomi, will take over as sales director. I have seniority. Fifteen years I've been with Grimshaws. Started when I was 21 as a sales rep, worked like a dog, I have. Always on target, never took a day off. And when Reggie made me a team manager, I didn't complain about the extra work. I just did it, and I got my people to do it, too. What's Naomi done?

Dropped her knickers. That's what."

"She's not been there long?" Joe asked.

"Five years. Came in as a sales rep, worked on my team, then she got promoted to Northern sales manager. Yet, you can see what'll happen when Reggie retires. She'll move up and muggins here will be under her thumb. The bitch."

Joe rolled another cigarette. "I can see why you're angry, but you know, it's only work. If it comes down to it, you can always get yourself another job. Or you can swallow it and carry on. Seems to me that if and when Reggie retires, he'll still have a hand on the tiller, and if she screws it up, there may yet be an opening for you."

"Not while he's taking advantage of the opening between…"

"I get the picture, sunshine." Joe interrupted. He looked up at the cathedral. "Twenty-four and a bit hours of the year left, and then we start afresh. You never know, lad. The New Year may bring new opportunities."

Joe turned back into the hotel and the Scampton Room where the DJ had already begun the evening's entertainment with John Lennon's *Imagine*, leaving the dance floor empty.

The chatter and clink of glasses sounded over the music. Sheila and Brenda had found a table and were in earnest conversation with the actor who had played Captain Wilson. George and Owen were hitting on two women, neither of whom Joe recognised, but who were dressed as bobbysoxers. Wendy Grimshaw was still in her corner, Reggie and Naomi sat with her this time, and there was a look of anger about the kitchen magnate's wife. She talked at both her husband and his sales manager, her virulent stare switching between them. She had been talking to Robbie Kendrew earlier, and Joe guessed she was passing on the whinges young Kendrew had made known at the door.

"Without the bed hopping," Joe said to himself.

"I am sorry, dollink, I didn't kvite ketch that."

Joe found the Countess Lucescu alongside him, holding a glass of what looked like champagne, her little finger extended.

"Zara Lucescu." Joe smiled. "You could drop that appalling accent."

"But, ziss iss how I speak, dollink."

He laughed aloud, then looked around to ensure no one was listening in, and dropped his voice to an audible whisper. "You do know that Varna is in Bulgaria, not Romania?"

"You're Joe Murray, aren't you?" The caricatured, Black Sea accent was gone, replaced by a slight cockney lilt. "Bugger," she said when Joe nodded. "Melanie warned us about you. Still, at least I can, how do you say, *drop ze phoney eccent.*" She smiled broadly, exhibiting fine, white teeth. "I'm Emma Pemberley, actress, waitress, scene shifter and part time Romanian countess."

"Waitress?"

"When I'm not scene shifting, rehearsing the others with their parts, I tend to keep the crowd topped up with booze."

"And yourself." Joe nodded at the glass.

"Spritzer, I'm afraid. Tiny dash of lime juice to make it look like shampoo." She sipped from the glass. "Do you know, I don't think anyone's ever rumbled the countess so quickly."

"My friend did." Joe nodded towards Sheila, still talking with Captain Wilson. "She was a school secretary for years. Clever woman. Very good with history and geography."

"She'll need to be with Billy."

Drinking from his glass of lager, Joe raised his eyebrows.

"Billy Norman. Plays Captain Wilson. Brilliant actor. Very devious, you know. He improvs most of the time, but he can run rings round the rest of us, including the famous Gerry Carlin, Melanie's blue-eyed boy." Emma drank more spritzer. "So who's the other woman? Your wife?"

Joe almost choked. "Hell fire, no. Sorry, I didn't mean that quite as it sounds. Brenda is one of my best friends, but the thought of marrying her…" He shuddered convincingly. "My wife has gone the way of all good women."

"Oh. I'm sorry."

"Don't be. There's nothing wrong with Tenerife."

A puzzled frown creased her brow. "But I thought you meant… Oh. You were taking the mick."

"Depends how you look at it," Joe said. "Most good women do want to go to Tenerife. Naturally, most of them come back. Alison never did." Joe considered the tale close enough to the truth for a stranger. "So, fake Countess Lucescu, what's your real story."

He was instantly impressed by the speed with which Emma dropped back into part. "Vell, dollink, there are zo many peoples not tellink it like it really wass. I tink I chust lay low for ze time beink. But if I vere you, I'd keep my eyes on zat McLintock."

With a broad smile, she ambled back across the room, and Joe moved to join his companions.

"Joe," Brenda greeted him. "Where have you been? This is Captain Christopher Wilson."

Joe nodded a greeting. "How are you? Getting over the shock of the old man's death?"

"You know how it is, sir."

For all that Joe recognised him as an actor, the tones were still the high, precise English of the Sandhurst military academy.

"You friends were telling me you cast doubt on the map. You have my assurances that it's absolutely accurate."

"My friends have misinterpreted me. There's absolutely nothing wrong with the map." Joe smiled evilly. "But it does call into question some of the information we were given during your debate."

The other man looked convincingly shocked. "Such as?"

Joe wagged a disapproving finger. "Oh, no. I promised your boss I wouldn't discuss it with anyone but her. But tell me something, Captain Wilson, if it wasn't Nazi gold, what was the secret of Chateau Armand?"

Wilson delivered a rueful twitch of the head and a cynical smile. "I was a junior officer, Mr Murray, and if they wouldn't tell seniors like the colonel, it's a certainty that they wouldn't tell me."

"It must have been something really vital to justify all those deaths," Joe argued.

The smile faded. "A bloodbath. But then, war is like that, isn't it?"

"I don't know. I've never been to war. One of your brother offices was shot by friendly fire, I believe."

The brow creased. "Hmm. Lieutenant Creasey. Wandering round in the dark. He was mistaken for a Jerry. Sad business, but these things happen in war." Defensiveness enveloped the captain. "We gave him a decent burial. Full military honours. More than some of our chaps got." He got to his feet. "If you'll excuse me, ladies, sir. I must circulate."

"Of course," Sheila said, and gazed in admiration at his departing back.

Brenda nudged Joe. "I think she's smitten."

"Don't be absurd," Sheila retorted. With a giggle, she added, "He is rather dishy, though, isn't he?"

"He's as transparent as glass," Joe announced.

"Now, Joe, no need to be jealous."

He laughed harshly. "Jealous? Do me a favour. He's told more porkies in the last few minutes than I've made steak and kidney puddings in the last year."

"Lee makes the steak and kidney puddings," Brenda pointed out.

"You know what I mean."

"We've talked at some length to him, Joe," Sheila said, "and he's put us on the right track. You're the one who has it wrong. Brenda and I had it right the first time." She leaned closer into them, and whispered conspiratorially. "It is Zara Lucescu."

"That's funny," Joe said. "She's just told me it's McLintock."

63

"Well she would deny it, wouldn't she?" Brenda observed.

"So would they all," Joe replied. "I know who it is, and I'll tell you one thing. It isn't the Countess Lucescu."

He gazed around the room and spotted Melanie alone, by the windows. "You're gonna have to excuse me, too. Like Wilson, I must circulate."

Taking his drink, worming his way through the dancers, he slid himself alongside Melanie.

"Hello, Joe. I notice you've been talking to one or two of our cast. Enlightening?"

"Hmm, yes. But it only confirmed my opinions."

There was a light-hearted air of challenge in Melanie's reply. "All right, then, let's have them."

He took out his notebook and laid it on the table. "Read it," he suggested. "That way no one will overhear."

While Melanie read, Joe looked out over the dance floor. George and Owen appeared to be getting on well with the two women, other couples were jiggling around to The Spice Girls, and there was a general air of good feeling threading through the room. At the bar, the staff were rushed off their feet trying to cope with the crowd, the actors were mingling freely with the guests, and when he checked the Grimshaws' corner, he found Reggie and Wendy, now alone, enjoying a laugh with Emma Pemberley.

The balm worked its magic on Joe, too. He could not recall the last time he felt so relaxed.

"If I didn't know better, I'd swear you'd sneaked a look at our scripts."

Melanie's words snapped him out of his reverie. "What? Oh. You mean I got it right."

"Not one hundred percent," she confessed, "but then you couldn't. We're not finished yet, and there are things to happen that you can't know about... unless you really have looked at our scripts." She smiled to show she was only joking. "But, honestly, Joe, I never realised we were that transparent."

"Don't beat yourself up. You're not." He finished his lager. "I've been talking to a lot of people tonight, and amongst my members no one has it right. No one has noticed the things I did. That's not a reflection on them, or on your work. It's me. My brain is wired up differently. I see things other people don't, and those notes were what I noticed while the drama was going on. I have more to add, yet."

Melanie finished her glass of wine. "How many murders have you investigated and solved, Joe?"

"A fair few. I said earlier, in real life, the perpetrators are a good deal less devious than this." He patted the notebook. "Like your players, they try to hide their crimes, but it's much more difficult with the real thing. The police have a huge army of science to back them up. Did you know they can even get DNA from a burglar breathing on a window?"

"Really? But I thought you usually show the police up as bumbling idiots."

Joe laughed. "Nothing like it. I usually come in with a different train of thought to them. They'd get there eventually, I'm sure, but I just see it quicker and that's because I pay attention to the trivia." He picked up his glass. "Let me get you another drink. House red, is it?"

Joe passed the next two hours between Sheila and Brenda, and Melanie when she was free of discussions with her cast. Drink flowed freely in the room, the party warmed up until by 10:30, the dance floor was packed.

Joe spotted Reggie and Wendy Grimshaw leaving the bar, Reggie carrying a tray with a teapot, two cups, and other items. Wendy appeared to be hanging back. Joe waved to them. Wendy waved back but Reggie had already left the bar.

A short while later, with the time just turned eleven, Joe was sitting with Melanie when Gerry Carlin approached.

"Excuse me, old son, Melanie, Billy and I are calling it a night. Don't forget we have to be on the ball early in the morning before the motley come down to breakfast."

"I'll meet you in the dining room at seven thirty," Melanie promised.

Carlin bid them both a friendly goodnight and wandered off.

"The rock upon which our success is built," Melanie assured Joe.

"He has a thing for Wendy Grimshaw, doesn't he?"

She frowned. "I don't think so. I know he knew her years ago. They were in Rep together, I understand. And I've known him a long time. He's not the kind to play around, especially with a married woman."

Joe beamed. "Y'see. I can misread the signs."

Melanie's smile faded quickly. "Listen, Joe, I have a proposition for you. It might make a little money for you. If you're interested, that is."

"I'll always listen to ideas where there's a profit involved. As long as it doesn't cost me a fortune."

"It won't actually cost you anything," Melanie told him. She checked her watch. "Difficult to talk here with all this noise, and I have to be up in the morning. Please don't misunderstand what I'm going to say, but why don't you pick up your computer and come along to my room at midnight? I can show you what I have in mind."

Joe cast a furtive glance across the floor to Sheila and Brenda, both of whom were preparing to leave. "All right. I'll escort my friends back to their room, collect the computer and be with you in, say, half an hour. How's that?"

Chapter Five

Sheila was in some considerable discomfort, clutching at her right side. "Gallstones," she announced as they waited for the lift. "That damned fish."

"Not to mention the booze," Joe said as the lift arrived.

The doors opened and George Robson stepped out. "Hey up, you lot. Cracking barney on the first floor. Someone just hit someone else with a tin tray."

Joe frowned. "How do you know?"

"Heard it as I was passing, didn't I? Walked that lass back to her room, gave her a goodnight feel, and as I was coming back to the lift, I heard the woman clatter this bloke over the head with the tray. At least I think it was a woman hitting a bloke. Can't see it being t'other way round. Went with a real crack, and I could hear him moaning. Bet he'll have a hell of hangover in the morning." George's laughter subsided as he noticed Sheila's pain. "You all right, luv?"

"Gallstones," she repeated. "Painful."

"Had mine done yonks ago," George told her. "Keyhole surgery, best thing ever. No trouble since. You need anything? Ibuprofen, or owt?"

"No, thank you, George. I have painkillers in the room."

"Oh well. Take care. Night all."

Two minutes later, Joe, Sheila and Brenda stepped out of the lift onto the richly carpeted corridor of the fourth floor, and by then, Sheila was almost doubled up in pain.

Their faces lined with concern, they helped her to the room she shared with Brenda, where she lay on the bed, clutching at her right side.

"You sure you don't want anything?" Joe asked. "I can get the hotel to call for a doctor."

"No, Joe," she gasped. "I'll be all right. It will pass in a little while. It always does."

Joe turned to Brenda. "I'm right across the corridor. If she gets much worse, shout me."

"Don't worry, Joe. I'm sure she'll be all right."

He nodded, left the room and crossed to his own. Retrieving his netbook from the wardrobe, he sat at the escritoire, looking out over the twin towers of the cathedral while he rolled a cigarette. From there, he returned to the lobby and stepped out into the damp night air, where he found actor Billy Norman smoking a cigarette.

"Your mate Gerry said you were hitting the sack," Joe commented, lighting up.

"We were supposed to, but he's pulled some woman and he's, er, otherwise engaged." Billy grinned. "Lucky bugger. We have an understanding. If one of us scores the other takes the prop room." He held up a key.

"Prop room?"

"We're a small outfit, Joe. For a weekend do like this, we get to stay in the hotel at reduced rates, but we still have to pay for the meals and stuff. In order to keep costs down and make sure Markham Murder Mysteries can still pay us our wages, we have to share rooms, but we take an extra, single room for the props. Since Gerry looks after the props, it's handy if one of us, er, strikes it lucky. Naturally, none of the aforementioned applies to her ladyship."

"Melanie?"

Billy nodded. "She sleeps alone."

"I'm the same with the Sanford 3rd Age Club outings," Joe told him. "The rest share, I always take a room alone."

Billy crushed out his cigarette. "Never know when you'll get lucky, eh?"

"Something like that."

"I'm just nipping to the bar for a last snifter. See you tomorrow. Oh, and keep your eyes on the Countess Lucescu."

"I will," Joe said after his departing back.

He gave the actor another few minutes, then stubbed out his own cigarette, made his way back into the hotel and up to the first floor.

Emerging from the lift, padding along the corridor, a loud and familiar voice came to him through a partially open door.

"You'd do well to mind your own business, old lad, but I'll be charitable and put it down to drink. Take my advice and sleep it off. I'll talk to you in the morning."

Joe had no idea who Reggie Grimshaw was talking to, but it didn't take much to work it out. He could imagine young Robbie Kendrew's angry (and drunken) face challenging the old man.

Tempted though he was to stay behind and listen to the argument, he did not want to keep Melanie waiting. He knocked lightly on her door. She opened it, let him in, and closed it behind him.

"Bit of a row going on over there between Grimshaw and one of his team," Joe said, unpacking his netbook on the escritoire and plugging in the mains adaptor.

"I find him a very disagreeable man," Melanie declared. "Brash. You know."

"He's certainly pushy," Joe agreed, switching the machine on, "but I suppose in his field you have to be."

"Who was he arguing with?"

"Dunno," Joe replied. "I fancy it's that young Kendrew kid. He was having a moan to me earlier about Reggie."

Melanie had discarded the dark blue jacket of the business suit she had been wearing in the dining room and bar, and perched on the edge of her bed, in a skirt and a pale cream blouse which showed her flowery bra beneath.

"Let's forget about them, Joe, and talk about Markham

69

Murder Mysteries. As well as the proprietor, producer and director, I'm also the head writer. It's my job to come up with new scripts, new angles, which we can play to audiences like this weekend's. The whisper is that you write up your cases, as you call them, and they're on the shelves of your café for your customers to read."

"And they're very popular. In the Lazy Luncheonette, at least."

"How detailed are they, and could I read one?"

He grinned. "So that's why you wanted me to bring the computer." He turned to the screen and ran his finger across the mousepad, opening the documents folder. In turn he double clicked on a file and the word processing software sprang to life. "There you go. It's an account of our stay at the Beachside Hotel in Filey, during the summer."

"Detailed?" she asked.

"Only the names have been changed," he told her. "Including mine."

Melanie moved to the wardrobe and took out a laptop. "May I copy it and read it through over the weekend?"

Joe took a memory stick from the netbook case, and inserted into one of four USB slots. "Are you going to tell me what all this is about?"

"Simple enough" Melanie replied, switching on her machine. "I want to turn your cases into murder mystery weekends." She smiled. "And I'll pay you for each one you let us transcribe."

***

Ever the soul of discretion, Billy Norman pressed his ear to the room door, and from within he heard muttered sounds of lovemaking.

With a wry smile, he stepped next door, took out the key and unlocked it. Stepping inside, he grabbed the mannequin, already dressed in Colonel Haliwell's clothes, from the bed and tossed it into a corner.

"Sorry, Colonel, but I need my beauty sleep."

He threw off his jacket, sat on the edge of the bed and yanked his boots from his feet.

With one ear cocked to the sounds coming from next door, he smiled again, and spoke once more to the dummy. "Don't sound like Gerry's gonna get much kip, though"

***

With the script copied, Joe removed the memory stick, his wrinkled brow creasing further. "I'm not sure what the legal position is, Melanie. I mean, these are not novels, you know. These are real murders."

"Aren't novels real murders, too?" Melanie asked taking the memory stick from him. "Murder is murder, Joe, and all novelists base their tales on the real thing, but you've already changed the names of the participants. Besides, we could leave the legal intricacies to solicitors. As a bona fide drama company, we would need the business on a formal footing anyway. You know: have proper contracts drawn up."

With her laptop ready to begin work, Melanie slotted the memory stick into a USB port, and Joe watched her slender, deft fingers working on the mousepad and keyboard to copy it over.

"We're not a rich company, Joe. We play on the popularity of murder mystery weekends, and we do some stage work… where and when we can get it. We couldn't pay you a fortune. You'd be looking at hundreds rather than thousands of pounds."

Joe hedged. "That's all right. I'm not a writer. I'm a cook. A businessman. I run a trucker's joint in West Yorkshire."

"And this is a business proposition," she reiterated, her eyes on the laptop screen. "I'm not interested in the quality of the writing, Joe. I'm interested in the case, your deductive processes, the way you arrived at your conclusions. And, of course, the murder itself. Gerry and I will deal with the script."

The job completed, she removed the memory stick and handed it back. Switching the laptop off, she put it to one side to let it go through its shutdown routine.

"You're a businessman. I'm a businesswoman. This is business." She laughed. "God, why do I sound like a mafia hood when I say that?" She studied his worried face and sympathised. "What's the problem, Joe?"

"Is it legal?" He tucked the memory stick back into the netbook case and, following Melanie's lead, shut down his computer. "Like I say, these were real murders, not made up."

"If there's anything illegal, it's you writing them down in the first place," Melanie pointed out, "and you already know it's not illegal. You changed the names. You're not identifying anyone. Of course it's legal, Joe. You own the rights to these tales as you've written them. I'm simply asking that you grant Markham Murder Mysteries the right to adapt and perform them, and let me pay you for that right."

There was a brief hiatus while Joe packed away the netbook and Melanie put away her laptop. Joe's natural, Yorkshire caution ran riot through his head, looking for some loophole, some hint that Melanie was out to take him for a mug, or land him with the blame if it all went wrong.

"Let me think it over while you're reading about our adventures in Filey," he suggested.

"Of course," Melanie agreed. "There's not much we can do this weekend, anyway. I'm in the middle of a job, and you're enjoying the New Year."

He picked up his computer. "Right. We'll talk later."

Joe stood, ready to leave.

"Just a minute, Joe. There's something else."

"What?"

Melanie took the netbook from him, placed it on the escritoire, then slipped her arm around his neck and kissed him.

***

Almost two hours had passed since Joe bid them goodnight at the door, and still Sheila was doubled up in agony.

Brenda had knocked on his door and got no answer. She tried his mobile and it was switched off. She had asked reception to telephone both his and his mobile room and they couldn't get an answer, either. In desperation, she had reception call a local doctor who examined Sheila while Brenda stood by, acting as a veritable chaperone and a responsible friend.

Once through with his examination, Dr Chowdury had not hesitated to call an ambulance. "Your friend may be right, Mrs Jump. It may only be gallstones, but I don't think we should take chances. We'll get her down to A & E and let them take a proper look at her."

Fifteen minutes after that, Sheila was on a trolley, being wheeled through the hotel, and Brenda was at reception.

"Keep trying Joe Murray, and make sure he gets the message."

"As soon as we can find him, Mrs Jump," the night duty manager assured her.

Brenda turned to follow the ambulance attendants, and almost bumped into a wobbly, reeling Robbie Kendrew.

"Get out of the way, you drunken idiot," she snapped.

Still furious with Joe, she rushed out into the night and climbed into the back of the ambulance.

***

Joe stared up into the darkness, mixed sensations of

satisfaction and guilt coursing through him.

Passion had never played any part in his life other than with regard to the Lazy Luncheonette and the Sanford 3rd Age Club, but over the last hour he had been consumed by almost uncontrollable lust and he felt guilty.

He was not so vain as to imagine that Melanie found him irresistible. She was making an effort to secure the performance rights to his cases. On the other hand, she had given as good as she got, so she can't have been faking it all… could she?

In a lifetime of tunnel vision focussed on the Lazy Luncheonette, Joe freely admitted he was clueless when it came to women. He did not have George Robson's easy going charm. In general, he was clumsy and awkward, and successfully masked it with outspoken irritability. His libido, such as it was, had never troubled him when he was married, and during the ten years since his divorce, he managed to suppress it in work.

And yet, here he was, sharing a bed with an attractive and demanding woman… an attractive, demanding and *sleeping* woman. Was that normal? Was it supposed to happen?

Joe asked no further questions of himself. He had no answers, and anyway, he was tired. His eyelids drooped, he yawned one more time, and fell into an untroubled sleep.

***

"I don't know where the hell he got to but when I've finished with him, he'll be singing soprano."

In deference to the taxi driver, Brenda had kept her voice low. Sheila, glad to be out of the hospital and no longer in pain, did likewise.

"He's not our servant, Brenda. He does have his own life to lead."

"His last words to me were, 'If she gets much worse, shout

me'." Brenda growled. "I shouted him and he wasn't there. I'll bet he went back down to the bar with that Melanie Markham and then out clubbing with George Robson and Owen Frickley."

Sheila patted Brenda's hand. "You were there, dear. And I'm all right now." She glanced at her watch, angling her wrist so she could see it in the flickering illumination of passing street lights. "A quarter to four. We won't get much sleep before breakfast."

"We can always catch up later." Brenda grinned savagely. "Then we can take Joe and his credit card shopping. Make him pay for ducking out on us like that."

***

With the time just gone seven, Billy tapped on the door. When he got no answer, he pressed his ear to it. Silence.

He turned his key softly in the lock and stepped in. Even in the dim light he could make out the shape of Gerry and the woman in bed together. He cursed under his breath, tiptoed across the room and nudged his pal.

"Huh? What?"

Billy put a finger to his lips. "Don't disturb your lady love, Gerry. It's turned seven, and I need to wash and shave before we're on."

Gerry glanced sideways at his bedmate, then grinned up at Billy. "Christ, what a night."

"Yeah, well you'd better get ready for the day..." Billy trailed off on seeing the woman's face. "You lucky old bugger. Wendy Grimshaw? Won't her old man notice she's missing?"

Gerry shrugged. "That's her problem... and his. Not mine."

***

Checking both ways along the corridor, Joe bid a

75

whispered, "See you later" to Melanie, and stepped out into the corridor. He had gone barely three paces towards the lift, when a familiar voice rang in his ear.

"Hello, hello, hello. What's all this here, then?"

Joe called the lift and smiled at Gerry Carlin and Billy Norman, making their way along the landing. Gerry was dressed in a shabby, double-breasted suit and faded white shirt, with a ragged, dark red tie fastened at the collar. He also sported a floppy trilby hat on his head and a theatrical scrub moustache above his upper lip. Billy wore the same dinner suit he had the previous evening, and was carrying a mannequin under his arm which was clad in the colonel's dinner jacket.

"How you doing?" Joe asked.

"We're fine, old son," Gerry said. "Inspector Jonathan O'Keefe at your service. And what have you been up to? Been entertaining the boss, have you?"

Joe felt his cheeks colouring. "I, er, well, er, you know. We had business matters to discus." *When in doubt, go on the attack.* The thought ran through Joe's head. It was a mantra by which he had lived most of his life. "I wouldn't fancy your chances of playing me in your new productions."

The lift arrived and the doors soughed open.

"Ah," said Gerry as they stepped in, "the boss has been negotiating with the famous detective. Tell me something, Joe, if I get the part of you, do I get to do a lot of bed-hopping?"

"Yes," Joe said, pressing the button for the fourth floor. "You get to hop out of bed at half past five every morning to start cooking hundreds of breakfasts for hungry truckers."

"Er, we were going down, Joe," said Billy.

"And you can, Billy. After I've gone up."

A few minutes later, certain that he had left the two actors pondering his irritation, he stepped into his room, put the computer away in his small suitcase, threw off his clothing and stepped into the shower.

The uncertainty of 2 a.m. had left him, and as he shaved,

76

he asked his reflection what was so appealing about his middle-aged wrinkled features. Nothing, was the conclusion he came to. For every Melanie Markham there was a Tanya Richmond or Sarah Pringle; women who found him too blunt to be of interest or women who inveigled themselves into his affections because they wanted something. Tanya Richmond made it plain that she didn't like him, Sarah Pringle had wanted to keep up with his investigation, whereas Melanie Markham had wanted to persuade him that granting her performing rights was the right move. The latter, he decided, was infinitely preferable, but why was he still questioning it?

Brenda, the epitome of the free-living merry widow, would have no trouble. Never as loose as some claimed her to be, Brenda nevertheless shared beds with a number of men, and had no qualms about it.

"You're a long time dead," she could often be heard to say.

And she didn't care whether the men found her attractive or not. If their only interest was sex, Brenda had no problem since it was her only interest in them.

With a day's trail round Lincoln ahead of him, comfort was the priority. Joe put on a pair of denims and a short sleeved shirt, slipped on his quilted gilet, and left his overcoat ready on the wardrobe door. He would come back to the room for it after breakfast and the next act of Haliwell's Heroes.

Not on top of the world, but better than halfway up, he stepped out of his room and locked the door.

"And where the hell were you in the early hours?"

Brenda's angry voice unpacked the deeper Joe, the one always ready to rise to an argument. "What?"

Locking the door of their room, Sheila ranged herself alongside Brenda. Both women were in their shopping clothes; dark trousers, warm jumpers, sensible, flat shoes, lethal handbags hanging from their forearms.

Dropping his key into the pockets of his gilet, Joe asked. "What are you on about?"

"Sheila was rushed to hospital at one o'clock this morning."

He looked to Sheila who nodded. "It's true, Joe."

"What... but... why the hell didn't you call me?"

"We did," Brenda assured him. "Several times, but you weren't answering your phone."

Because it was switched off. The thought bounced into Joe's mind. He had not wanted to be disturbed while he was with Melanie.

"Well, at least you're all right."

"How would you know?" Brenda jabbed at the lift button.

"They let you out." Joe answered Sheila rather than Brenda.

"Yes, and a fat lot of use you were."

Joe was stung into retaliation. "I'm not your father, nor your husband. Neither of you. I do have a life away from you both, you know." Pulling in a shaky breath, he concentrated on Sheila. "Did they find out what it was?"

"It was as I said, Joe," Sheila reported. "Gallstones. Probably something I ate or drank last night. They gave me some stronger painkillers, and I'm fine now, but they've advised me to see my doctor when I get home. My gall bladder needs cutting out. Like George told us."

They stepped into the lift.

"So where did you get to?" Brenda demanded. "And don't tell me you were elbow bending in the bar. I checked, and you weren't. I suppose you were out boozing with George and Owen."

"Brenda, it's none of our business where Joe got to."

"Correct," Joe said. "It is none of your business, but as it happens, it was business. If I'd known Sheila was that bad, I would have called it off and been with you, but I didn't know."

"Business?" Brenda asked as if she had not heard the rest of Joe's words. "The only business I understand at one o'clock in the morning is usually done under the duvet."

Joe glared. "Brenda, keep your nose out."

Settling into the dining room a few minutes later, they

found the cast of Haliwell's Heroes at their joint tables, talking between themselves. Gerry Carlin was missing, his place taken by the mannequin, but the young woman playing the colonel's biographer was also absent.

Brenda was still grumbling over Joe's absence during the night when the waitress served them with cereal, followed by a full English breakfast, which Joe ate with gusto while Sheila only picked at hers.

Casting an eye around the dining room Joe marked the Grimshaws down as absent, and some of his crew, particularly Robbie, looked badly hungover.

"He was well tanked up this at one o'clock morning when I saw him in reception," Brenda said, "as I was taking Sheila to the hospital."

"Will you for God's sake shut up about that?" Joe grumbled.

"To be frank, I wish you'd forget it, too, Brenda," Sheila said.

"Not until I know what he was up to that was so important he could forget his best friends."

At that moment, Melanie entered the dining room, glanced around, spotted him and made her way across. "I've read about half of that, Joe, and I think we can do business. Can I catch up with you later?"

"What? Oh, sure. We'll be sight-seeing round Lincoln's shops, but I reckon we'll be back mid-afternoon."

Melanie left with a smile and Joe found Brenda's face split into a broad grin.

"So that's where you were. You randy old sod."

"I told you. I was discussing a business proposition."

"What? She charges?" Brenda laughed. "Game old bird, isn't she? She won't get many punters at her time of life."

Brenda, he realised, would not shut up until she knew exactly what the business was. Helping himself from the toast rack, he explained the situation to her. "It means," he concluded, "that I might actually make a few quid from all the work I've done helping to wall up killers."

"Course it does, Joe, and I understand why you were missing. I take it all back. I'd go through the roof if someone disturbed me on the legover just because a friend was taken ill."

Joe groaned and buttered another slice of toast.

On some unseen cue, Melanie appeared at the dining room entrance with her microphone.

"Good morning, ladies and gentlemen," she began. "I hope you had a great party last night, and I hope our little drama has got you thinking. We're about to pick up now where we left off after dinner yesterday. After this act, the cast will be about the hotel all day so you can question them. I'm going to drift into the background now, and leave it up to the police officer in charge."

To a polite round of applause, Melanie moved to the camera, the lights came on and Gerry entered.

***

"I am Inspector Jonathan O'Keefe of Scotland Yard," the newcomer announced. "I gave instructions over the telephone that no one was to leave the room. I was also told that there were nine people present at the dinner and yet, including the dead man, I see only eight of you. Who is missing?"

"Kerry," said Wilson. "Kerry Dolman. She's the colonel's biographer. She felt unwell after seeing him dead. My wife gave her a sedative and we put her to bed."

"Probably a wise move, sir. And you are?"

"Captain Christopher Wilson. I'm a business associate and an old army chum of the colonel's. This is my wife, Valerie. She's a doctor."

"And you pronounced the colonel dead, madam?" asked O'Keefe.

Valerie nodded. "I checked his glass. Prussic acid, I think, but your forensic people will confirm it."

"Of course," said O'Keefe. "Now, my information is there were one or two disagreements over dinner. Is that correct?"

"Skirmishes," Crenshaw declared. "The usual sort of arguments one finds at a party of this nature."

"Especially," said McLintock, "when one guest is apt to dismiss the medical infirmities of another."

"Now look here, McLintock…"

"All right, gentlemen," O'Keefe interrupted. "We're here to ascertain the circumstances of Colonel Haliwell's death, not pick up our personal vendettas."

"We were here to celebrate his birthday, but Crenshaw here, forgot about that," McLintock argued.

"And who are you, sir?" O'Keefe demanded.

"McLintock. Patrick McLintock. I'm a stockbroker. I handle most of the colonel's investments." He glowered at Crenshaw while gesturing at Theresa. "I was also engaged to his daughter until Crenshaw showed up."

"And you broke the engagement off, did you, miss?" O'Keefe asked.

She looked from Crenshaw to McLintock and back, and then back to the inspector. "I, er, yes. I'm afraid I did."

"Tell the inspector the truth, Theresa," McLintock insisted. "You broke it off because your father ordered you to." He, too, addressed O'Keefe. "The old man preferred his daughter to marry a military man. Someone he could push around."

"I resent that," snapped Crenshaw.

"It's the truth," McLintock retorted. "He treated you like a bloody batman, and that's just what he wanted in his daughter's husband. A damned ADC."

"All right, all right, that's enough." O'Keefe broke into the argument again. "You were not in the army, Mr McLintock?"

"Medically exempt," the stockbroker replied. "I have a minor heart condition."

81

O'Keefe turned his attention to the countess and consulted his notes. "And you, madam. Countess Zara Lucescu. A Romanian refuge."

"Zat iss correct. Inspector, I would prefer it that I say nothink here, but zat I speak with you alone."

"You have something to hide?" Sadie Haliwell asked.

"I haff nothink to hide, Mrs Haliwell, but there is informations vitch I will discuss only with der inspector."

"Very well, madam. So that only leaves Ms Dolman. Would someone care to go to her room and bring her?"

McLintock stood up. "I'll get her." He scowled at Crenshaw. "I need the fresh air."

He left the room and O'Keefe busied himself studying the layout of the table.

"Are you all where you were during dinner?" he asked.

"Yes," Wilson replied. "The empty chair between the colonel and me was Miss Dolman's."

"I have to ponder, you see, who could have dropped cyanide into the colonel's glass. It would have to be someone sitting close to him."

"Not necessarily, Inspector," Crenshaw disagreed. "You see, the colonel pulled the ashtray very close to himself."

"He always was a selfish old bugger," Sadie pointed out.

"Most of us were smoking," Crenshaw went on, "and we had to lean across to use the ashtray."

"That's right," Wilson agreed. "And the colonel's glass was close to the ashtray."

"In that case," O'Keefe said, "it could be any of you, so we need to establish who had the greatest motive for killing the colonel."

Crenshaw cast a sour eye on McLintock's empty seat. "If you want my opinion, you don't need to look far."

"But your opinion is coloured, isn't it, dollink?" Zara suggested. "You hate Mr McLintock."

"I don't particularly like you, Countess, but I'm not

82

accusing you."

"Vy?" screamed Zara. "Vot haff I done to you?"

"You were a Nazi sympathiser. Captain Wilson and I spent six years fighting your sort."

"Iss not true. I voss…"

The door burst open, interrupting Zara, and McLintock hurried in.

"Kerry," he gasped almost out of breath. "She's dead. Shot in the head."

***

The lights dimmed and the cast received a warm round of applause before Melanie took centre stage again.

"Thank you ladies and gentlemen. I trust we're engaging and frustrating your little grey cells. The next act will be performed at one thirty, during lunch, but for those of you who don't come back to the hotel, like all our scenes, it will be recorded and you'll be able to watch a rerun of it on video before the third and final act of the day. In the meantime, as I said earlier…"

Melanie trailed off and looked behind her.

From the lobby came the sound of running feet. The door crashed open and Wendy Grimshaw burst into the room. Her face was white with shock, there were tear streaks on her cheeks and she was shaking.

Melanie looked perplexed and all her cast were similarly intrigued. Joe realised at once that this was not part of the show.

"Reggie," Wendy cried. "Reggie is dead. Someone shot him."

Chapter Six

The room sat in sudden, stunned silence. Joe guessed that some of the guests were wondering if this was part of the entertainment, but even if he had thought so, the shocked face of Melanie would have told him different.

Wendy was on her knees weeping. Joe got hurriedly to his feet. "Brenda, Sheila, see to her." He rounded on the Kendrews. "What room were they in?"

"One, ... er one-oh-four."

"I'll go check it out," he said to Sheila and Brenda as they helped Wendy up and to their table.

A burst of conversation spread rapidly through the room. Stirring from her shock, Melanie asked, "Shouldn't we call the police?"

"I'll check it out first and let the management bell them." Joe scanned the room and raised his voice above the chatter. "Listen to me, everyone. It's important that you stay put for the time being, until we've checked this out."

"Who gave you the authority...?" Robbie Kendrew began, only to be cut off by Brenda.

"Just listen to him, boy. He knows his stuff."

"Thanks, Brenda." Joe smiled. "If you all stay here, I'll see what I can find out." He hurried from the dining room and out into reception where he collared Cliff Denshaw and quickly explained the situation.

"Hadn't we better call the police?" The manager's face worked worriedly as he unconsciously echoed Melanie.

"And have them turn up to find that she's drunk and

Reggie is enjoying a cup of tea in bed?"

Denshaw blanched.

"Grab your key, son, and let me into that room."

The manager called on one of his staff to man the desk, then grabbed a key from the rack and followed Joe.

When they arrived at the room, Denshaw's hands were trembling so badly, he could hardly get the key into the lock. Eventually Joe took over, turned the lock, pushed the door open and stepped in, automatically reaching for the light switch.

His legs, too, were shaking. He reminded himself sternly of the times he had been in this position before. He had come across the body of Edgar Prudhoe just moments after he was killed, and he had seen the man's wife dead the morning after. He had been shown photographs of Jennifer Hardy after her head was caved in and Ursula Kenney after she had been hanged. There was nothing to fear in this room.

He did not need the lights. The curtains were open and in the dull light of a foggy morning, the dead man stared up at the ceiling as if hypnotised.

Reggie Grimshaw lay where he had died, in bed, a neat hole in the side of his head, a large blood stain spread across the pillow. He was wearing pyjamas and Joe noticed that the right hand side of the bed, next to Reggie, was undisturbed.

Denshaw turned away unable to look.

"Not pretty," Joe said. "Murder never is."

Gingerly, he pressed his finger to the neck. No pulse, the skin cold.

On the cabinet alongside him were the teapot, an empty cup and a small, metal container holding individual portions of milk and sachets of sugar.

"Looks as if he'd had his bedtime cup of tea and then gone to sleep," Joe said. "The killer probably woke him."

Denshaw looked around. "I'll check the bathroom, see if the other tea things are in there."

"No. Don't touch anything," Joe barked. "The cops will want everything as it is. Undisturbed." He fished into his pocket for his mobile. "Come on. There's nothing we can do here. I'll call the law from outside."

They stepped out onto the first floor landing, Denshaw leaning back against the wall, visibly shaken.

"Lock the door," Joe ordered. He dialled 999 and pressed the mobile to his ear. "Police," he barked when the operator answered. He waited again, and smiled in what he hoped was a reassuring manner at Denshaw. "You'll be all right, son. When we get back downstairs, step outside and get yourself a breath of fresh air." The phone came alive again. "My name's Joe Murray. I'm a guest at the Twin Spires Hotel, Lincoln, and I want to report a suspicious death." He paused to listen for a moment. "We have a man in room 104, who has been shot in the head." He paused again. "Of course he'd dead, you idiot. Here. Hang on. I'll put the hotel manager on."

He passed the phone to Denshaw.

"Hello? This is Clifford Denshaw, duty manager at the Twin Spires." The manager's voice trembled as he spoke. "I'm afraid Mr Murray is telling exactly what we have just found in room 104." Now he paused. "Yes. Yes, we've locked the room and most of the guests are in the dining room, at breakfast." Another pause. "Very good. We'll wait downstairs with them."

He killed the connection and handed the phone back to Joe.

"They say we have to keep everyone in the dining room until they get here."

"Standard procedure," Joe grunted as he led the way along the corridor to the lift. "There's a lot about this that doesn't make sense."

"There's a lot about it that's scary," Denshaw muttered as they entered the lift.

"You know a woman called Yvonne Naylor?" Joe asked pressing the button for the ground floor.

"I know of her, certainly. She was a section manager in reservations for some years."

"She was general manager at the Palmer when we were there at Halloween. She was a lot tougher than you when we found a dead MP and his wife there."

"I'm responsible for how I behave, Mr Murray, not other people, and I find it difficult to believe that..." he trailed off and for a moment Joe thought he would burst into tears.

"Yeah, yeah. All right."

They stepped out of the lift, Denshaw heading for reception, Joe moving back into the dining room where he found the place a sea of murmured conversation.

"Listen up everyone. Can I have your attention please?" he called out.

The noise shrank and silence fell.

"We have a dead man in room 104. The police have been called and they're on their way here as I speak. They've asked that we all stay here until they arrive."

The room became a sea of conversation again, and Joe had to raise his voice to be heard. "I would suggest that you all make a note of our movements between ten thirty last night and now. It's the kind of thing that the police will want and it may just help them piece together what happened."

"At least you and I don't have any trouble accounting for ourselves," Melanie whispered to him.

"Depends how long he's been dead," Joe said, and then grinned at her. "It's all right. He looks like he was killed late last night." He chewed his lip. "There's some stuff that doesn't make sense."

"The famous Joe Murray mind at work," Melanie commented. "Do I get to see you solve the crime?"

Joe shrugged. "The cops may or may not ask me to help. I'll carry on shoving my oar in, whether they like it or not, and that starts right now." He looked at the forlorn figure of Wendy Grimshaw. "But she's in no state to talk. Not yet." His eyes travelled beyond Sheila, Brenda and Wendy, settling on Robbie Kendrew. "And there's a boy who has some explaining to do."

Billy Norman left the cast's table and confronted Joe. "Can we not even step outside for a smoke?"

"Not up to me to stop you, Billy, and I could do with a fix, myself. It just complicates matters when the cops get here." Joe pondered the matter. "I suppose if we go outside together, we can vouch for each other. Come on."

After informing Sheila and Brenda, he accompanied Billy from the dining room, through the lobby and out into the murky morning, where Billy offered a cigarette. Joe shook his head and took a little time rolling one.

"Bit of a bummer, this," Billy commented as he lit up.

Joe noticed that the actor's hands shook as he fumbled with the lighter. He was relieved to find that his own nerves were quite steady.

"I don't suppose Reggie Grimshaw is having much of a ball, either."

"What? Oh. Sorry. Yes, I see what you mean." Billy blew out a large cloud of smoke. "I suppose it's the end of the Murder Mystery Weekend."

"Not necessarily. We have a large number of people here in the hotel, and the police are likely to restrict our movements. Best way to do that is to keep them entertained." Joe nodded at the road and the flash of blue lights making their way through the early Saturday traffic. "Cops are here now. Listen, Billy, let me ask you where you were last night, and whether anyone can vouch for you."

"Well, I was here, with you, smoking until I went back to the bar. I had a last drink. That takes me to maybe a quarter past midnight, and then I went back to our room. Gerry and his girlfriend were both still at it when I got there, so I spent the night in the prop room next door." He smiled thinly. "I went back to our room first thing, and they were still sleeping it off. He's a randy old sod, that Gerry."

Joe filed the information in his mind. "Reggie was still alive when I joined Melanie," Joe said. "I heard him playing hell with someone. Robbie Kendrew, I think. That was about midnight-ish."

Two patrol cars and an unmarked saloon swept into the drive and came to a crunching halt on the gravel. Uniformed officers climbed out and began to put on forensic overalls. A young, blonde-haired woman got out of the saloon, and drew her winter coat closer about herself as she hurried to the entrance.

"You the detective in charge?" Joe asked as she made to pass him.

"I'm Detective Sergeant Idleman," she announced. "Who are you?"

"Joe Murray. I called you."

Puzzlement struck across her young features. "You work here?"

"No. I'm a guest. The manager wasn't feeling too well when we checked the body."

There was no mistaking the contempt in the detective's pretty face. "Whereas you're made of sterner stuff?"

"I've been through this before," Joe assured her.

"You're a police officer?"

Her attitude got to him. "No, I'm not and I never have been, but I will tell you this, lady. I'll get to the answer before you." Joe took a deep drag on his cigarette. "The dead man is called Reggie Grimshaw, and he's in room 104. Cliff Denshaw, the manager, will give you the key. You'll find him on reception. That's the large flat thing on your left as you go in. Looks like a shop counter."

With a final curl of her lip, Detective Sergeant Idleman carried on into the hotel, while Joe and Billy watched the uniformed officers gathering their equipment alongside the vehicles.

"You're taking a risk aren't you, Joe?" Billy asked. "Chewing her out like that?"

"She was the one taking the risk… with my temper on a chilly Saturday morning." Joe sucked on his cigarette, realised it had gone out, and relit it. Dropping his Zippo lighter back into the pockets of his gilet, he went on, "Listen, Billy, you can give Gerry and his girlfriend an alibi, but can they give you one?"

"Shouldn't think so. I didn't go into our room last night. They were, er, at it. You know. And they were both spark out when I went in this morning."

"Why did you go in?"

Billy ran a hand under his chin. "Shower and shave. I had to wake Gerry up. He can sleep for England when he's had a few snifters and his legover, can our Gerry. We were down for an early breakfast. But you know that, don't you? You saw us."

"And the girlfriend?" Joe asked.

"What about her?"

"Who was she?"

When Billy did not answer, Joe pressed him.

"Come on. The cops will ask you the same question."

"Sorry, Joe, no can do."

"She wasn't a regular girlfriend, or you'd have no problem telling me."

"No," Billy admitted. "I'm practically sure Gerry doesn't have a regular girlfriend."

"So who was she?"

Billy checked his shoes, pulled out another cigarette and lit it, then checked his shoes again, before looking out into the mist as if he were seeking the spires of Lincoln cathedral.

"Come on, Billy. The police will want to know."

"It's not really my place to say, Joe. It's up to Gerry to volunteer the information."

"It's up to you to help the cops as much as you can," Joe insisted. "Now who was she?"

Billy took another drag on his cigarette, blew out the smoke, then filled his lungs with damp air. When he finally spoke, it was with an air of enforced resignation.

"Wendy Grimshaw."

***

Arriving back in the dining room where Gerry Carlin kept the audience entertained with a stand up routine of monologues and one-liners, Joe found Wendy sat between Sheila and Brenda, her eyes unfocussed, staring into space.

"No joy?" he asked.

Sheila shook her head. "She's in shock. Was it bad?"

"Murder is never pleasant, is it?" Joe clucked irritably. "I need to speak to her, too." He glanced at Gerry raising thin laughter amongst the crowd. "Either her or him."

Something about his words or the way he spoke them seemed to telegraph the situation to Brenda. "They were together last night?"

Joe nodded. "That's one of the things I found odd. I heard Grimshaw tearing a strip off young Kendrew – I think – at midnight. It didn't occur to me at the time, but would he have permitted such an argument if his wife was there? Well, maybe, given that he had a big mouth. But, if he was shot during the night, how come she didn't wake up and raise the alarm then? It's not the kind of thing you'd sleep through, is it? Just now, Billy told me she spent the night with Carlin, in the room he shared with Billy."

Brenda tutted. "Bit brazen with another man in the room."

"Billy was next door in the prop room." Joe replied and went on to explain the arrangement as Billy had described it to him.

"According to Billy, they were still out for the count this morning."

Sheila clutched Wendy's hand tightly. "Poor woman. And

91

then to go back to the room this morning and find..." she trailed off, not wanting to put it into words. "What's the situation now, Joe?"

"Police have just arrived. Officious looking woman. A detective sergeant. I thought they always put an inspector on a job like this."

"She'll be the advanced guard," Sheila said. "Get the job going. The inspector will probably be along shortly."

"What are our chances of getting out today?" Brenda asked.

"They'll need statements, I should imagine," Sheila replied. "It depends how long that takes."

Melanie crept across the floor and crouched at Joe's side. "May I ask, will the police let us carry on?"

"Billy asked me that," Joe told her, "and I see no reason why not. But these people are going to be held in this room for a few hours. It may be an idea to bring your schedule forward."

Her brow creased. "To do that, I need to make some, er, exterior arrangements. Do you think they'll let us out into the grounds?"

He shook his head. "I doubt it. At least, not yet. Not until they've searched the area."

The door opened and a large, square-shouldered man stepped in.

He had a brief word with Gerry, who stopped his impromptu floor show and backed off, then the big man faced the room.

Somewhere in his forties, his straw hair combed neatly into place, his suit bagged on him as if he had recently lost weight. His fierce eyes stared under near-invisible brows and when he spoke, his voice carried the stentorian bellow of the parade ground.

"Ladies and gentlemen, your attention please." He waited for quiet. "I am Detective Chief Inspector Philip Grant. As you are aware, we have a suspicious death on our hands, and anyone of you may be a material witness. For that reason, I need statements from you all. I have a team of officers to do the job, and they'll get through it as quickly as they can. For the moment, however, I need you all to stay on the ground floor, in this vicinity. If you need to smoke or you need to visit the toilets, check with my officers first but please, do not return to your rooms."

Towards the back of the room, Les Tanner stood. "Excuse me, Chief Inspector, but my good lady, here, is diabetic. What do we do if she needs her medication?"

"Under those circumstances, sir, obviously you would be permitted to go to the room, but you would have to be accompanied by one of my officers."

"Chief Inspector," Melanie called out. When she had his attention, she went on, "I'm Melanie Markham, the director of this weekend's entertainment, and I need to speak with you fairly urgently on where we go from here." She waved regally at the room. "These people have paid a lot of money…"

"If you'll forgive me, madam, I have more important matters to attend to right now, but once I have things organised, I'll speak to you. Give me, say, half an hour."

Melanie nodded.

"I'd like to speak to Mr Joe Murray, please," Grant said.

Joe stood up. "I'm Joe Murray."

"Would you come with me, sir?"

For all the civility of his tone, there was no doubt that the request was an instruction, and Grant's use of the word 'sir' in no way indicated any subservience to Joe.

Grant led Joe next door to the Scampton Room, where uniformed officers were already arranging seating for interviews and stacking statement forms on the tables. Detective Sergeant Idleman was seated to the right, just inside the door. Grant took a seat next to her, and invited Joe to take the chair opposite them.

"It's not often we get a lucky break on this kind of crime,"

Grant said, "but when I heard your name, I almost called in at my local church to offer a prayer of thanksgiving."

Perplexed, wondering whether he was being complimented or accused, Joe shrugged.

"You reputation precedes you, Mr Murray, or may I call you Joe?"

"Please do," Joe invited.

"My name's Phil. You've already met Detective Sergeant Idleman, I believe."

Joe scowled. "We exchanged pleasantries at the main entrance."

"Good," said Grant, but the look on Idleman's face indicated that she thought it was anything but good. "You're well known to the police in Yorkshire and Lincolnshire, Joe, and Frank Hoad, in Chester, spoke very highly of you. I'm aware that not much gets by you. I have to say, I welcome your thoughts, your observations, but please bear in mind this is a police matter."

"Obviously," Joe agreed.

"Sergeant Idleman has already spoken to Mr Denshaw, the duty manager, and he tells us that you and he were first on the scene. Can you give us your account of how that came about?"

Over a cup of tea, Joe gave them a detailed résumé of what had happened, pausing occasionally to answer Sergeant Idleman's questions as she sought to clarify one matter or another. When he had finished, Grant studied his sergeant's notes.

"So it was Mrs Grimshaw who found the body and raised the alarm."

"Yes," Joe agreed, "but you won't get much out of her. She's with my friends in the dining room and she's totally out of it." He toyed with his teacup. "Look, Phil, I don't wanna lead your investigation, but there are some things you really need to know."

"Go on?" the chief inspector invited.

"First, I know that Reggie was alive at midnight. I passed his room about then, and I heard him arguing with someone."

"Someone? You don't know who?"

As he answered, Joe noted that Sergeant Idleman was consulting a list printed on several sheets, all stapled together.

"No. The door was open. I only heard Reggie's voice"

"And you're sure it was him?" Grant asked.

The sergeant now ran her finger along one line of the list, then flipped back several pages.

"I'd recognise that voice anywhere," Joe replied. "I only met the guy yesterday, but there was no mistaking him. Brash, noisy. You know."

"Mr Murray," Sergeant Idleman interjected, holding up her stapled documents. "This is a list of the guests and their room numbers. You are in room 404. May I ask what you were doing wandering past room 104 at midnight?"

"I had a business meeting with Ms Markham, the lady who runs Markham Murder Mysteries."

"A business meeting? With a woman? At midnight? On a Friday?" Idleman's staccato series of questions spelled out her increasing disbelief.

"That's correct. As far as I'm aware, it's not illegal and we are both over twenty-one." Having made his position clear, Joe turned his attention back to Grant. "So I know Grimshaw was still alive just after midnight. But just before I joined Ms Markham, I was having a smoke at the main entrance with Billy Norman, one of the actors. He told me his roommate, Gerry Carlin, the clown who was putting on the improvised show when you came in the dining room, had scored and was with the woman in their room. That woman was Wendy Grimshaw."

Idleman's lip curled. "Scored?"

Joe shrugged. "Scored, trapped off, got his legover, fixed up an assignation. I don't care how you write it down, as long as you know what I mean."

Again he concentrated on the senior officer who appeared to find the exchanges between Joe and Idleman amusing.

"Billy also told me, just before you people arrived, that Gerry and Wendy were still snoring their heads off when he went back to their room at seven this morning for a shower and shave."

"So Mrs Grimshaw spent the whole night there," Grant murmured. "That explains why she didn't raise the alarm until this morning. You seem pretty sure of the times, Joe."

"To within five minutes, yes," Joe said, and went on to explain how Sheila had been taken ill the night before and how he had emerged from Melanie's room and met Gerry and Billy as they left theirs earlier in the morning. "So, you see, I can be reasonably confident of the times."

Grant considered the information for several moments, during which the first of the guests were brought in to give statements. Amongst the first dozen, Joe noticed Alec and Julia Staines, Les Tanner and Sylvia Goodson, and he would bet a week's takings that Tanner had badgered the police into bringing them in early. He could imagine the captain playing on Sylvia's diabetes and lactose intolerance. To Joe's way of thinking, both Sylvia's problems were more psychosomatic than physical, but even he had made use of them in the past.

"The doctor hasn't given us a time of death, yet," Grant said, "but we can assume, then, that it was sometime between, let's say, half past midnight and nine this morning, which was several minutes before Mrs Grimshaw arrived in the dining room. It also explains why the right side of the bed was undisturbed. Grimshaw had slept alone all night."

Joe nodded. "I also thought it might explain why the curtains were open. I figured Wendy may have come back and opened them before realising that Reggie wasn't asleep, but dead."

"Possibly," Grant agreed, "but I don't think that's particularly important." He rubbed a huge hand over his chin as if checking for stubble. "It would be interesting to know who Grimshaw was arguing with last night."

"Well, again, I don't wanna lead you astray, but I talked to one or two of his people yesterday, and not everything in the Grimshaw Kitchens' garden was as rosy as Reggie made out. One of his people, a man named Robbie Kendrew, was telling me some tale about Reggie and a woman named Naomi Barton. She and Kendrew are rivals for the top job when Reggie retires..." Joe caught himself with a sheepish grin. "When Reggie would have retired. Kendrew seems to think Naomi had the edge because she was doing the business with Reggie."

Idleman's lip curled again. "Doing the business with him?"

"What is it with you, Sergeant?" Joe demanded. "Were you trained at the school of politically correct terminology? Would you rather I'd said fornicating? Or sha..."

"No." She cut him off.

"I was going to say sharing a bed," Joe told her.

"Involved in an affair would suffice," Idleman retorted.

"I come from Sanford, not Oxford. We don't have affairs in Sanford; we do the business." Still irritated, Joe turned to Grant once more. "I'm not saying Kendrew killed Grimshaw, but I distinctly heard Grimshaw refer to whoever he was arguing with as 'old lad'. That's pure Yorkshire and it tells me he was obviously talking to a man. Maybe Kendrew got mad and shot him. I don't know. But there are other possibilities aren't there? Maybe after arguing with Kendrew, Reggie called Naomi and told her she wouldn't get the job. So maybe she killed him. Maybe it was another member of his party. Kendrew's wife didn't like Reggie. I heard her say so yesterday afternoon."

"I take your point, Joe," Grant agreed. "The only person we can properly eliminate is Grimshaw's wife."

"Assuming she really was with Gerry all night, and Billy wasn't lying about it."

"Why would he lie?" Idleman asked.

Joe shrugged. "He and Gerry are old pals. Maybe he was giving them a cover story. I don't know why he would lie, but human nature makes us all liars sometimes."

The sergeant put down her pen. "You do realise that applies to you, too, Mr Murray. We have only your word that you spent the night with Ms Markham, and even if she backs up your story, it may be that you both colluded on it."

"True enough," Joe agreed, "but hell, I'm used to being a suspect."

Idleman's eyes almost popped. "You are?"

Joe nodded. "People have been accusing me of putting dog meat in my steak and kidney pies for years."

Chapter Seven

When Joe left the Scampton Room, it was with Sergeant Idleman alongside him, going to the dining room to collect Wendy Grimshaw for questioning.

"It's not compulsory to dislike me you know," Joe told Idleman as they left the Scampton Room.

"I don't dislike you. I'm quite ambivalent towards you."

It was obvious to Joe that she was uncertain of the extent of his vocabulary, for she immediately translated.

"I don't have any feelings towards you one way or the other. It's just that I believe there are certain matters which are not the province of the general public."

"Like investigating a murder?"

"Correct."

Joe held the dining room door open for her and she passed in.

Following her, he said, "There are advantages to being an ordinary citizen. I can ask questions you can't. I don't have a set of procedures to follow."

"You can also get your head bashed in, Mr Murray, and even I wouldn't like to see that happen."

"I have a niece who's the same rank as you," Joe said. "Detective Sergeant Gemma Craddock of Sanford CID. She thinks I'm a pain in the backside, too, but it doesn't stop her coming for advice when she's stuck."

"I'll bear it in mind."

Wendy Grimshaw was a little more responsive, willing to speak and answer questions, and after a few moments of gentle encouragement from Sergeant Idleman and Sheila, she allowed herself to be led from the room.

Joining a short queue and helping himself to a cup of tea from the counter, Joe rejoined his companions.

All around them, the large TV screens had been switched to Sky News, the volume turned down, the mutter of subdued, concerned conversation running through the air. From the ceiling hung the festive decorations, casting an air of good cheer which now seemed wholly inappropriate; almost in poor taste. The staff went about their business, clearing away crockery and cutlery, placing fresh cups, sachets of sugar and sweetener, individual portions of milk on the service counter, and chatting amongst themselves. Joe did not know where they took their breaks, but he knew there would be only one topic of discussion.

With the arrival of the police, Gerry had ended his stand up routine and at the front table, the cast of Haliwell's Heroes were as much in mufti as the rest of the room, talking amongst themselves. Melanie sat with them, her face urgent, determined, trying to make some point to them, while one or two members of her cast argued back.

Every table was the same. People argued, debated, chattered, but few were smiling. At the table immediately behind Joe and his companions, Robbie and Fliss Kendrew and Naomi Barton were in the middle of what appeared to be a heated discussion, and Joe uncharitably assumed they were arguing on who would take over now that Reggie was dead.

Even Sheila and Brenda had fallen into the same routine, talking about the killing, speculating on how it could have been done and whether it was a hotel guest, member of staff or someone who had come in from the outside, carried out the deed and then left.

Speculation. Vital from some angles, but so wasteful when it was as generalised as this.

In an effort to distract them, Joe asked, "How are you

feeling, Sheila?"

"I'm fine, thank you, Joe, and right now we have more important matters to consider, don't we?"

"No, we don't. Not until we have more information." Stirring his tea, Joe leaned forward on the table and kept his voice down. "Right now everyone in this room knows who did it or how it was done, and most of it is twaddle. I just heard you two speculating on whether someone from outside could have come in and killed him. It's bloody nonsense. Whoever shot Reggie was inside the hotel all the time, and the likelihood is it's someone from his own party."

"And you accuse us of speculating," Brenda snorted.

"It's not speculation," Joe argued. "It's logic. How do you suppose anyone from outside could have got past reception or avoided the CCTV outside? Don't you think Cliff Denshaw would have said something? Even if they managed to get in, how did they know what room Reggie was in and how did they know he was alone? No. This was someone inside, someone who knew Wendy was getting it on with Gerry Carlin, and that Reggie would be on his own. Now ask yourself, who knew Reggie and Wendy well enough to know that she was playing away? Alternatively, could it be that someone knew Reggie was alone because Reggie had asked to see him or her? Either way it was someone from inside the hotel, and the odds are on one of his salespeople."

"And you're going to start questioning them?" Sheila asked.

Joe shook his head and sipped his tea. "Not yet. I told Grant I'd help, and he doesn't seem to mind." He grinned. "But his sergeant doesn't like me."

Brenda, too, smiled. "Now there's a girl with some taste."

Ignoring her, Joe concluded, "When we have a better picture of what happened, then I might shove my nose in."

"Tell you what's odd," Brenda said. "He was shot. Just like the woman in the play."

"Coincidence," Joe argued.

"But you don't believe in coincidences," Sheila pointed out.

It was true. Joe had spent most of his life arguing the point. When it came to crime, coincidences were often anything but coincidences.

"All right," he said after giving the matter some thought. "Let's imagine this was premeditated…"

"It could have been a spur of the moment thing," Brenda interrupted.

Joe fumed. "Brenda, you do not bring a gun to a do like this without giving the matter some thought."

"Oh. I never thought of that."

He shook his head and drank more tea. "Shooting Reggie actually brings other issues up, if you think about it. Most murders are by strangulation, like Ursula Kenney, or the traditional blunt instrument, like Jennifer Hardy. For someone to bring a pistol to this weekend, means they either intended to threaten or murder Reggie. And why a gun? Because this is a murder mystery weekend, and these plays usually involve a gun."

The women stared blankly at him.

"Yes? And?" Sheila prompted.

"The intention is to cast suspicion on the cast of Haliwell's Heroes. Either that or to bring an air of confusion to the problem."

"Or it really is a member of the cast and they couldn't think of any other way of doing it," Brenda suggested.

Joe glared at her. "A member of the cast? Why would any member of the cast want to shoot a man they met only twenty-four hours ago? Oh. I know. Reggie had already solved Haliwell's murder so they shot him to stop him letting the cat out of the bag."

Brenda's temper approached boiling point. "I was only putting ideas forward, you crabby old sod. And if you'd spent half the night at the hospital with your best friends instead of rogering that old sow, your brain might be in better working order."

"And talking of rogering, the only member of Markham Murder Mysteries who knew the Grimshaws was Carlin, and he was busy elsewhere; with Mrs Grimshaw."

Brenda pushed her cup and saucer away. "All right, so it's one of Reggie's salesmen..."

"Or women," Joe interrupted.

"Women don't use guns," Brenda argued, and Sheila giggled.

"Stop winding him up, Brenda. Of course women use guns."

"Correct," Joe agreed. "Or don't you read James Bond?"

"Then how come no one heard the shot?" Brenda demanded. She stared pointedly at Joe. "Well, we know why you didn't hear it. You were busy firing your own bullets into Melanie Markham."

Joe was about to protest, but Sheila beat him to it.

"Guns don't make as much noise as you may imagine. I remember Peter telling me about it after he'd been on a firearms training course. The report is not particularly loud, nor distinctive, especially when you're dealing with a small calibre pistol. Someone in the next room, either side, or someone passing in the corridor may have heard it, but they wouldn't necessarily equate the noise with a pistol shot."

"And there are ways of muffling the shot," Joe added. "A pillow over Reggie's face, a book, or something soft like that, pressed to the end of the barrel. In any case, it would depend what time he was shot. If it was in the really early hours, most of us would have been asleep."

Brenda's lip curled. "Some of us weren't. Some of us had just got back from Lincoln County Hospital."

"Some of us should have stayed at Lincoln County Hospital, and invested in a mood transplant." Joe drummed his fingers on the table top, his mind wandering. He played with his cup and saucer, allowing free rein to his imagination, running the various scenarios, rerunning them, running them backwards. "There's something I should be thinking of. Something that happened last night."

"Was it between the time you put a hand on her knee and the moment you pulled her knickers off?" Brenda asked, her finger pointing first at Joe, then Melanie.

Keeping his voice to a low hiss, Joe snapped, "Will you, for God's sake, shut up about me and Melanie. Are you just plain jealous or what?"

"Yes," Brenda replied. "Not because she got you, but because I didn't get anything last night and you did."

Joe took out his tobacco tin and rolled a cigarette. "Like dealing with a bloody child."

Unwilling to release her grip on his irritation Brenda said to Sheila, "I wonder where he keeps the condoms hidden."

Joe almost dropped his rolling machine. "Now that is an interesting question."

Brenda stared, her face agleam with humour. "I was joking, Joe. I didn't mean…"

"No, not you and your stupid remarks," he cut her off. "I mean our killer. Where did he hide the gun? See, we have the place crawling with cops, and at some stage they will narrow down their suspects and insist on searching them and their possessions. So what has he done with the pistol? He can't afford to be caught with it, can he?"

The two women lapsed into silence and Joe knew that, like he, they were pondering ways and means of getting rid of a gun in a busy hotel.

"He could have walked out of the hotel and thrown it into the bins," Sheila suggested.

Joe shook his head. "CCTV. Remember? The grounds are covered. Even if he walked out pretending to have a smoke or something," he held up the completed cigarette to emphasise his point, "he would still have been caught near the bins. No; he'd have to be more inventive than that."

"Do you remember *The Godfather*?" Brenda asked. "Al Pacino dropped the gun in the restaurant when he shot those baddies."

"In that case the cops should already have it," Joe pointed out. "I never noticed it and Grant didn't say anything."

The door opened, Les Tanner and Sylvia Goodson came back in, and Sheila and Brenda were called out. Shortly after, Alec and Julia Staines entered, George Robson and Owen Frickley were called. Two more officers entered, Naomi Barton and other guests, not members of the Sanford 3rd Age Club, were called out.

Joe glanced around the room and guessed that there were still 80 or more people to interview. At this rate, it would be well into the afternoon before they could get out.

Then Sergeant Idleman came back with Wendy Grimshaw.

In contrast to her earlier disposition, Wendy was wide-eyed and furious, her face flushed with colour, eyes popping, looking around the room until they homed in on someone behind Joe.

"You bastard," she screamed and rushed towards Joe.

Momentarily thinking he was the target, he cowered. He felt the rush of her movement past him. Looking up and round as Sergeant Idleman hurried in pursuit, he saw the woman launch herself at Robbie Kendrew.

"Murderer," she screamed. "You killed him. You killed my Reggie."

Sergeant Idleman grabbed her arms and dragged her off the startled young man.

"Mrs Grimshaw, please," Idleman begged as she wrestled with the distraught widow.

"Get the crazy cow off me," Kendrew shouted.

Idleman echoed his sentiments. "Help me, someone."

Joe hovered. It would not be seemly to leap up and grab Wendy by the waist. While he dithered, Melanie Markham hurried across, Fliss Kendrew got to her feet and between

105

them and the sergeant they managed to save Robbie Kendrew from Wendy's fury.

"I'll kill you," she screamed as the three women dragged her away. "I'll see you fry in hell."

Melanie and Fliss sat her down away from Robbie. Idleman stood for a moment, getting control of her breathing, and then spoke to Robbie.

"I'm sorry about that, sir. Is it Mr Kendrew?"

He nodded. "Someone should lock that mad cow up."

"She's just been widowed," Joe pointed out.

"And you can mind your own bloody business, too," Kendrew retaliated.

"Stop it," Idleman ordered before Joe could pick up the argument. "Mr Kendrew, would you come with me, please? We need to ask you some questions."

Straightening his tie in an effort to regain his aplomb, Kendrew glowered at the room, reserved a final glare for Joe, and followed the detective out.

Joe got to his feet. "If anyone asks, I'm outside, having a smoke."

Busy trying to soothe the distressed woman, Melanie nodded, and Joe ambled out of the dining room, explained to the constable on duty where he was going, then passed through to reception where he paused at the desk to talk with Cliff Denshaw.

"You have CCTV running day and night out in the car park, don't you?"

"We do, Mr Murray, but the police have already asked for the recordings."

Joe grunted and carried on out into the damp and misty morning.

There was an ornate, metal bench just outside the entrance. In deference to the wet surface, Joe perched on the edge of, fished out his Zippo and lit his cigarette.

Uniformed police officers wandered around the grounds

peering into planters, checking the bushes around the perimeter. The trees opposite were barren, stripped of their summer foliage, and through them he could make out the East tower of the cathedral, its uppermost reaches lost to the fog. In just over twelve hours, the place would be packed with worshippers welcoming in another year. Traffic along the road was light, almost non-existent, but Joe could imagine, further down the hill, the town centre packed with shoppers even at this hour. New Year's Eve was never as busy as Christmas Eve, but it was still a heavy trading day.

Back home in Sanford, Lee, his nephew, and wife Cheryl, standing in for Joe, Sheila and Brenda, would be rushed off their feet in an effort to keep pace with the rush of shoppers, overspill from the nearby Sanford Retail Park.

Normality. Joe loved it, and right now, in direct contrast to his feelings the night before, he would give anything to be up there with them, clad in his whites, listening to the chime of the cash register and the chink of change dropping into it, working to the hum and bubble of the tea urn boiling up the water, giving vent to his irritability and the background orchestration of the customers' chatter.

Instead, here he was, 80 miles from home wrapped up in another gruesome crime, his movements (and those of his friends) restricted by the initial investigation, a distressed, newly widowed woman letting out her fury on a man who had to be the prime suspect, and a thousand questions rattling round his head.

"Having five minutes, Joe?"

Chief Inspector Grant's words brought him back to grim reality.

"Arguments all over the shop in there," Joe replied as Grant sat alongside him and lit a cigarette.

"Has the famous Joe Murray any ideas?"

"Hundreds, but nothing I could pin down." Joe dragged on his cigarette. "You?"

"We're questioning Kendrew. It's routine. Nothing to suggest he had any part in it, but after what you told us, and the way Wendy Grimshaw reacted when we put it to her, we thought we'd better put the screws on him. I've left him with Hayley."

"Hayley?"

"Sergeant Idleman," Grant explained. He laughed sharply. "She's good at questioning men."

Joe smiled ruefully. "Bit of an Amazon, is she?"

"She's a good copper, even if she is slightly motivated by gender politics. Don't get me wrong, Joe, if she's confronted with a woman suspect, she gives no quarter." He narrowed his eyes in an amused fashion. "You do know you're still a suspect, don't you?"

"Gar." Joe took another irritable drag on his cigarette. "You know damn well it isn't me. Have you spoken to Melanie Markham yet?"

"No. I'm planning to interview her after we're through with Robbie Kendrew. I'm sure she'll give you a good reference."

"Yes, and when she's through, she'll give you a roasting." Joe chuckled at Grant's surprise. "She was trying to tell you earlier. We've all paid a lot of money for this weekend and she'd like to go ahead with the entertainment."

"The show must go on, eh?"

"Yes, because otherwise she'll have to give us all our money back." Joe crushed out his cigarette and indicated the uniformed officers. "You're looking for the gun?"

"Not specifically," Grant said. "We're looking for anything that may throw light on the matter, but yes, at this moment in time, we're wondering where the gun is."

"Any indication of the type of firearm?" Joe asked.

Grant shook his head. "Too early for that, mate. All the doc will say is it's a small calibre. Possibly a two-five or a thirty-eight."

Joe smiled again. "Ladies' gun."

"Sorry?"

"Private joke," Joe returned." How soon will we be able to get away?"

Grant was puzzled. "You're not thinking of going home?"

"No, no, but I know my two friends, Sheila and Brenda... Mrs Riley and Mrs Jump. They'll want to get a look at Lincoln sometime today."

"Oh, that's no problem. You've been interviewed, so you're free to go, and the minute they've given a statement, your two friends can do as they please, too." Grant took out his mobile. "Give me your number and take mine. Helps us to keep in touch."

Joe pulled out his notebook and scribbled down his number. When he had Grant's he transferred it immediately to his mobile directory.

"So you don't object if we get a look around Lincoln?"

"Beautiful city, Joe, so help yourself, but remember; don't leave town without letting us know."

Joe stood up. "Will do, and thanks."

***

When Grant returned to the makeshift interview setting in the Scampton Room, it was to find an agitated Robbie Kendrew facing Sergeant Idleman. The young man could not sit still. He fidgeted constantly; with his tie, with the buttons of his jacket, he ran a finger round his collar regularly, and his right foot jittered on the carpet, causing his knee to jog rhythmically.

He took his seat alongside his junior colleague, giving Kendrew a smile of threat-filled assurance, Grant took Idleman's notes and read through them.

"We won't keep you much longer, Mr Kendrew, but there are some issues I'd like to clear up." Grant consulted the notes again. "You left the bar after midnight, went to your room and stayed there, and your wife will verify that?"

"That's correct."

Grant sat back, maintaining an air of total relaxation. When he spoke, it was with a nonchalance that matched his ease. "How did you feel about Mr Grimshaw?"

The knee jerking started up again. "Reggie? He was all right, bit of a tartar, but hell, we had to bring in the business. He was bound to get tough when we missed targets."

"According to Mrs Grimshaw, he was going to retire next year and control of the sales division would fall on either you or Ms Barton."

The knee began to move faster. "Really? I hadn't been told that."

Grant sat forward again, with a menace that took Kendrew by surprise. "But you must have been, Mr Kendrew, or how could you have complained to Joe Murray about it last night?"

The knee stopped. Then started again. An old hand at the game, Grant waited patiently for Kendrew to work out his next move. Whatever it was, Grant had more up his sleeve.

"Oh, well I'd heard the rumours, naturally, but nothing official from Wendy or Reggie."

Grant would not let go. "I find that hard to believe, too, sir, because I believe that's why you were in Mr Grimshaw's room arguing with him at midnight last night."

"What? No. That's wrong." Colour rushed to Kendrew's cheeks. "I wasn't... I never went anywhere near Reggie's room last night."

"I have a witness who overheard an argument between you and Reggie Grimshaw at midnight or thereabouts."

"It's not possible. I wasn't there. I was..."

Kendrew trailed off and looked frantically around the room at the small army of uniformed officers talking to other guests.

"You were what, Mr Kendrew?" Grant demanded.

"I was not in Reggie's room. My wife will verify where I was. With her. All night."

Still leaning on the table, Grant tapped his palm on Idleman's notes. "It's my belief, sir, that almost everything you have told my sergeant is a tissue of lies. Wendy Grimshaw told us you were bending her ear yesterday, trying to convince her to persuade her husband that you should be promoted, not Naomi Barton. In the end she got so sick of it that she told you to clear off, and she later took the matter up with both her husband and Ms Barton. I also have a witness who heard you arguing with Grimshaw at midnight. In short, Mr Kendrew, it doesn't matter what you or your wife tell us, you cannot satisfactorily account for your movements between midnight and breakfast this morning, and that fits the time span during which Mr Grimshaw was murdered."

Kendrew rallied briefly. "I am not a murderer. I was never in Reggie's room last night. And all right, so I was hassling Wendy Grimshaw, but you don't know that cow, Naomi. She's the one you should be looking at. She was sleeping with Reggie; trying to make sure she got the job, not me. But Reggie didn't work like that. He wouldn't give her the job just because she was opening her legs for him. And if he told her so, she could have lost it and killed him."

"I accept that," Grant agreed, "but so far, Ms Barton has accounted for her movements last night. At least as well as everyone else in the hotel. She hasn't lied about being alone. You, sir, are the only person who has tried to mislead us, and that places you top of my list of suspects." The chief inspector relaxed again. "You can go, but we will need to speak to you again. In the meantime, I suggest you think about what you were doing last night, and when we interview you again, tell us the truth."

Kendrew scraped his chair back, leapt to his feet and marched briskly out.

"Well?" Grant asked.

Idleman put down her pen. "He's the front runner for now, sir."

"I agree." Grant's frown deepened. "The problem is, Sergeant, Joe Murray didn't actually hear Kendrew arguing with Reggie. He only heard the old man ranting and we're just assuming the row was with Kendrew."

His partner tapped her pen repeatedly, absently on the table. "If you'll forgive me, sir, I did say we shouldn't be relying on civilians."

"And if you recall, Sergeant, I said we weren't, but Joe's evidence could be crucial to nailing our man." Grant checked his list. "Melanie Markham was giving me some earache earlier, so we'd better get her in next."

Chapter Eight

"My problem, Chief Inspector, is that I have getting on for one hundred people who have paid for a weekend of entertainment," Melanie said. "I appreciate you have a real murder on your hands, and I also accept you have to restrict our movements, but I believe we can help you by keeping the guests entertained."

"And I have no problem with that, Ms Markham," Grant replied. "But I do have a problem with your people wandering round the outside of the hotel."

"It's a necessary part of the play," she urged.

"Perhaps after uniformed have completed their search, sir?" Idleman suggested.

Grant checked the time. "Fair enough. I anticipate our officers will be through by about three o'clock. Would that be early enough for you?"

Melanie considered it a moment. "We can probably work with that. There are other scenarios we can run indoors until we're free to go out." She half stood. "If there's nothing else?"

"There is, Ms Markham," Idleman said. "If you'd stay where you are for the moment."

Uncertain of herself, Melanie sat down again. Across from her, Idleman shuffled through her statements until she came across the one she was seeking.

"We spoke to Joe Murray earlier. He told us he spent the night with you. Could you confirm that?"

Melanie balked at the question. "Is it really any of your business?"

"Yes," Idleman asserted. "As we speak, almost everyone in the hotel is considered a suspect. If you spent the night with Mr Murray, then you are confirming his alibi, subject to the pathologist confirming the time of death, and by turn, he will confirm your whereabouts."

Melanie tutted. "Mr Murray and I did spend the night together, yes, but forgive me. I didn't know it was against the rules, and as I'm sure you'll appreciate, establishing an alibi for the murder of Mr Grimshaw was the last thing on my mind."

"You'll have to forgive Sergeant Idleman's scepticism, Ms Markham," Grant apologised. "We're not remotely interested in what you and Mr Murray were doing, only in confirming your whereabouts and his during the hours we suspect Mr Grimshaw was killed. May I ask, do you own a pistol?"

"A pistol? Of course not… well, that is, I don't own one personally, but as a company, Markham Murder Mysteries owns a few replicas. They're necessary for our productions, you understand."

Her reply piqued the interest of both officers, and Melanie went on the defensive.

"They can't be fired," she assured them and again, she immediately corrected herself. "That is, they can fire, but only blanks. The barrels are not fully drilled out. Gerry Carlin is designated as the person responsible for them. We're fulfilling all our responsibilities under the Firearms Act and the Health and Safety at Work Act."

"I'm sure you are," Grant replied. "However, we'll need to take a look at those guns you have with you."

"We have just the one for this show," Melanie told him. "I think it's a thirty-eight calibre pistol."

Again the two officers exchanged concerned glances.

"In that case, we really will need to take a look at it," Idleman declared.

Feeling uncomfortable under their intense stare, Melanie shuddered. "Of course. I'll get Gerry to bring it down for you.

We'll need it anyway. It's one of the items we like to hide in the bushes outside for the guests to find."

"Once we've cleared it," Idleman insisted.

***

"Thank you, Mr Carlin," Grant said, after examining the replica Mark IV Webley, and learning that the barrel, as Melanie had promised, was not drilled out. "You can carry on with your show now, but bear in mind we still need a statement from you. One of the uniformed officers will get to you."

"Whenever they're ready, old son," Gerry said slipping the revolver in his pocket.

Watching him leave, Grant fished into his pocket for his cigarettes. "Time for another smoke and a chat with our favourite sleuth, I think."

"Murray?"

Grant nodded and Idleman scowled.

"I really don't like him shoving his nose in, sir."

"That, Hayley, is because you're not thinking straight. You're thinking Joe Murray is running the show, but he isn't. Think about it. What is it we need most when we're on this type of investigation? The public's help. Am I right?"

Idleman nodded. "We need them to tell us what they may have seen, certainly."

"Which is where a man like Joe Murray really comes into his own." Grant chuckled. "He fancies himself as a detective. Truth is, he probably couldn't detect a smell in a bunged up lavatory. In reality, he's a keen observer. He notices things; the little things the rest of us miss, and in amongst those little things, Sergeant, will be something that may give us a pointer."

"Well, my money is still on Kendrew," Idleman said.

"So is mine." Grant got to his feet. "And that's precisely

why I need to speak to Joe Murray. See if he's noticed anything that may point to Kendrew; something more concrete than Kendrew moaning about Naomi Barton. Back in a little while."

He left the bar and wandered out of the hotel where he found Joe and Brenda sat on the metal bench.

"Hello, Joe," he greeted. "And is this Mrs Riley or Mrs Jump?"

"Brenda Jump," she introduced herself. "It's easy to tell Sheila and me apart. I'm the sexy one."

Grant laughed and lit his cigarette. Perching next to Joe, he said, "I want to talk to you about Robbie Kendrew."

"A very unhappy lad," Joe said. "Even less happy now that Wendy Grimshaw has accused him outright. Can't say I know much about him, though."

"You only had the one conversation with him?" Grant asked, and Joe nodded.

Brenda volunteered more information. "He was griping about Joe taking control this morning."

"Perhaps he's heard of Joe's reputation," the chief inspector suggested.

"What? As a detective or a lover?" Brenda grinned at Joe's irritation.

"Take no notice, Grant," Joe advised. "She's only trying to wind the pair of us up."

"And with good reason." Brenda pointed an accusing finger at Joe. "He was AWOL in the early hours of this morning. Busy giving Melanie Markham a good seeing to when Sheila took ill…" Her face lit up in surprise. "Oh. That's a point."

"You've remembered something, Mrs Jump?" Grant asked.

"Kendrew. He was wandering about the lobby when the ambulance came this morning. I had to tell him to get out of the way. I mean, I'm not saying…" Brenda trailed off, unsure of what she was not saying.

"What time was this?" Grant asked.

"I dunno. About one this morning. The hotel management should know. They called the ambulance on the doctor's orders. And if they don't, the ambulance service would."

"Where exactly was he?"

"In the lobby. Looked like he'd just come in from out here."

"He'd probably just had a smoke," Joe suggested.

"Perhaps," Grant agreed, "or perhaps he was out here disposing of the weapon."

Joe waved at the grounds, now devoid of uniformed officers. "I thought your people had checked everywhere."

"Yes, Joe, but there's nothing to say he got rid of the gun in the hotel grounds." Grant pointed across the road, beyond the gates of the Minster. "Who's to say he didn't wander over there and dump it?" Grant drew on his cigarette and crushed it out underfoot. "I think it's time I had another word with our Mr Kendrew."

***

"You were seen in the lobby area at about one this morning. Mrs Jump saw you while she was taking her friend, Mrs Riley to the hospital. She did not see your wife."

Kendrew was in slightly better shape than he had been an hour earlier, but Grant's declaration reduced him once more to nervy, jerky movements of his hands and feet. "Oh, er, that's my mistake. I'd forgotten about that. I went for a cigarette. I'd had a trying evening, what with one thing and another."

"You went for a cigarette?" Idleman asked, suspicion bursting through her words.

Kendrew controlled his jerking leg. "You can't smoke in the rooms. It's illegal."

"And how long were you gone, sir?" Grant asked.

"Hard to say, really. Half an hour, forty-five minutes, I can't remember exactly."

"That's a hell of a long smoke break," Grant observed.

117

"So I smoked more than one cigarette." Kendrew raised his voice. "I was at the door, finished my smoke and came back in. What the hell's wrong with that?"

"Nothing," said Sergeant Idleman. "Provided that's all you did."

"For the last time, I did not kill Reggie Grimshaw, and I don't own a pistol."

Grant studied Kendrew's previous statement. "That last time we spoke to you, sir, about an hour ago, you told us you went to bed, and you said your wife could confirm that. You said the time was about after twelve. Now, based on other information, from yet another source, you admit that you didn't go straight to your room with your wife."

"I forgot," Kendrew pleaded. "I was half drunk."

"And what else might you have forgotten?" Grant demanded. "The argument with Mr Grimshaw in his room?"

"I told you earlier, I did not get into an argument with Reggie. He left the bar at about ten thirty as far as I can remember, and I didn't see him after that."

"In that case, Mr Kendrew, you won't object if we search your room, will you?"

Kendrew's alarm increased. "Search my room? What for?"

"A pistol? Ammunition? Or just to clear your name." Grant smiled with sufficient menace to make his position clear to Kendrew. "And if you refuse, I'll get a warrant, but I can assure you, you will not leave this hotel until I'm satisfied that you are innocent."

The kitchen salesman shook his head. "Don't bother with your warrants. I've nothing to hide. Shall we go up now?"

***

"What is with you, Joe?" Sheila asked. "Why so glum?"

"Leave him alone, Sheila," Brenda suggested. "He's probably fed up that we've left a murder behind at the hotel

118

and made him go shopping."

Following them through the Lincoln branches of famous names of the High Street, Joe could have confessed that Brenda was right, except that she wasn't. He was more than happy to leave the investigating to the police, but there was something nagging away at the back of his agile mind, and it would not make its way to the front.

The key, he knew, was to think about something else. Let his mind wander off along more pleasant routes and it would come naturally to him. But he did not consider shopping with Sheila and Brenda to be a pleasant distraction. He enjoyed their company, but not their habit of passing hours ambling from shop to shop, only to return to their start point where they bought the goods (usually clothing) that took their fancy.

"And I don't know why you bother," he had griped when they came out of British Home Stores empty-handed. "It's not like I give you enough time off to go anywhere in all this clothing you buy."

As far as Joe was concerned, visiting shop after shop after shop had only one advantage. It kept him out of the overcast and damp chill of the day. The streets of Lincoln city centre were crowded; far busier, Joe guessed, than a normal Saturday, but not as busy as they would have been the week before, on Christmas Eve.

And yet, everyone had that same, indefatigable Christmassy cheer about them. They greeted total strangers, like Joe and his companions wishing them Happy New Year for no good reason other than they were there.

"I wonder how they'd speak to me a fortnight next Wednesday," Joe grunted as they passed on into Laura Ashley.

"One of these days, Joe, you'll wake up on Christmas morning and have a Scrooge-like epiphany," Sheila promised. "You'll open the curtains, then the window and shout down to a little boy asking what day is this."

"And then I'd give him a guinea to go to the butchers on

Pontefract road and buy the biggest goose... Got it!" Joe snapped his fingers.

Brenda smiled. "Well here's hoping you didn't catch if off Melanie Markham."

"No, you idiot. I mean I've got what was bothering me." He dug into his pockets for his tobacco and mobile phone. "You two carry on. I'll be outside having a smoke. I need to speak with Grant."

He stepped back out into the street and after wandering up and down for several minutes, eventually found a seat on a bench packed with people the same age as his club members. Rolling a cigarette, he jammed it between his lips and lit it, then dialled Grant's number.

After ringing out for a time, it eventually cut him off and directed him to Grant's voicemail. He tried three more times before Grant finally answered.

"I'm questioning a suspect," Grant grumbled after Joe complained to him.

"Yeah? Well, get this. The curtains in Grimshaw's room were open. Do we know yet if his wife opened them?"

"Can't say as I've asked her. I told you earlier, I don't think it's important."

"It may just be, though," Joe argued. "I don't think Wendy opened them. I think the killer did. I think he opened the curtains, then the window and dropped the gun out. Get your people round to the side of the hotel. There are flowerbeds and planters and stuff all over the place. See if they can find the gun, or if not, possibly signs of one having been dropped there."

"Clever stuff," Grant agreed. "And thanks, Joe. I'll get someone onto it right away."

Joe cut the connection and dropped the phone back in his pocket feeling pleased with himself. All it took was that little distraction and Sheila prompting him.

"I'll buy them both afternoon tea," he said to himself.

But by the time his two companions emerged from the shop fifteen minutes later, carrying more purchases, the gloom had descended upon him again. Whatever it was that troubled him, it was not the open curtains and window of Grimshaw's room.

He took it out on the two women. "I think you only buy all this stuff because you want the brand name carrier bags."

"That's right, Joe," Brenda assured him. "We're working our way up to really high quality carriers. C&A."

"Woolworths," Sheila put in. "And the Famous Army Stores."

Brenda rounded off their taunts. "And a genuine, top of the range, Lazy Luncheonette."

"Signed by Joe Murray," Sheila suggested.

"Come on," he ordered. "Let's find somewhere for that cup of tea."

***

In a hastily arranged change of schedule, the Markham Murder Mysteries players took their places at the front of the dining room just after one o'clock.

On the board behind the players, convincing photographs of the now deceased Kerry Dolman and her room, had been pinned up

Standing before her audience, the first thing Melanie noticed was the absence of Joe and his two companions.

"Ladies and gentlemen," she said into her microphone. "Because of the terrible events of this morning, the police have asked us to continue with our little drama, so what we've arranged is by way of a question and answer session. Inspector O'Keefe will question the suspects here in front of you all, and I will then throw the floor open to questions from you, our sleuths. I also hope you will forgive us, but some of the events in Haliwell's Heroes mirror the awful crime which took place here last night. Unfortunately, we didn't have sufficient time to change them." She took a step back, and held out her right arm. "I give you, Haliwell's Heroes."

There was a round of polite applause. Leaving the camera to Danielle McMahon, who had played Kerry, Melanie backed out of the dining room, into the lobby, where she collared Cliff Denshaw.

"Do you have any idea where Mr Murray is? I wondered if he was still with the police."

"As far as I'm aware, madam, he and his two lady friends were going shopping in Lincoln."

"Ah. Right. I'd better not ring him, then. If you see him would you tell him I've been asking for him?"

***

Inspector O'Keefe checked his notes. "It seems that Miss Dolman has been shot in the temple by a small calibre pistol. Do any of you own such a weapon?"

"I have a Webley Mark IV," Wilson volunteered. "Thirty-eight calibre. It's my old service revolver."

"I see, sir," said O'Keefe. "And do you have that pistol with you?"

"Well, yes. It's in my room."

O'Keefe looked suspiciously on the captain. "May I ask, sir, what possessed you to bring it with you?"

"Well... well, when the colonel invited me, he told me old Mickey Crenshaw would be here, and I assumed it would be a regimental reunion. Good Lord, Inspector, I even have my mess dress in my room."

"I see. Would you like to fetch that pistol, sir?"

Wilson appeared relieved at the request and hurried from the room to obey.

"And you, Mr Crenshaw? Do you own such a revolver?"

"As a matter of fact, I do, Inspector," Crenshaw replied,

"but it's not here. It's at home, and home is a hundred miles away. Birmingham."

O'Keefe paced irritably around the table. "What can you tell me about Miss Dolman?" he concentrated on the recently widowed Sadie. "Madam?"

"I know nothing about the girl, Inspector," Sadie replied. "Gregory had decided it was time to write his memoir, and he commissioned her to do the research and write it on his behalf. That is all I know."

"There's no question, then, of a, er, liaison between the colonel and Miss Dolman?"

O'Keefe's provocative query produced a howl of protest from Theresa, the two men and Valerie Wilson.

"Be quiet," Sadie ordered and silence fell at the table. "Do you all take me for a fool? I know all about Gregory and his dalliances. However, my husband was also a terrible snob, Inspector, and I doubt very much that he would have involved himself with a common librarian, which, as far as I'm aware, was Dolman's calling before he appointed her."

"Thank you for your honesty, Mrs Haliwell. We're left, then, wondering about the motive for both killings. Why should anyone wish to murder the colonel and, more to the point, why would anyone wish to murder his biographer?"

The door opened and a worried Captain Wilson burst in.

"Well, sir?" O'Keefe asked.

"It's gone. My revolver is gone."

***

Sat at the rear of the room, Les Tanner, Sylvia Goodson, and Julia and Alec Staines applauded as enthusiastically as anyone.

"We could do with Joe here," Alec said.

"If Murray can work it out, I'm sure we can," Tanner objected. "I must say, their research is good."

"Really, Les?" Julia asked.

"Hmm, yes. The Webley thirty-eight was one of two variants carried by British Officers in World War Two. And that Captain Wilson spoke of mess dress. Spot on. A lot of people would refer to it as number one or number two dress, but its proper name is mess dress and it's different to numbers one and two. Short, cutaway jacket."

At the front of the room Melanie took the microphone. "And now, ladies and gentlemen, Inspector O'Keefe and the dinner guests are open to your questions."

Tanner stood immediately. "Captain Wilson, may I ask was your revolver loaded?"

"Yes," Wilson replied. "But the ammunition was old. Left over from the war. I doubt that it would have fired."

"Who else had access to your room?" Alec Staines demanded.

"I don't know. No one, I suppose, but someone must have been in there to steal the revolver."

"If I may venture at this point," O'Keefe interrupted. "If anyone should find the revolver, would they hand it to me, please. There is a reward for its discovery."

From across the room, Owen Frickley pointed to the board with photographs of the dead woman. "Inspector, who opened the window in Kerry Dolman's room?"

"It was open when we entered the room, sir. Forensic did check it for fingerprints, but the only ones found on it were Miss Dolman's. We assume the lady preferred fresh air."

"Is that significant, do you think?" Julia muttered to the table. "I mean it's bloody freezing outside."

"Yes, Julia, but remember this is a play, and we were told that it's set in 1950," Sylvia reminded her. "But we don't know the time of year."

"Ah. Right. Sorry. Forgot."

Alec stood up again. "Inspector, earlier on, Countess Lucescu asked to speak to you in private. Could you tell us what was said in that discussion?"

"I'm sorry, sir, I can't divulge the nature of the information. I can, however, say that Madam Lucescu is not a suspect."

The question and answer session went on for a further twenty minutes, during which time, Les Tanner made copious notes, the Staineses only a few. Eventually, Melanie took centre stage again, and called the session to a close.

"The video recording of this scene and the questioning of Inspector O'Keefe will continue to run for the rest of the afternoon, to let you seek any pointers. Finally, may I just say that the reward for finding the revolver, as mentioned by Inspector O'Keefe, will be a bottle of champagne."

While the rest of the room applauded, two tables in front of the Sanford 3rd Age Club members, Robbie Kendrew, jumped to his feet and marched out.

***

Kendrew stood at the Twin Spires' entrance chain smoking, and chewing spit on his grievances, made worse, according to him, by the suspicion that he was a murderer.

"I'm one of those fools who would never hurt a fly," he protested to Gerry Carlin and Billy Norman.

"I'm sure they'll clear you eventually," Billy said in an effort to soothe the younger man's irritation.

"To do that, they have to find who really shot Reggie. And this isn't one of your damned plays. This is for real."

"Buggered up our entire schedule," Gerry said. "Anyway, if you'll excuse me. Things to do, you know."

To Kendrew's surprise, Gerry did not go back into the hotel, but stepped out into the grounds and moved to the right hand side of the hotel. "I thought the cops had banned us all from going out there."

"Special dispensation, old flower," Billy replied. He laughed. "Shouldn't really be telling you, but we have things

125

we must do outside." He crushed out his cigarette. "Catch you later."

***

It was turned two when Joe settled into a side seat at the front of the service bus running on a circular route from Lincoln City Centre up around the Minster and back down again.

"We could have walked it in twenty minutes," he grumbled as he paid their fares.

"Up that hill?" Sheila asked. "Carrying all this?" Sat with Brenda on the double seat adjacent Joe, she gave a passing nod to her own carrier bags and those of her best friend.

"Sherpa Tensing made it up Everest carrying more than that," Joe pointed out.

"That's because there were no buses running up Everest," Brenda riposted.

The bus driver pulled away and the vehicle roared along the inner ring road, turning left up the steep hill on the A15.

After the two women had finished their shopping, Joe treated them to tea and scones in one of the many cafes around the High Street before boarding the bus. He was glad to be on their way back to the hotel, and he had a sneaking suspicion that the same applied to his two friends. Events at the Twin Spires, and Sheila's overnight illness had taken the edge off their normal gusto for retail therapy.

"So, have you worked out what's nagging you, Joe?" Sheila asked as the bus plodded up the hill away from the city centre.

He shook his head. "As usual it's something tiny, and insignificant. It'll come to me before the weekend is out. I'm sure it will."

"Is it about the real killing or the pretend one?" Brenda asked.

Joe studied her cherubic features. She appeared deadly

126

serious, but the slightest twitch to the corner of her mouth gave her away.

"I told you, I've already solved the murder mystery weekend. And I'm not wrong. No, no. It's the real thing. There's something… but I can't quite put my finger on it."

"I bet you managed to put your finger on it last night."

Joe fumed. "You're not gonna let that go, are you?"

"I think we're surprised, Joe," Sheila said. "It's so unlike you."

"So what do you think I've been doing since Alison left?" he demanded.

"I don't know," Sheila retorted, "and quite frankly, I don't want to know."

"Whereas I'd love all the gory details, Joe." The twinkle was back in Brenda's eye.

He shook his head, glaring comic defiance at her. "I'm not one to kiss and tell."

"No. You probably kiss, steal their purse and run like hell."

Ten minutes later, back at the hotel, Joe spotted Gerry Carlin making his way from the side of the building to joined Billy Norman near the entrance, where he lit a cigarette. Puzzled, Joe nodded to the men as he passed, and left the two women to retire to their room while he sought out Chief Inspector Grant.

"Sorry, Joe, but you were wrong. We checked the outside, under Grimshaw's window, and there was no sign of the weapon."

"Me? Wrong?" Joe grinned "It has been known to happen." More seriously, he asked, "So you're no further forward."

Grant shook his head. "Chief suspect is definitely young Kendrew, but we don't actually have anything on him, so we're keeping an open mind."

"Searched his room?"

"Clean," Grant confessed. "It would help if we could find the weapon. These acting bods have one, but we've looked at it. Movie gun. Barrel isn't even drilled out. It can fire blanks, but nothing else."

"Oh, hey, talking of the drama group, I thought you'd banned everyone from wandering around the grounds, except for the car park. Only I've just seen one of them coming from that side of the building." He pointed to the left.

"I gave them permission, Joe. It's part of the act."

"Oh." Joe grinned. "But you're not gonna say what?"

Grant grinned back. "No. I swore I wouldn't. It's up to you master sleuths to work it out."

"Well, if there's anything else I can do to help, let me know."

"There is," Grant admitted. "Look, it's New Year's Eve, Joe, and we're all going home shortly. I'd appreciate it if you just keep your eyes open and ear to the ground. We're all supposed to be off tomorrow, but you have my number if anything turns up."

Joe felt gratified by the request. "You can count on me."

Still puzzled by Gerry's actions and the overall planning of the drama, Joe made his way into the dining room. The crowd had thinned out considerably, and he guessed the police were nearing the end of the interview process. The players, minus Gerry and Billy, were seated in a group to his left. Les Tanner, Sylvia Goodson and the Staineses still occupied their table at the back of the room and were arguing quietly over something. The fictitious murder mystery, Joe guessed. In front of them Robbie and Fliss Kendrew were deep in debate, and over to the right, Naomi Barton sat with other members of the Grimshaw party. Wendy Grimshaw was noticeable by her absence and as Joe walked in, Owen Frickley and George Robson made their way out, giving their chairman a nod of greeting as they passed.

Joe joined Tanner, Sylvia and the Staineses.

"Girls took you shopping, did they, Joe?" Julia asked.

He nodded, one eye firmly on the TV screens. "Anything

happen here?"

"Tons of stuff," Alec replied, "but most of it in the play, not in real life."

"Do you know whodunit, Joe?" Sylvia asked.

"What? The play or the murder of Reggie Grimshaw?"

"Either? Both?"

Joe took out his tobacco tin, and still keeping an eye on the developing drama on screen, said, "Yes. I know whodunit it in the play, and yes I know who's favourite for bumping off Reggie Grimshaw."

He transferred his gaze to Kendrew's back, then as the young man sensed it, he switched quickly back to the TV screen where Inspector O'Keefe was now answering questions from the audience.

"Well don't keep it to yourself, Murray," Tanner said. "Who is it?"

"Who killed Grimshaw? Oh I couldn't tell you that, Les."

Tanner fumed. "Not Grimshaw. Who killed the colonel and his biographer?"

Joe laughed. "I can't tell you that, either, because I'm sworn to secrecy, but I can tell you what I've just seen." He leaned forward and lowered his voice. "What do you make of Kerry Dolman's window being open?"

"Owen asked O'Keefe the same question, and O'Keefe said it was open when they entered the room." Julia pointed to the TV screen where O'Keefe was answering Owen's query. "We thought she might be a fresh air fiend."

"With a missing gun?" Joe asked. "And I've just seen one of the actors around the side of the building." He sat back. "Work it out for yourself."

Satisfied with their puzzled features, he took out his tobacco tin and began to roll a cigarette.

To this surprise, Robbie Kendrew leapt to his feet and rounded on him.

"If you have anything to say, Murray, why not say it to my

face?"

Joe felt a rush of anger and anxiety. Kendrew was taller, fitter than him, and he was twenty years younger. "Calm down, son," he advised. "No one was talking about you."

The younger man took a pace forward. Joe shrank into his seat.

"Robbie, no," Fliss barked.

Kendrew backed off and his wife narrowed dagger eyes on Joe. "We're not stupid, Mr Murray."

"No? You're doing a passable impression."

Kendrew lost it, hurtled forward and grabbed Joe by the shirt. The tobacco tin fell to the carpet, spilling its contents.

"Get off me, you idiot," Joe protested.

Tanner and Alec Staines leapt to their feet, two of the younger actors of the drama group moved to help, Fliss Kendrew joined them and dragged her husband back.

"Robbie, this won't help," she cried.

The younger man calmed down and released Joe. Tanner collected the tin and as much of the tobacco as he could gather.

Fliss gazed defiantly round the room. "My husband has killed no one. I know you all think he's guilty, but he's not. Now why don't you leave us alone?"

His face flushed bright red, Kendrew, too, glared round the room, then marched out, quickly followed by his wife.

Tanner shook his head at the door as it soughed softly shut. "I always knew your lip would get you into trouble, Murray."

"For speaking the truth?" Joe demanded, taking his tobacco back. "She was being stupid, and so was he."

Trying again to roll his cigarette, he noticed his hands were shaking. In a lifetime of speaking his mind, of blunt, often rude opinions, it was the closest he had ever come to physical violence, and it had unnerved him.

Across the room, Melanie was signalling to him with her eyes. He crossed to join her, nodding a greeting to the members of her cast gathered around the table.

"Are you all right, Joe?"

"Yeah, yeah. Just a bit shook up, that's all. The guy on reception told me you were looking for me earlier."

"Hmm, yes. The, er, manuscript you left with me last night. Brilliant piece of detective work. I think we can do business. I wondered if we could find some time to talk. If not tonight, perhaps tomorrow."

"You think you can work on it?"

"I'm sure we can."

Joe smiled. "That's the first bit of good news I've had all day."

Chapter Nine

Fliss squeezed her husband's hand tightly. "It'll be all right, Robbie. Believe me. No matter what these morons think of you, the police will realise you're innocent."

"Billy and I tried to tell him earlier, old lass."

Fliss looked around and noticed, for the first time, Gerry Carlin sat on the bench by the entrance, smoking a cigarette.

"Excuse me, Mr Carlin, but I'm trying to hold a private conversation with my husband."

Gerry crushed out his cigarette in a planter. "Pardon me for being so supportive."

Ignoring him, Fliss moved closer to her husband. "They weren't talking about you, you know."

His face a picture of dejection, Kendrew raised his head, and looked over his wife, to the barren busy roads beyond the hotel. "Who?"

"Murray and the other old fuddy-duddies. That irritating little man's trouble is his mouth is too big."

"Why do you think I wanted to punch him in it?"

She laughed, a tiny, soft chuckle. "I understand that, but it doesn't make it right. All you would do is draw attention to yourself. Anyway, that's not what I meant. When he was supposedly whispering to his pals, I could hear every word he said, and he wasn't talking about you. He was trying to hint to them that the gun used in the play had been thrown out of the biographer's bedroom window."

Gerry crushed out his cigarette and stood up. Sidling past Fliss, he said, "Do excuse me. I have people to entertain."

Fliss glowered at his departing back. "Another annoying fool." She turned to Kendrew again. "Murray can't tell his people directly because he has some agreement with that director woman, Melanie, so he could only drop hints. You heard her. There's a bottle of champagne for the person who finds the gun."

Kendrew's spirits appeared to lift slightly. "Oh, that's easy. I saw him, that Carlin bloke, and his mate, the one playing the captain, out here earlier. Carlin wandered off along that side of the hotel." With a nod of his head, he indicated to the right. "He'll have hidden it in one of the planters."

Fliss, too, felt invigorated. "Come on. Let's see if we can find it."

She hurried along the front with her husband close behind, and turned up the side of the hotel.

Long tubs were sited at intervals along the bottom of the hotel walls, filled with shrubbery, the evergreen leaves looking decidedly drab in the poor winter light. Fliss looked up at the windows rising in straight lines above them.

"If they're going to pretend that the killer dropped it out of the window, the logical place to look for it would be directly under one, but we don't know which room she was supposed to be in."

She began to poke and search through the nearest planter, while her husband prodded the foliage in the next one.

Having no joy, they moved further along the side, and suddenly, Fliss spotted the dull glint of metal amongst the greenery. "It's here."

Kendrew joined her and reached down into the shrubbery, feeling his way through the bare thorns and damp foliage until he grasped the pistol by the butt.

Pulling it out, he broke the revolver and checked the chambers. "Empty. This is it all right." For the first time in hours, he smiled. "Come on. Let's claim that bottle of champagne."

133

They made their way back into the hotel and the Gibson Room, where they confronted the Markham Murder Mysteries players and Joe.

"I owe you an apology, Murray," Kendrew said. "My wife tells me you were not talking about me."

"You should always make sure of your facts, son," Joe told him, "but there's no harm done. Let's forget it." His eyes fell on the gun, and for a brief moment, Joe looked worried. "What's that?"

Kendrew smiled at Carlin. "Inspector O'Keefe, I've found your murder weapon." Holding the pistol by the barrel, he offered it.

Dropping easily into part, Carlin dipped into his pocket and came out with a handkerchief. "Thank you, sir. Ms Markham will announce your reward at this afternoon's session before dinner." He dropped the revolver in his pocket.

Joe tapped his hands together in a small round of applause. "Congratulations. Where did you find it?"

"In the shrubbery on…" Fliss paused a moment to get her bearings, then pointed through the dining room door. "On that side of the hotel."

"I'm sure you'll enjoy your champagne," Melanie said, "and I'm certain it won't be long before the real police clear up this real mess."

***

While the Kendrews wandered away, Joe got to his feet. "Well, it's nice rapping with you luvvy dahlings, but I've other things to think about. Melanie, we'll talk later."

Having decided that the police had allowed Reggie Grimshaw's murder to drift for long enough, and convinced that the Kendrews had just lied, he looked around the dining room, and his gaze lighted on Naomi Barton, sat alone, reading a paperback novel.

Joe hovered over her. "Mind if I join you?"

She closed the book, and Joe noticed it was a copy of Barbara Taylor Bradford's *A Woman of Substance*. "I wondered when you'd get round to me. Well, I've nothing to say to you, Mr Murray. I already gave a statement to the police."

"I know you did. But there are other questions on my mind, and since Wendy Grimshaw is too shocked to answer them, and Robbie Kendrew thinks I have a downer on him, you're the next best option."

Without waiting for Naomi to offer an invitation, Joe sat down, and picked up the book, skimming through its pages. "Role model?"

"Who? Barbara Taylor Bradford, or Emma? Both, as a matter of fact."

"I'm old enough to remember the TV series, you know."

Naomi took the book back. "So am I. Now what do you want?"

"Grimshaw Kitchens," he declared. "Now that Reggie is out of the picture, who gets to run the company?"

The dark eyes became pinpoints of anger. "You've been talking to Kendrew."

"No. I've been *listening* to Kendrew. He insists you were using your, er, feminine wiles to get at Reggie to ensure that you were promoted when he retired."

"You mean he claims I was sleeping with Reggie." She leaned forward, forearms on the table, heavy breasts resting on them. "Whether or not I was has bugger all to do with you or anyone else. And if I was, it had nothing to do with the prospects of promotion. Reggie didn't work like that. The people he promoted were the best. Simple as that. He gave people who could turn in the business the chance to show how they could improve returns in others. I could have been laying Reggie until the cows come home, but he would never promote me to sales director unless my results as northern area sales manager prove I can handle the job. Satisfied?"

Joe maintained an easy air. "I'll take your word for it. But as I asked originally, what happens now that Reggie is no longer with us? Presumably the decision will fall on Wendy."

"Yes." Naomi sat back and took a deep breath. When she spoke again the irritation had faded a little. "Wendy has never had anything to do with the business. What she knows about making or selling kitchens you could write on a postcard and still leave enough room to tell mum how good a time you were having. She's about ten years younger than Reggie, and when he married her, she was a trophy wife. A glamour girl." Some of Naomi's cynicism returned. "An out of work actress if the truth be told. Thirty years or so with him, and she still doesn't have a clue about Grimshaw Kitchens. My guess is she'll probably sell to one of the big players in the market. Midland Kitchens put in a bid last year, so there's an option for her to realise her assets and clear off to live in the South of France."

"My wife did that," Joe said with a smile. "Tenerife, not the South of France, but you know what I mean."

"Well since we're in the realms of telling it like it is, let me tell you about Reggie and Wendy. He was a prick, plain and simple. He bullied his employees relentlessly, and he bullied Wendy, but only in private. Outwardly, theirs was the perfect marriage, but he's had more bits on the side than any dozen celebrities you could bring to a drugs party. And Wendy always forgave him. Know why?"

"Because she had her bits on the side?" Joe asked.

"She's had one or two encounters, for sure," Naomi agreed. "There was one last night, if the rumours are to be believed. But her real reason for standing by Reggie was much simpler and much more mercenary. Thanks to his bullying ways he was a millionaire a few times over, and Wendy was determined to stay home where she could raid the piggybank as often as she liked."

"Funny. I got exactly the same feeling about my ex-wife. Only the piggybank was better guarded and I'm not a millionaire. And I don't bully my staff." Joe chuckled. "If anything, they bully me."

"But once again, if the rumours flying round this hotel are anything to go by, you're just as bad when it comes to bed hopping."

Joe let out a long sigh of resignation. "Looks like I'm never gonna live that down. And let me remind you, lady, there are a fair number of rumours about you making the rounds. Or did Reggie bully you into bed?"

"No he did not," she snapped. Heads at several tables around them turned their way. In deference to them, Naomi lowered her voice again. "I earn over fifty thousand a year, Mr Murray. If I slept with Reggie, and I stress, 'if', it was because I saw it as expedient, and not because he brought any undue pressure to bear."

"Expedient? That's a new name for it." Before Naomi could react to Joe's calculated dig, he dragged them back on topic. "So, if Wendy decides to sell out and leave for the South of France, what happens to you and the rest of Grimshaw's sales force?"

She shrugged. "Lap of the gods. And it depends on who takes over. There are those companies who don't approve of the high-pressure techniques we use. They won't offer the kind of discounts we do for a spot decision. My team would need retraining in more up to date, softer selling techniques. Some companies may decide to keep some of us on, because we can bring contacts with us. Others would just retire the lot of us. For Kendrew and me, it's even more complicated. Our potential buyers already have area and regional sales structures. If another company decided to keep us on, it would be as salespeople, not managers. That would mean a step down and a considerable kick in the bank balance for me, and for Robbie."

"And that would be a problem?"

Naomi denied it. "Not for me. I live alone. I'm careful with my money. I have plenty saved and some good investments which would tide me over for a while. Kendrew is not in the same position, unfortunately."

"Oh?"

"Big house out in the country, mortgaged to the hilt. The fifty grand a years he's earning now wasn't enough, so no way could he make ends meet on less money."

Joe gathered together his belongings. "Interesting."

"You think so?"

"Hmm." He stood up. "Doesn't sound to me like a man who would want to see Reggie dead, unless he had some hold over Wendy that would persuade her to keep the company going."

***

Checking the time and surprised to learn that it was after four, Joe looked through the windows to confirm it. Beyond them the sky was dark.

"Doesn't time fly when you're having fun, Joe," Cyril Peck commented as he passed.

"I'll let you know when I'm having some fun."

"Plenya pubs in the town," a half drunk Mavis Barker said as she passed along with Cyril.

Noticing that Gerry Carlin was making his way out of the room, Joe once again joined Melanie.

"We're back on again at six, Joe. Gerry and the crew are going off for something to eat and to freshen up a little before they turn it on. And it'll be a late night, tonight. We all have to greet the New Year."

"As long as they don't look at me for first footing," Joe replied.

"Why not? You're dark haired."

"Yes, but I'm not tall enough." Joe delivered his favourite, self-deprecating smile. "I'm away to my room to shower and shave for dinner. What time do you want to get into negotiations? Before or after midnight?"

She laughed. "I'm not likely to be sober enough for business talk after midnight. Can I see you in the bar about nine-ish before the DJ begins his stint?"

"Sure."

Wondering how he could ensure a repeat of the previous night's pleasures, Joe left the dining room and called at reception for his key. As he made for the lift after collecting it, Gerry Carlin joined him.

"I thought you guys were getting an early meal before your next stint."

"I'll wait until after," Carlin replied, leading the way into the lift and pressing the button for the first floor. "Just been for a quick smoke. You know how it is. Need the fix, old lad."

Joe pressed the button for the fourth floor and the doors closed. "I understand. You know, I own my place, a trucker's café in Sanford, and I'm not even allowed to smoke on my premises."

"Health and safety, old son. Can't beat them."

"Nanny State, you mean."

The doors opened again and with a nod, Carlin left and Joe continued to the fourth floor. Letting himself into his room, he suddenly felt very tired. He stood for a moment looking out from the window, over the twin towers of the cathedral, lit up against the night sky, and wondered what more the coming night would bring.

Eventually, deciding that the shower and shave could wait, he set the alarm on his mobile phone, and lay on the bed. In minutes, he was asleep.

***

"Are you jealous, Brenda?"

Sitting before the dressing table mirror, carefully applying a

139

pale lipstick, Brenda picked up Sheila's reflection in the mirror. As usual, her best friend had opted for conservatism; an ankle length evening gown in dark chocolate, with a white, sleeveless wool top, which buttoned at the neck. Brenda had chosen a simple black skirt, and an opaque chiffon blouse in pink, decorated with roses.

"Jealous? Of what?"

"You mean of whom," Sheila corrected. "Joe, of course. Or Joe and Melanie, to be precise."

Brenda laughed. "Good heavens, no. Whatever gave you that idea?"

Sheila slipped her feet into a pair of dark brown, high-heeled courts, and studied the effect in the full-length, wardrobe mirror. "You've been niggling at him all day over it."

"That's revenge for all the times he's had a go at me." Studying Sheila's reflection again, Brenda went on, "you have some black, wet look slingbacks that will go better with that dress."

Sheila kicked off the shoes again. "You're probably right. Those heels would be killing me by ten o'clock." She dug into the wardrobe and came out with the lower heels. "I worry about Joe, you know. I worry that he works too hard, and doesn't get enough enjoyment out of life."

"Well, he can hardly complain about last night. Melanie got her hooks into him early on and he probably had a ball. Or she had a pair of…"

"Yes. Thank you, Brenda. I get the picture."

Lipstick applied, Brenda put away her makeup pack and turned on the seat so she could look at Sheila. "Joe is one of those men who will drop dead within six months of retiring. You know that, don't you? He lives for that café."

"And the club." Sheila pulled on the glossy slingbacks and again admired the effect. Satisfied with it, she closed the wardrobe.

"Correct. I think that last night was the best thing that's

happened to him in years, and he really needs more like that. Not necessarily jumping into bed with someone, but just enjoying himself." Brenda grinned broadly. "I keep hinting; one night with me and he wouldn't know what had hit him. He'd be a changed man for the rest of his life. And it wouldn't cost him a penny."

"I know you're always ribbing him about it."

Brenda laughed again. "Who's kidding?"

Sheila was surprised. "Would you? Would you really?"

"Of course." Brenda became more serious. "I know you won't even look at other men. Your whole life was dedicated to Peter and the children. And when Colin was alive, there was no way I'd even consider another man. But we had an, er, *active* relationship, Sheila. When I eventually got over his death, I saw no reason to deny myself that which I'd always found so pleasurable. If I'd gone first, Colin wouldn't have taken holy orders, you know. Joe is more like you. After Alison left him, I think he just switched his sex drive off."

"I never thought she was the right woman for him, anyway," Sheila commented. "But even if I had been working for him at the time, I wouldn't have said anything. I don't think it's our place to interfere with anyone's life."

"Or, to look at it another way, it's every man's – and woman's – right to make a mess of his life in the way he chooses. But my point was, Joe bottles up all that, wossname, testosterone, and lets it out in his moods." She grinned lasciviously. "I can think of better ways of getting rid of it, and my guess is, Joe would be dynamite."

Sheila giggled in a teenage manner. "Dynamite on a very short fuse most of the time."

"I hope you're referring to his temper," Brenda said with mock severity. "Personally speaking, I've never had sight of his fuse."

Sheila loaded her belongings into a clutch bag. "You dated him not long after we all left school."

Brenda, too, picked up her bag. "Yes but I never looked. I just had fun." She giggled and checked her watch. "Half past five. Shall we make a move?"

***

After the two women collected Joe, they entered the dining room just as the Markham Murder Mysteries players were taking their places for the early evening's entertainment.

More photographs had joined those already on the display board, this time of the revolver, taken from a number of angles. The weapon itself lay on the table encased in a polythene bag. The actors were dressed as they had been earlier in the day, but Carlin, as Inspector O'Keefe, had dispensed with his overcoat while still wearing his trilby.

Melanie appeared, microphone in hand, and as the room settled into quiet, she went into her introduction.

"Good afternoon, ladies and gentlemen. The drama is developing. Earlier this afternoon, the missing revolver was discovered in the hotel grounds. Our congratulations go to Robert and Felicity Kendrew, who found the pistol."

Melanie led the room in a round of polite applause as the couple went forward to receive a bottle of champagne.

When the Kendrews had returned to their table, Melanie went on with her introduction.

"The pistol is now in the hands of Inspector O'Keefe but he has some questions he needs to ask the colonel's dinner guests. So without further ado, let's get back to Haliwell's Heroes."

***

To a smattering of applause, the lights came up and O'Keefe placed the revolver, encased in a polythene bag, on the table.

"Captain Wilson," the inspector began, "can you identify this pistol as your service weapon?"

Wilson picked up the bag and examined the pistol. "Hard to say. It could be mine." He made to open the bag. "If I could just…"

"No, sir," O'Keefe interrupted. "Don't take it out of the bag. There are no fingerprints on it, and I don't want to get yours all over it."

Wilson put the bag down. "In that case, all I can say is that it looks like mine."

"We've run checks on it, sir, and the War Office records confirm the serial number matches that of the pistol issued to you. I simply needed your confirmation."

Wilson shrugged. "It must be mine then."

"Thank you, sir. Now do you recall saying to me earlier that your revolver was loaded with old ammunition?"

"That's correct," the captain confirmed.

"And we know that only one shot has been fired," O'Keefe carried on. "And yet, the chambers are empty. There is no ammunition in the gun."

The announcement caused consternation at the table.

"That's not possible," Wilson insisted. "I checked it yesterday as we packed our bags to come here. Val will confirm it."

His wife agreed. "I remember asking him why he was bringing it, Inspector, and he muttered something about the war. And I do recall him breaking the gun to check that the chambers were loaded."

"Men," Theresa Haliwell complained. "Will they never let go of the damned war?"

"It's in the nature of the beast, Theresa," said McLintock, with a scowl directed at Crenshaw.

"Oh, do shut up, McLintock," Crenshaw protested. Concentrating on the policeman, he asked, "What are you driving at, Inspector."

"I'm formulating a theory, Mr Crenshaw. Someone stole the weapon from Captain Wilson, and removed the old, dud ammunition, replacing it with a single, live round, which he – or she – then used to murder Miss Dolman. The question is who, and what did he – or she – do with the old ammunition?"

"Well it seems to me, then, that the prime suspect is Wilson himself," McLintock declared.

The captain rounded on him. "How dare you –"

"That will do, sir," O'Keefe interrupted. "Yours is an interesting observation, Mr McLintock, but it's not strictly true. Captain Wilson is a likely suspect, but he's not alone." He laid a gleaming eye on Crenshaw. "It wouldn't be too difficult for anyone with a military background to secure thirty-eight calibre ammunition."

Crenshaw half rose, but the determined eye had moved on to McLintock.

"As would anyone with widespread contacts in the City; especially when one of his business partners is a member of a local gun club." O'Keefe rounded on Zara Lucescu. "Foreign nationals, too, may find it easier to obtain this kind of ammunition than your everyday British citizen."

Zara's shrill voice filled the room. "You haff the audacity to accuse me of killink my friend, Colonel Haliwell?"

"No, madam. We're talking about the death of Kerry Dolman. Where the colonel's death is concerned, each and every one of you had the opportunity, and the motive to administer the cyanide." The inspector's dangerous gleam took in the entire table. "One of you is a double murderer, and I will not rest until I know which one."

***

The scene rambled on for a further fifteen minutes before Melanie finally brought it a close amidst generous appreciation

144

from the audience.

Joe had made several pages of notes, and as he ran through them, adding or subtracting information, he listened in on the debate between Sheila and Brenda.

"I think it's Crenshaw," Sheila declared.

"Really?" Brenda sounded genuinely surprised. "Why do you say that?"

Sheila skimmed back through her notes, shorter than Joe's, but more detailed than Brenda's. "In the very first scene, yesterday, we heard McLintock describe him as being, er, under the colonel's thumb." Sheila rifled back through her notes. "A damned ADC, was the actual description. I think McLintock was right, and I think Crenshaw resented the way the colonel put him down for not being on the front line on D-Day."

"But why did he murder the biographer?"

"That's not clear yet," Sheila said, "but I think O'Keefe will learn something tonight or possibly tomorrow, that will give us a motive. Who did you have in mind?"

"The countess. There's some secret she's told O'Keefe, which we haven't heard yet. My guess is that the colonel was guilty of war crimes, or something like that, when he led the assault on Chateau Armand. I don't think she's a Romanian countess at all, but she's one of the vigilantes they had after the war, who went round the world seeking war criminals."

"But the inspector said she wasn't a suspect," Sheila protested.

Brenda grinned. "Maybe she did a Melanie Markham on the inspector." She checked to see if Joe would rise to her dig, but he was still writing, so she turned back to Sheila. "In fact, I wouldn't be surprised to find that the colonel conspired with the Nazi commanders at Chateau Armand, and that the gold was real, so they split it between them, and massacred the rest of the German forces there." This time Brenda nudged Joe. "What do you think?"

Joe folded away his notebook and dropped it in his pocket. "I think most of what you've just seen is smoke." He stood up. "And talking of smoke, that's exactly where I'm going before they serve dinner. Back in a few minutes."

***

The night air hung heavy with damp. The upper reaches of the cathedral towers, just a hundred or so yards away, were hidden in the gloom, and the roads were deserted.

He found Gerry Carlin outside, enjoying a smoke, still dressed as Inspector O'Keefe, the floppy trilby on his head, lending him the appearance of a latter-day American gumshoe from a 1950s B movie.

Lighting his cigarette, Joe sat with him. "Depressing."

Carlin blew a large cloud of smoke out into already polluted air. "What? The show?"

Joe laughed. "No. I meant Christmas and New Year. Short, dark, damp days, and I don't know about you, but I live alone. Without my friends at the club, I'd have no one... well, a loopy nephew whose heart is in the right place, but who doesn't have the brains or manual dexterity to go with it."

"At least you have roots, old lad. More than I have." Carlin crushed his cigarette under foot and immediately lit another. "I'm a gypsy. Wandering all over the country playing silly buggers in hotels like this, or living in digs while I'm appearing in some theatre."

"Nowhere to call home?"

"Nope. I come from your part of the world originally. Little place called Rothwell. Between Leeds and Wakefield."

"I know it," Joe said. "So how does a son of Rothwell end up treading the boards?"

"Drama school, old son. Got myself a scholarship to the Central School of Speech and Drama down in the big smoke. Did a year and a half there, then dropped out, landed a part in

146

Rep at Birmingham, and I've never really stopped working…
or travelling." He puffed on his freshly lit cigarette. "One of
these days, I'll look back and say to myself, 'what a complete
waste of a life'." He chuckled sadly and removed the trilby.
Rubbing a hand across his hairline, he went on, "If I'd
followed my old dad down Lofthouse pit, I'd probably have a
wife and two point four, and a nice semi in South Leeds."

"You'd also be out of work," Joe told him. "Most of the
mines are long gone. And take it from me, following in your
dad's footsteps isn't all it's cracked up to be. I worked for my
old man when I left school, and because my brother had the
good sense to move to Australia, I took over the café when he
retired. It's all I amount to. I spend seven days a week there. I
even live above the bloody place."

Joe too, drew on his cigarette and discovered that it had
gone out. Taking out his engraved, brass Zippo, he relit it.

"So how did you team up with Melanie?" he asked when it
was satisfactorily glowing again.

"Through the theatre, naturally," Carlin replied. "Met her
while she was on placement in Nottingham, then bumped
into her later. Nottingham again, as I recall. She was the
assistant set designer and we were putting on an adaptation of
Billy Liar. I played Stamp. We got chatting during rehearsals
and she told me she had this idea for a travelling troupe
putting on murder mystery weekends." He beamed proudly at
Joe. "I was her first recruit, in at the very beginning, and I've
been with her ever since." He sniffed and dragged on his
smoke again. "Keeps me in beer and condoms, and it's better
than some of the work I'd tried."

"Such as?"

"Stand up comedy, for one. Hell's bells, I was awful. You
probably noticed if you were watching while we waited for the
cops to come this morning." He delivered another, self-
deprecating laugh. "I'm an all-round entertainer, Joe. My act
was a mishmash of improvisation, one-liners, monologues

147

and, believe it or not, the odd song. Went down about as well as one of your pies at a slimmer's convention."

"So you weren't cut out for comedy?"

"Not the stand up variety, no." Carlin heaved a sigh. "I suppose I have to be grateful, old lad. I've never been out of work during the last twenty years, and even if I'm not making a fortune, at least I'm making more than scale."

Joe had heard the word before. "Scale?"

"The minimum amount an actor can be paid as agreed between the union and representatives of the various media; radio, theatre, TV, films."

"Ah. Like the minimum wage?"

"Y'see, even you're a better comedian than me. Yes, it is like the minimum wage, but a little more generous." He stubbed out his second cigarette, stood up and stretched. "Oh to be one of life's Reggie Grimshaws, eh? Pots of money and no worries."

Joe grunted. "A live Reggie Grimshaw."

"Ah. Yes. See what you mean." Carlin stood. "Well, old lad, mustn't hang about. Face to feed, elbow to bend, clues to dish out to the never-ending queue of sleuths." He put the hat back on. "Catch you later."

Chapter Ten

It was 7:30 when Joe returned to the Scampton Room to discover that the right hand wall of the Gibson Room, the wall without any decoration, had been slid back and open to turn the whole dining/bar area into a huge, single, open plan room. Hotel staff were laying out trestle tables with food in the dining area.

Above the bar, a sign read *Free bar 7:30-9:00*, and the area was already packed; mostly with the Sanford 3rd Age Club. Joe knew enough about his members to be sure that they would not pass up such an opportunity. Even the more middle class members like Les Tanner, or the near-teetotallers, like Sylvia Goodson, would not hesitate to take advantage of free drink.

Sheila and Brenda were sharing a table with Tanner and Sylvia and the Staineses, and sat with them was the young woman playing Theresa Haliwell. Other members of the cast were dotted around the room, chatting with guests, and he noticed George Robson laying a line of chat on Tanya Richmond, the actress playing Valerie Wilson, the same woman who had given Joe such short shrift the previous evening. Melanie was on the podium in the far corner talking to the DJ, and the air was thick with the approach of New Year.

He joined his friends who promptly introduce him to the actress.

"I'm Olivia Anderson," she said, "and as I'm sure you've noticed, I play Theresa Haliwell."

"Joe Murray, private detective extraordinaire..." he introduced himself. "When I'm not making steak and kidney pies."

Olivia laughed. "So I've been hearing. Are you going to question me on the real murder?"

"Do you know anything about it?" Joe asked. She shook her head, and he concluded, "In that case there's no point me questioning you, is there? Tell you what, though, I do have a question for Theresa."

She appeared disappointed but hid it behind a cheery smile. "Go on, then."

"You're engaged to Crenshaw, but you were engaged to McLintock. How much influence did daddy really have in the switch?"

She scowled convincingly. "Lots, if you must know. He didn't like Patrick, er, McLintock, at all. Daddy always said that McLintock got out of serving in the war thanks to his money. He was born to it, you know. His father was a stockbroker, too. Frightfully rich, of course."

"So how did the colonel persuade you to settle for Crenshaw?"

"Threatened to cut my allowance off. He said I wouldn't need it if I married new money. The Crenshaws, on the other hand, are old money. Related to royalty, so they claim, and Michael is a decent sort, but he's so... I don't know. Boring. You know?"

"And old money is a euphemism for being near broke, isn't it?"

"Hmm. I never thought of it quite like that, but yes, I suppose so. They don't have much in the way of hard cash. Michael is always counting the pennies. But they do own a frightful lot of land."

"Would McLintock be angry enough to pop your father off?" Joe wanted to know.

"I shouldn't have thought so. Of course one can never really

150

tell, can one? I suppose he is a bit miffed, but he's not the violent type."

"And what about Crenshaw. Would he be up to shuffling daddy off the mortal coil so you could inherit?"

The actress chortled convincingly. "Wasting his time if he did. Everything goes to Mummy. All I get is my allowance. A measly thousand a year."

"One last thing, Theresa," Joe pressed. "How did your father make his money?"

"Haven't a clue. I only know how to spend it. Haven't the faintest idea how one goes about making it. You'd have to ask Mummy."

Joe gave her a small round of applause. "You're a very capable actress, young lady."

"Thank you, Mr Murray."

"And now, tell me, not as an actress, but as Olivia Anderson, did you know Reggie Grimshaw or any of his crowd before this weekend?"

Olivia appeared thrilled to be asked. "Gosh, no. Do you really suspect one of our people? Because there are those who knew him, you know."

Joe's eyebrows rose. "Really?"

"Oh yes. There's Gerry for one. Well, I don't know that he knew Mr Grimshaw, but he certainly knows Mrs Grimshaw." She leaned into Joe and lowered her voice. "Knows her in the biblical sense."

Disappointment seeped through Joe. He'd been hoping for something different to the scuttlebutt. "Yeah, right. Thanks, Olivia. You get yourself off with the other young people and enjoy the party."

He picked up his glass and surveyed the room. The DJ was already playing background music, most of it easy instrumental, to which Cyril Peck and Mavis Barker were already dancing. The Grimshaw Kitchens crowd had already split up and were circulating around the room, including

Wendy Grimshaw, who appeared anything but the grieving widow. Joe noted that she kept her distance from the Kendrews, who were the only couple out of step with the rest of the room. The party mood had already begun to spread, but they sat at a table, deep in discussion, Kendrew moody and anxious, his wife serious and urgent as she spoke to him.

"Charm not working tonight, Joe?"

Alec Staines's question brought Joe back from the meanderings of his mind.

"I notice the bint you trapped off with last night is chatting up the DJ." Alec pointed to the podium where Melanie was still talking with the entertainer.

Joe groaned. "Don't you start, Alec. I've had enough with Sheila and Brenda."

"Not like you, Joe. Everyone's commenting on it. When they're not talking about old Grimshaw or Haliwell."

"Grimshaw and who… Oh. Right. I get you." In the day's confusion, Joe had temporarily forgotten that there were three murders to solve, even if two of them were fictitious. "If you're angling after tips on the murder mystery play, forget it. I promised I wouldn't."

Alec chuckled. "No, mate. Not worried; I think Julia has it cracked anyway."

"Brenda and Sheila think the same, but they're both wrong."

"So you say." Alec took a long drink of beer. "And what about Grimshaw? Any progress?"

Joe shook his head. "Early days, yet. Favourite is still yon fella." He pointed at Robbie Kendrew and, at that moment, Kendrew looked up and around, his gaze settling on Joe, who quickly diverted his finger to point at the bar.

Alec laughed again. "If looks could kill, Joe, you'd be skewered now." His face settled into something more serious. "Tell you what, though, I wouldn't be surprised if it was an irate customer who murdered the old git."

Toying with his glass, Joe invited, "Go on."

"Have you ever seen a Grimshaw kitchen?"

"Never even heard of them until yesterday," Joe admitted.

Alec, a self-employed painter and decorator, snorted derisively. "Utter crap. I was on a job on Leeds Road coupla months back. Old girl wanted the place tarting up afore Christmas. Full monty in the living room; you know. Paper and paintwork, fresh coat of paint on the kitchen ceiling, all the woodwork. She lived on her own and the kitchen was one of Grimshaw's. I've never seen such a mess. Doors hung out of true, hinges coming out of their MDF backing, worktops loose, and a couple of drawer fronts that kept coming off. It was a bloody disgrace. She'd had more grief with the fan oven than you get from Brenda Jump in a year. I guessed it was all years old, but she told me it had only been in two years, too. I told her she should be giving them what for, but she said she'd complained a dozen ways from Sunday, and they just ignored her."

"That bad, huh?" Joe asked. "Reggie told me they were the dream of every housewife."

Alec laughed. "Dream? Nightmare more like." He shook his head and drank more beer. "Makes you wonder why the daft old sod turned down the offer from Midland Kitchens."

In the act of lifting his glass to his lips, Joe paused. "Midland Kitchens? That's twice I've heard them mentioned."

Alec nodded. "Course, you won't know because you're not in the game, but it was in all the trade papers. Midland Kitchens are one of the big players in this part of the world. Part of the International Group. They're from Bromsgrove. We're talking big boys. They offered Reggie Grimshaw ten million or something for a complete buyout. He told them where they could stick it."

"He must have been doing well to say no."

"That's the funny thing," Alec said. "According to reports, Grimshaw's was... well, not exactly struggling, but not cutting it the way they once did." Alec finished his beer. "Have to get a refill before they start charging again."

Joe checked his watch. "There's no rush, Alec. It's not eight o'clock yet, and the free ale lasts another hour."

"Never look a gift horse in the mouth, Joe. Not when you can kick its teeth in."

"Hang on. I want to know more about this takeover business."

"No more to tell. Home improvements, mate. Played out. Kicked in the bejeebers by the big DIY merchants." Alec took his glass to the crowded bar, leaving Joe to contemplate the story.

He scanned the room, seeking a target. Robbie Kendrew? No way. The only thing Kendrew would be willing to discuss would be Joe's funeral arrangements. Wendy Grimshaw, too, was out. She was not exactly playing the grieving widow, but she would be unlikely to welcome intrusions on her husband's company.

Settling for Naomi Barton, he grabbed his empty glass and made for the bar.

After spending the better part of ten minutes trying to get served, he eventually pulled rank on George Robson and Owen Frickley, and secured fresh drinks for himself and his two lady friends. Delivering them the table, he then moved closer to the DJ, carefully dodging round Mavis and Cyril who were taking up most of the dance floor jiving to the them tune from Chariots of Fire (Joe often called into question the sanity of the pair), he hovered above Naomi, who was deep in discussion with the other saleswoman from the Grimshaw party, a redhead named Nikki Taplow.

Eventually, Naomi registered his presence and looked up, her eyes filled with blatant loathing. "What do you want?"

"You. But not you personally, if you see what I mean."

"Go to hell?"

Joe smiled viciously. "Ladies first." He crouched down on

his haunches so that his head was level with hers. "YOU mentioned a bid from Midland Kitchens earlier today. Tell me about Reggie and them."

"There's nothing to tell," Naomi snapped. "They offered, he told them where to shove it."

"So I understand, but whose advice was he taking when he told them to stick it? Yours? Kendrew's?"

"I don't know and I don't care," Naomi snapped. "Now why don't you go away and leave me alone?"

Joe ignored her demand. "Y'see, I've just learned that what Grimshaw claimed was a top notch product was actually as cheap and nasty as all the others. Just twice as expensive. So I get to thinking that when Midland Kitchens offered Reggie a princely sum, maybe he thought he could hold out for more. And maybe you saw that as a threat, and you saw Wendy as being easier to persuade to keep the company going. If I look at it that way, it makes sense for you or Kendrew, or the both of you to want Reggie out of the way. With him dead, Midland Kitchens may come back with another offer, but it'll be no more than a quarter of the previous one, and you can persuade Wendy she'll make more by keeping the business going... with you in charge, naturally."

Naomi leaned closer to him. He could smell the drink on her breath. "For the last time, Murray, bugger off."

Joe smiled and stood up. "That's better. Now you're showing your true colours. Behind all the expensive clothes and fancy accents, you're as common as pit muck used to be in Sanford."

Satisfied that he had touched a nerve, he moved away, and made for his friends again. Crossing the floor, he bumped into Den Ellerby.

"Oh, hey, Mr Faction," Joe said, "I wanted a word with you."

"About Normandy?" Ellerby asked.

"No, not about Normandy," Joe replied. "About Grimshaw

Kitchens."

"Don't know anything about them. I work for them, that's all, and I'm only doing that until I get through my Open University course."

"On Normandy?"

To Joe's surprise Ellerby nodded. "Not specifically Normandy, but French history from the time of Richard, Coeur-de-lion."

"Must be riveting," Joe said mustering as much disinterest as he could. "And I'd love to hear about it sometime, but right now, tell me what you know about Midland Kitchens making a bid for Grimshaw's."

Ellerby gave an easy shrug. "What's to tell? They made an offer, and Reggie turned it down. I can tell you this, though. The reports were wildly exaggerated. Either that or the people at Midland Kitchens are a set of numpties."

"How so?"

"According to the rumour factory, Midland Kitchens bid ten million. I reckon the company was worth no more than about two or three."

"And you'd know about these things?" Joe challenged.

"Of course," Ellerby replied. "It's common sense. The only thing the company had of any value was the machinery at the factory and the stock of raw materials. And maybe the designs, but hell, they were twenty years old. Salespeople like us are ten a penny and since we're dealing in home improvements, there's not much in the way of repeat business. You see? Homeowners only tend to do up their kitchen every five or ten years, and quite honestly once you've had one Grimshaw kitchen, you wouldn't want another."

"Not good?"

"Rubbish," Ellerby replied frankly.

"Reggie said different," Joe argued.

"Reggie would. Face it, Mr Murray, most people could go to one of the big DIY stores, buy the kits and either do it

156

themselves or get a local joiner in to do it for them. And the big stores offer a design service free of charge. They'll cut all the panels and worktops to size, even number them for you. Hell, they'll even arrange to install it for you if you pay the extra. And they charge a fraction of the price Grimshaw's are asking." Ellerby shrugged again. "If you think about it, Grimshaw's was worth nothing like ten million. I'd go no higher than three, but you don't have to take my word for it. You know how to use the internet?"

Joe suppressed an acid response. "They covered it on our pre-retirement course."

"They did? Good. It's great, you know. Anyway, if you go on the Web and Google it, you'll find it all on there. See ya."

The gears of his mind meshing, Joe made his way back to his friends. "Do me a favour will you?" he asked with one eye on the covered food tables. "When they uncover the spread, put me some to one side before the locusts strip it."

"Why?" asked Sheila. "Where are you going?"

Brenda nudged her. "He's scored again and he's nipping upstairs for a quickie."

"You're right," Joe agreed, and turning on his heels marched away, his mind's eye filled with an image of Brenda gaping after him.

Waiting for the lift, he was surprised when a breathless Melanie arrived alongside him.

"I wondered where you were going," she said as the lift doors opened. "I thought we'd agreed to chat about your casebooks."

"We did," he said, holding the doors open, "but something has just come up and I need to get on the Web to check on it."

"Oh. Right." Melanie stepped into the lift with him. "Would you like to use my laptop and we can kill two birds with one stone?"

Joe shrugged, his finger hovering over the 4th floor button. He moved it down to the 1st floor and pressed it. "As long as you're okay with that."

"Okay with it?" She smiled at him. "It's my pleasure... I hope."

***

With the time on his watch reading 9:15, Joe rolled from Melanie's bed and padded across the carpet into the bathroom where he washed and dressed. As he came back into the room, Melanie passed him carrying her clothing, and he made for the laptop on the escritoire.

"I could get used to this," he said.

"Used to what?" she called back.

"Jumping into bed with you." He switched on the laptop. "But we all have to go home the day after tomorrow and I have a string of murders to solve."

"I don't live far, Joe," she said. "Only Nottingham."

With the private reservation that Nottingham was still too far when he had to be out of bed at 5:30 every morning, Joe rolled a cigarette and concentrated on the computer.

When it finally booted up, he called up the internet browser and Googled *Grimshaw Kitchens Midland Kitchens*.

There were hundreds of results, but the first was the one he was seeking: *Grimshaw rejects Midland bid*.

The link took him to the website of *Home Improvement Digest Online*, and a photograph of Reggie beaming brashly into the camera.

Reginald Grimshaw, known affectionately as Reggie, the sole proprietor of Sheffield-based multi-million pound firm, Grimshaw Kitchens, has rejected a takeover bid from Midland Kitchens, a subsidiary of the International Group.

"My business is not for sale," Mr Grimshaw told our reporter, "and even if it was, they'd have to dig deeper into their pockets than they have already."

A spokesperson for Midland Kitchens confirmed that the bid, believed to be in the region for £3-4 million, had been rejected, but insisted the offer was generous. "It seems Mr Grimshaw has a vastly inflated sense of his own importance and the value of his company. Both his product and his methods are outdated and unsuited to a better-informed, 21st century customer base."

Mr Grimshaw, however, was unrepentant. "We are Midland Kitchens' biggest competitors on the east coast from The Wash as far North as Teeside, and our order books are full. Insofar as I can judge, all they're after is closing the business down to give them a free hand."

Midland Kitchens denied this, insisting that they are seeking a better location for their Northern and Eastern regions. "Our main factory is in Bromsgrove, and we're looking to open another manufacturing plant. Sheffield is ideally situated for the purpose and we would have been more than happy to take on the Grimshaw factory and its employees."

Expensive perfume assaulted Joe's nostrils, and he looked up from the computer to find Melanie seated alongside him.

"Ah," she said as she glanced at the screen. "You're looking into Reggie's business."

Joe turned the laptop to her so she could read. "When you're investigating a murder, you always look first at the victim. Learn all you can about him, and you should be able to identify a motive."

After reading quickly though it, Melanie passed the screen back to him. "And have you?" she asked. "Identified the motive, I mean?"

"Hmm, no, not really." Joe shut down the internet browser. "Young Kendrew is our front runner, and Naomi Barton told me that now Reggie is dead, Wendy is likely to sell up. She also reckons that she and Kendrew will be out of work because of it. Or at the very best, demoted. Either way, they'll take a kick in the pay packet. From that point of view, Reggie was worth much more to him alive."

"Unless he – or whoever murdered Reggie – had a deal

with Midland Kitchens which would cushion him."

Joe's wrinkled brow creased further. "Could a guy like him negotiate a deal like that?"

"Possibly," Melanie said. "How much do you know about direct selling?"

"They're a pain in the butt."

She laughed. "Quite true, but there are negotiating skills involved, Joe, and they're exactly the same negotiating techniques big companies and large corporations use when they're putting a deal together. If Kendrew can sell to householders, then I'm sure he can haggle with a company like Midland Kitchens."

Joe strummed his fingers on his lips.

"Look," Melanie insisted, "you and I are about to get into negotiations for the rights of your casebooks. I'm quite comfortable with that, and so are you. But if I were talking to a movie producer about the rights to my murder mystery scripts, I'd be just as comfortable. All his millions of pounds wouldn't worry me. Well, Kendrew may be of the same mould." She mimicked a proposal. "'Guarantee me a top job and I'll make sure Reggie signs on the dotted line at the price you want'." Reverting to her normal voice, Melanie went on, "You heard him arguing with Reggie late last night. Maybe he was trying to persuade Reggie, and the old man finally had enough of the pressure and told him to go to hell."

Joe cleared his throat. "Y'see, I'm all right when the big boys are trying to sell me something. I'm quite happy to tell them to take a long walk off a short pier, but I don't think I could sell them anything."

"That's because you work in a staple industry. Food. You don't have to actually sell, people come and buy. Kendrew, on the other hand, has to sell. He has to persuade, to negotiate. It's meat and two veg to him, the same as meat and two veg is meat and two veg to you."

Joe shut down her laptop. "Enough about Reggie bloody

160

Grimshaw. Let's negotiate the Markham Murder Mysteries, stroke, Joe Murray agreement."

***

It was turned ten when they finally returned to the Scampton Room to find the party in full swing. The dance floor was crowded with couples mimicking the hand and body movements of the DJ to the sound of Black Lace and *Agadoo*, prompting Joe to complain, "I thought this was a holiday number."

"This is a holiday," Melanie told him. "Get with it, Joe."

"Thanks," he replied, "but I'm happier without it."

Melanie rushed onto the dance floor to join her friends, and Joe made his way to his table, currently unoccupied, where he found a covered plate of snacks and savouries close to his long-since, flat beer.

Casting his gaze around the room, he was not the only one sitting it out. In her corner by the bar, Wendy Grimshaw sat talking earnestly with Gerry Carlin, and a few tables along from them, the Kendrews were still deep in discussion. A couple more tables from them and the subject of occasional glances from Fliss Kendrew, Naomi Barton was immersed in her book.

While he ate and collected a fresh drink, his friends, indeed most of his members, left the dance floor only occasionally to rattle him. For the most part, they stayed up there, dancing the evening away to *The Macarena, Staying Alive, I will Survive*, Sinatra singing *New York, New York*, a selection of Beatles, Rolling Stones and Abba (Joe's personal favourites, but he still refused to dance). As the time wore on towards midnight, the DJ, sensing he had the cut of audience's jib, ran some Rock 'n' Roll, a little Glam Rock, and a few tracks from Queen, Madonna and more modern boy and girl bands, successfully intermingling them to keep all happy.

Sitting on the sidelines, the determined wallflower, Joe enjoyed the music and as the heat in the disco rose, he drank more and more beer until, by ten minutes to midnight, he was rolling and ready to dance. By then, the tempo had slowed with Sinatra, again, singing *My Way*, Engelbert Humperdink warbling the *Last Waltz*, to which Joe complained the celebration was supposed to be New Year, not a wedding. He nevertheless wandered around the floor with Brenda and Sheila in turn, before sitting out Queen's *We Are the Champions* on the grounds that he could not understand the relevance and in any event, he could barely stand up any longer.

As midnight approached, people looked at their watches with increasing frequency.

"We're into the last thirty seconds of the year, folks," the DJ yelled into his microphone. "Get ready for the big countdown."

People stood all around the room and began to link arms. Joe, the room beginning to spin before him, nevertheless kept his eye on his targets. Wendy was with her team, including Naomi Barton, and Gerry Carlin and Melanie had tagged onto them. The Kendrews were off to one side with members of the Sanford 3rd Age Club.

The DJ led the countdown in the final ten seconds, until he reached zero and a huge cheer went up. Somewhere in the distance outside a bell chimed the hour, fireworks lit up the sky and the hundred or so people in the Scampton/Gibson Room began to sing the first of three verses of *Auld Lang Syne*, each faster than the preceding one.

Hugs and kisses were exchanged all round. Brenda and Sheila had tears in their eyes. Joe knew why, but when he checked on the Kendrews, they looked no happier now than they had done five minutes previously. Wendy Grimshaw showed no emotion other than pleasure. His two companions had been widows for about six years, Wendy for less than twenty-four hours, and yet Brenda and Sheila still missed their husbands more.

The party would go on for another hour before Joe, weaving from an excess of alcohol he had not taken for many a year, escorted his two best friends back to their room and, bidding them goodnight and a final Happy New Year, returned to his own room, threw off his clothing and hit the mattress.

Minutes later, he was asleep.

Chapter Eleven

When Joe arrived in the dining room at eight the following morning, it was immediately obvious that New Year's Eve had claimed many casualties.

The stalwarts of the Sanford 3rd Age Club were there. It would take more than fast-flowing drink and extended opening hours to put the likes of the Staineses, Les and Sylvia, George, Owen, Mavis and Cyril, off their breakfast. The cast of Haliwell's Heroes were gathered next door, in the Scampton Room, so Joe could not account for them, but the Grimshaw Kitchens party was now down to three: Fliss Kendrew, Den Ellerby and Nikki Taplow. Wendy, Naomi and Kendrew were all missing.

Joe's tongue felt the like the inside of an unwashed fleece when he arrived in the dining room, and he realised instantly that he wasn't alone. Many people greeted him with a churlish, "Happy New Year" and he grunted by return. It did not take much to work out that hangover was the theme of the morning.

Brenda, too, looked worse for wear, but Sheila was one of the few not to suffer.

"All things in moderation," she said.

"Yes, well, you had your do on Friday night, didn't you?" Joe pointed out as he helped himself to cereal and a cup of sweet tea.

"Odd, too," Sheila said tucking into a bowl of porridge. "Fish doesn't normally trouble me. It's usually only fatty foods."

Joe ran an appreciative eye over her. Like him, she was razor thin. Unlike him, she looked younger than her 55 years. "Not something that troubles you, is it? Fat?"

"I do wish you two would stop talking about food," Brenda complained.

"Very well, dear," Sheila agreed. "We have other matters to debate, don't we?"

"If you're gonna ask me for a solution to Haliwell's Heroes, don't," Joe warned. "I'm not saying another word about it."

"We have more serious investigations than that, Joe," Sheila replied, pushing her bowl away.

"Yeah, well, I'm not much wiser on Reggie Grimshaw's death, either."

"I'm not talking about Reggie Grimshaw, either." There was an accusative twinkle in Sheila's eye. "Last night you asked us to save you some food because you had to nip upstairs for, quote, a quickie. Melanie Markham wasn't far behind you, and neither of you came back until after ten. What the devil were you up to for all that time?"

Across the table, Brenda cackled and then winced as her hangover bit back. Trying desperately to maintain a light-hearted tone through the headache, she said, "You randy old sod. I never knew you were that good, Joe. Any bloke who can make it last for an hour and a half can't be all bad. Or did you fall asleep after a ten minute roll on the rug?"

Brenda pushed the plate away, Sheila picked at hers and Joe tucked in before answering Brenda.

"For your information, I was checking something on the Web."

"I've seen those sites myself," said Brenda, keeping up the ribaldry. "They normally charge."

"I'm surprised you're not on most of them," Joe riposted, and before Brenda could take umbrage, he detailed the story Naomi Barton and Den Ellerby had given him, and what he had learned on his web search.

"I must say, it doesn't sound like a motive for murder," Sheila commented as the Markham Murder Mysteries crew began to take their places.

Noticing that Billy Norman (Captain Wilson) and Emma Pemberley (Zara Lucescu) were missing, Joe watched Gerry Carlin, again dressed as Inspector O'Keefe, push his trilby hat back while he pinned up fresh photographs on the board. They were covered in white tissue so their contents could not yet be seen, and he guessed they would be revealed during the next set. Satisfied with his work, Carlin reset the trilby to shade his eyes and joined his fellow cast members at the table.

Ignoring the work of the players, keeping his voice low, Joe explained his reasoning to his two companions.

"It still sounds thin," Sheila whispered. "In fact, I should judge young Kendrew had a bigger reason for keeping Reggie Grimshaw alive."

"That was my feeling until Melanie explained the alternative," Joe agreed.

Brenda picked up the admission immediately. "Oh, so it was Melanie's idea."

"You know, Brenda, I don't know how you put up with it."

"Put up with what?" she asked.

"People have been giving you stick for years about your, er, adventures. I've had less than forty-eight hours of it and I'm fed up already."

Before Brenda could rise to him, Melanie took centre stage again.

"Good morning, ladies and gentlemen. Well, that was a wonderful party last night, wasn't it? I hope your hangovers are not too severe this morning, because the inquiry into the murders of Colonel Haliwell and Kerry Dolman is about to become a little more complex. As usual, this scene will continue to play on the TV screens throughout the morning, and the cast and evidence table will still be there for your inspection. So without further ado, I'll hand you over to

Inspector O'Keefe and his investigation into the murders of Haliwell's Heroes."

***

"I asked you here, ladies and gentlemen because I have questions to ask of you all," O'Keefe began, "and yet, Mrs Wilson, I notice your husband is missing. May I ask where he is?"

"He went to fetch Zara Lucescu," Valerie Wilson replied. "She wasn't here, and Christopher, my husband, feels you need to speak to her more than you need to talk to the rest of us."

O'Keefe appeared surprised. "And why is that? Or didn't your husband tell you?"

"I should have thought that was obvious," Crenshaw declared before Valerie could reply. "Damned woman is a closet Nazi. And if you ask me, the colonel was about to expose her in his memoir, and that's why she killed Kerry Dolman, too. She was afraid the colonel had already dictated those passages to Kerry."

The inspector paced before the table. "We've looked into Miss Lucescu's past quite extensively, Mr Crenshaw, and I can assure you we have uncovered no connections with the Third Reich."

"She will have covered her tracks," said McLintock, for once siding with Crenshaw.

"An interesting theory, Mr McLintock. She did indeed cover her tracks, but she's not alone. So have a number of you." O'Keefe glared at McLintock. "Including you, sir."

The younger man almost exploded. "What? Are you suggesting I… How dare you…"

"It's very simple, Mr McLintock," O'Keefe took over from the blustering stockbroker. "You were educated at Warmingdale, an exclusive private school in Surrey, I believe, and won a blue on the track at Cambridge."

"Yes. What about it?"

"Prior to your graduation in 1938, sir, there was no mention of a heart murmur in any of your school or university medical reports."

McLintock opened his mouth to protest, but the inspector carried on.

"We also note that your father arranged for your family doctor to examine you at the outbreak of war, and it was that same doctor who pronounced you medically unfit for active service."

McLintock was suitably outraged. "Are you suggesting…"

"I'm not suggesting anything, sir. I am stating that your supposed heart condition was a ruse, arranged by your father to ensure that you were not called up during the war."

Crenshaw's lip curled in contempt. "I always knew you were a fake, McLintock."

"Yes, Mr Crenshaw, but let's look at your case, shall we?" O'Keefe suggested. "You were a lieutenant with the service corps in the second wave of landings on Sword Beach, weren't you?"

"Yes. In the bloody thick of it. Not sitting at home counting the profits."

"Indeed not sitting at home counting the profits, sir," O'Keefe agreed. "Instead, you were sitting in Bayeux counting the profits made from selling off army rations to the local population at black market prices."

Crenshaw controlled his anger. "That's a scandalous lie."

"What you mean, sir, is that it was never proven. And neither was the disappearance of two, fully fuelled four-ton trucks, dispatched, according to your records, to supply units gathering round Caen, but which travelled to a chateau some distance from the city according to the account of one driver, who was subsequently killed in action during the battle of Caen in July, 1944."

"There was nothing wrong with my reports," Crenshaw

insisted. "If those four-tonners were diverted, it was not on my orders."

"Quite," O'Keefe said. "We'll see about that." He swung to face Valerie Wilson. "And now, Doctor Wilson."

She wriggled uncomfortably in her seat. "What about me."

"I wonder, madam, could you be the same Doctor Valerie Wilson who was suspended in 1948 after misdiagnosing a myocardial infarction as indigestion, and who, it subsequently transpired, made the mistake because she had attended work while under the influence of alcohol. And that incident, Mrs Wilson, wasn't the first, was it?"

"Now look…"

She was interrupted by the sound of running feet coming from beyond the door. Captain Wilson burst into the room, breathless. "Zara," he gasped. "Inspector, you'd better come. She's dead. Strangled."

***

To generous applause, the lights were dimmed once more. Joe continued to write, Sheila and Brenda compared notes.

"Joe was right all along about us being wrong," Brenda commented.

"I'm always right about you being wrong," Joe said.

Melanie appeared at the front once more.

"The plot thickens, ladies and gentlemen, the clues are coming in fast. Have you yet worked it out? Our next scene will be at one o'clock, and the final act will take place at six this evening. The full solution will be given at breakfast tomorrow morning, and I must have your summaries by midnight tonight if you are to be included in the competition."

As she reached the close of her little speech, Joe signalled to her, and when she stepped down to a round of applause, she crossed to him and crouched alongside him.

"I owe you dinner," he said, purposely keeping his voice down, much to the annoyance of his companions.

"I don't know that you've got to within five percent of the solution," Melanie said.

Joe chuckled. "I need a little more information, and I'll give you my notes at lunchtime. Now where do you want to dine tonight?"

"You like Italian food?"

"Nope, I prefer Yorkshire to Umbria, but if you want Italian, that's fine."

"Gino's. It's about two hundred yards down from the hotel. On the same side. Reception will give you the number if you want to make a reservation."

Joe nodded. "Eight o'clock?"

Now Melanie nodded. "That's fine, Joe."

Satisfied with his arrangements, even more satisfied that he was irritating Sheila and Brenda by not telling them what he was up to, Joe took out his tobacco and as he relaxed in his seat, he half turned to cast his eyes about the room.

Behind their table, Fliss Kendrew sat alone, making notes, occasionally pausing to sip her tea. Her brow was knitted into a semi-permanent frown, and Joe felt for her. Ever since their arrival, or certainly since the first night, she and her husband had been the centre of attention, and the subject of whispers.

"A little worse for wear this morning is he, Mrs Kendrew?"

She looked up from her notes. Joe got the impression that if her eyes were daggers, he would have been impaled.

Fliss made effort to modulate her voice. "He's unwell, Mr Murray. I don't think he could stand the backstabbing any longer."

"I'm sorry," he said.

"You should be. You're the one who started the rumours."

If her husband was a man on the edge, Fliss was exactly the opposite. She was in total control. She simply no longer cared who heard or what anyone thought of her. As one who had never really cared about other peoples' opinions, and therefore did not care who heard him, Joe understood at once. But that understanding did not preclude defending himself.

"If you take a step back, I think you'll find it was your husband who stoked the fires himself."

Fliss folded away her notebook, drank her tea and stood up, gathering her belongings. "That may be, but it didn't take you long to fan the flames, did it?" Holding her head high, she marched to the door.

She did not make it. Before she could get there, the double doors crashed open and her husband staggered in. Dressed in his business suit, his shirt collar open, tie awry, he was unshaven, his hair scattered about his head, and tears were streaming down his cheeks.

"Naomi," he cried to his wife. "She's dead."

***

Silence engulfed the room. Joe felt all eyes turn from Kendrew to him. With a sigh, he stood up. "Sort him and her out, will you?" he ordered his companions, and while Sheila and Brenda moved to gently guide Kendrew to his table, Joe addressed the whole room. "Right, ladies and gentlemen, we appear to have another, er, situation. If you'll all stay put, I'll check it out."

He left the dining room with a good deal less speed than he had after the announcement of Reggie's death, and walked to reception, where Cliff Denshaw was on the phone. Seeing Joe, he ended his call, put the receiver down, and smiled a greeting. "Good morning, Mr Murray. How may I help you?"

Joe jerked a thumb back at the dining room. "We've just been told there's another body."

Denshaw continued smiling. "I assume you mean the Countess Lucescu from Haliwell's Heroes?"

Joe sighed again. "No I do not. I mean Naomi Barton.

Christ, man, didn't you see Robbie Kendrew just now?"

The colour drained from Denshaw's face. "I noticed him, yes, sir, but I was on the telephone. I didn't take much notice."

"Well, he says Naomi Barton is dead. We need to check her room."

His hands shaking, Denshaw searched the key rack. "She's in 107," he muttered and took the appropriate key. Handing it to Joe, he went on, "I'm not sure, er, I can, er you know... handle this, Mr Murray."

"Listen, sunshine, I need someone in authority up there as a witness. You're the man in authority."

"Yes, but it's... could you not find someone else?"

The sigh this time was one of pure exasperation. "Get the key, come with us. I'll ask Sheila or Brenda." He marched back into the dining room where he found his companions now seated one table back trying to calm the distraught Kendrew. "Sheila, could you come with me?"

"What's wrong with the manager? Denshaw?"

"No bottle," Joe reported as Melanie arrived at his side. "You and I are made of sterner stuff, and Brenda is still suffering from last night's booze, but I need a witness to confirm I don't touch anything I shouldn't."

"I'll come with you if you wish," Melanie said.

Joe eyed her. "Are you sure you can cope with it?"

"I won't throw up or faint at the sight of a body if that's what you mean."

Joe agreed and led the way back out where Denshaw was waiting by the lifts.

Once on the first floor, the manager opened the door for them and stood back while Joe and Melanie entered the room.

It was much worse than Reggie. The room had that foul odour of death, offset by the damp of the day coming through the open window. Naomi lay on the carpeted floor, the signs of a struggle all around her; a table lamp knocked over, chair laid flat on its back, the telephone receiver dislodged from its hook and hanging down, a glass and a bottle of water spilled at the bedside, which had showered onto her Barbara Taylor Bradford novel, which in turn was strewn on the carpet.

Her empty eyes stared up, her face was pulled into a rictus grin of torture. Her face was livid, her body paler, and a long, narrow gash showed under her chin. She wore only a pair of thin, cotton pyjamas, the top torn open leaving her breasts bared.

"We should cover her." Melanie made as if she was going to remove the duvet.

"No," Joe barked. "You mustn't disturb anything. Grant will want to see her and the room exactly as it is."

He crouched and pressed a tentative finger to her wrist. Cold, no pulse. He did not know why he had bothered. One look at her was enough to confirm that she was not breathing, and if it were not, the livid weal about her neck, red and coated with dried blood, would.

"Someone cut her throat," Melanie gasped.

Joe shook his head. "No. She's been strangled." He indicated the colour of her face and then her body. "Cyanosis," he said. "No oxygen to the body; turns it pale, almost blue. And whoever did it, used fine wire. Look at the way it's bitten through her skin. Come on, Melanie. There's nothing we can do here." He led her from the room, took out his mobile, and dialled the chief inspector. While waiting for the connection, he ordered Denshaw to lock the room. "Phil? Joe Murray at the Twin Spires. You'd better get your people out here. We have another killing."

***

Joe stepped out at the front entrance, rolled a cigarette with trembling hands, and lit it. Melanie, now wrapped in a warm coat, joined him.

"You'll catch cold," she said.

"I needed the fresh air."

"Me too. Joe, I'm worried."

He snorted. "About me catching a cold? I'm a tough old boot, Melanie."

"Not about you catching cold. It's the method of these murders that worries me."

Joe took a long drag on his cigarette. "Go on."

"First, tell me why the window is open in Naomi's room. Was she simply a fresh air fiend?"

He shrugged. "I know nothing about the woman, but coincidentally, the window was open in Grimshaw's room yesterday, and I thought the killer might have dropped the murder weapon out. Grant had his people check and he said not. If it's the murderer leaving it open, then it might be designed to screw up the pathologist's estimates of the time of death."

Melanie's face screwed up into a puzzled mask. "Again?"

"It's forensic science, and I don't understand much about it," Joe admitted. "It's December... pardon me, January, darkest, coldest time of the year. Most of us have the heating on. The police doctor will take the body's temperature, and they have a formula for working out the time of death. But if the room temperature has been screwed up, by someone opening the window and turning off the heat, it affects the post mortem processes, and that can mean the estimate of the time of death is little more than intelligent guesswork. That's when the investigating officer needs the testimony of reliable witnesses. On Friday night, I confirmed that Reggie was still alive at midnight. This time, I'm not reliable. I was well oiled last night and I can't say what time I last saw Naomi. Probably midnight."

"And I wasn't taking any notice," Melanie admitted.

"Someone will have seen her after that." Joe was less certain than he sounded. "Anyway, what is it that's worrying you?"

"These murders mirror Haliwell's Heroes." Her tones

changed, carrying an air of resignation. "I didn't want to say any of this, but you've already guessed ninety-five percent of the solution anyway, so here goes. Kerry Dolman was shot in the head with a small calibre pistol. In real life, Reggie Grimshaw was shot in the head with a small calibre pistol. You don't know it yet, but in the next scene, Valerie Wilson will pronounce Zara Lucescu's death, declaring it be strangulation, using the electricity cord from the bedside lamp. And we've just found Naomi Barton strangled."

"Yes, but not using the electricity cord from a bedside lamp."

Melanie smiled wanly. "Our play is set in 1950, Joe. Electricity cables back in those days were more flexible, more like rope. Besides, as you'll learn, Valerie has it wrong. Zara was strangled with …well, do you know what a cheese wire is?"

Joe stubbed out his cigarette in a nearby planter. "Of course I do. Every good kitchen has one. It's a long length of fine wire used for cutting cheese."

"Yes, but in World War Two, commandos carried one as a weapon for silent killing. Once round the victim's neck, it bites into the skin and there is no way the victim can get his fingers underneath it to pry it free." Melanie's eyes burned into him, willing him to understand her concern. "I thought of it right away when you said Naomi had been strangled with fine wire. Joe, someone is copying our play."

Joe's lightning mind had got there ahead of her. "But they're carrying out these murders before they've seen the drama, and that means it's someone who has seen Haliwell's Heroes before."

Melanie nodded. "That's one possibility. There is another."

It was obvious that Melanie did not want to say it. Joe looked beyond the hotel, along the main road. In the distance, he could see the headlights and flashing blue emergency lights of police vehicles hurtling towards them. He felt relieved. At least Grant could take over now.

Joe looked Melanie in the eye. "That it's one of your crew."

As Idleman's saloon, quickly followed by Grant's, shot into the car park, Joe pressed Melanie. "Tell me who."

"That's the problem. I don't know. Gerry knew Wendy years ago, and that meant he knew Reggie."

Joe shook his head. "We know where they were on Friday night, and they weren't killing Reggie. No one else?"

"No one that I can think of. You have to understand, Joe, I know my people well, but I don't know anything of their past histories. I only know about Gerry and Wendy because… well, because I've known him for so long."

"Keep thinking about it," he instructed her, and rose to meet the two police officers.

He gave Grant and Idleman a quick round down of events. With the scientific support team following them, they disappeared into the hotel, ordering Joe and Melanie to return to the dining room and wait with the others.

While Melanie rejoined her cast and crew, Joe made the announcement to the room, and then strode to where his two companions sat with the Kendrews. He gazed down on the sad, broken man, and then switched attention to his wife. "A word, Mrs Kendrew."

"I've nothing to say to you, Mr Murray."

The muted hum of concerned conversation dried up as Joe deliberately raised his voice.

"You may want to think again, lady, before Phil Grant comes back down here and carts him off to the nick." He pointed at Robbie Kendrew.

Reluctantly, Fliss followed Joe to the empty table ahead, the one vacated by Sheila, Brenda and Joe himself. Around the room, conversation picked up once more.

Joe leaned on the table, his head low, his voice not much above a whisper. "Where was your husband last night?"

"With me," she insisted. "All night. The same as he was on

176

Friday night."

"Why was he not at breakfast this morning?"

"I told you…"

"Not good enough, young lady. He was missing, a woman is dead. Now where the hell was he?"

"In our room. He was unwell. He's been vomiting all night. Like your friend was on Friday night. And I notice you haven't accused her of murdering Reggie Grimshaw."

"Because I know where she was," Joe snapped *sotto voce*. "What was wrong with your old man? Bad beer, bad food? What?"

"I don't know. All I know is we left the bar just after midnight, and he began projectile vomiting about fifteen minutes after we got back to our room. Personally, I think it's the stress of this last two days." Her bright blue eyes bored into him. "You think he's done it, don't you? You think my Robbie is a murderer."

"It doesn't matter what I think. It's what the police think that will count. I will say this, though; I'm not half as convinced of his innocence as you are." He paused a moment to let his forthright opinion sink in. "Take a bit of advice, Mrs Kendrew. When the cops talk to you, tell it like it is. Don't try to flannel them in an effort to clear your husband's name. Grant is no fool. Lie for your Robbie and you could both end up in court."

Grant appeared in the doorway, announced that everyone would, for the time being, be kept in the room, and then escorted Kendrew away.

Leaving Fliss Kendrew to contemplate her situation, Sheila and Brenda rejoined Joe, and he gave them a rundown of Melanie's worries.

When he was through, Brenda, keeping her usually stentorian voice as low as she could, said, "There's something not right about all this."

"Two people are dead," Joe pointed out. "That's what's not

right."

"Not that, you dork," Brenda grumbled. "I'm talking about Robbie Kendrew. Look, Joe, you never get emotional except when someone tries to part you from your money. Sheila and I are not like that. We recognise when someone is genuinely upset, and that young fella was definitely feeling the strain."

"Yes. The strain of guilt."

"I disagree," Sheila said. "I think you've got a downer on him, Joe, because he attacked you yesterday. Like Brenda, I think he's genuinely hurt by this killing. Good lord, have you not noticed how he's been going steadily to pieces all weekend?"

"Yes, because his plans are going astray. And why? Because he's up against me, is why."

"I think that's what we love about you, Joe," Brenda commented. "Your modesty."

Chapter Twelve

"Strangled," Grant said, "A long thin wire by the looks of it, but the doc will confirm it once he's made his initial examination."

"Exactly as I said when I first saw her." Joe stroked his chin. "Like a cheese-cutter?"

Puffing on a cigarette outside the hotel entrance, the chief inspector's eyebrows rose, and he exchanged serious glances with his sergeant.

"What makes you say that, Mr Murray?" Idleman asked.

Joe explained how the murder mystery drama had developed over breakfast, and the things Melanie had said to him. He concluded by saying, "The last two killings in the murder play have been a shooting to the head, and strangulation by a cheese wire. Now we have two *real* murders carried out in exactly the same manner *but...*" he paused to add emphasis. "The real murders were carried out before we saw the fictitious ones. We got to know about Kerry Dolman's murder at breakfast yesterday, but Reggie Grimshaw was killed in exactly the same way, in the early hours of the morning. In other words, several hours before we were told of the fictitious murder. We learned of Zara Lucescu's murder at breakfast today, and Naomi Barton was murdered overnight, and Melanie has told me that we'll learn at lunchtime how she was really killed... with cheese wire. In other words, several hours before we're due to learn of the fictitious murder. Someone is following the plot of the play, but *in advance* of the play and the only thing we're missing is the murder of an old army officer with poison."

"Because poison, the real McCoy, is hard to get hold of," Grant muttered. "This points at one of the actors."

Joe shook his head. "Melanie said that, but not necessarily. Y'see, I'm only speculating on this but I spoke to her when we first got here on Friday, and she told me it's possible that others have seen this play before. She has ways and means of rooting them out when it comes to awarding the prizes."

"And that could be someone in the Grimshaw party," Idleman said, "which still leaves Kendrew firmly in the frame."

Joe nodded urgently. "I agree. He did find the movie pistol yesterday, and to me that indicates he's seen this play before and he *knew* they'd hide it in the bushes under the victim's window."

"I think it's time we spoke to Kendrew again, sir," Idleman suggested.

"No. Not yet." A deep frown etched Grant's brow. "The Kendrews found the movie gun?"

"Yes," Joe replied. "It's all part of the plot. Only in this case, it's like the real life do, too. Kerry Dolman is shot through the head, just like Reggie Grimshaw, and the gun can't be found. That Inspector O'Keefe, Gerry Carlin, offers a reward for the person finding the gun. Then, when they take a break, Carlin goes out into the grounds and hides it. Kendrew found it pretty quickly, too, according to my information."

"What have they done with the gun?" Idleman asked.

"It's on the display table in the dining room."

"Let's take a look at it." Grant crushed out his cigarette and strode back into the hotel.

"I thought you'd already seen it?" Joe demanded as he hurried to keep pace with the two police officers.

Grant stopped and turned on him. "Where do you hide a tree, Joe?"

"In a wood. But… Oh, my god you don't think…" as the lift doors opened, Joe doffed his cap. "That's the first time I've ever had a cop one step ahead of me."

They hurried into the dining room where everyone was still in mufti, talking amongst themselves, the cast of Haliwell's Heroes gathered at their table.

Grant studied the objects on the table, and picked up the gun, still in its polythene bag. Much to the consternation of the Markham Murder Mysteries cast, he held it up to the dull light coming through the windows, and peered into the barrel. With a satisfied nod, he handed it to Idleman.

"Get it bagged up properly and off to Scientific Support. I want it dusted for prints, and I want a ballistics report on it twenty minutes ago."

Idleman dug into her pockets for forensic gloves. "Yes, sir."

Joe raised his eyebrows.

"I saw the prop gun yesterday," Grant reported. "That barrel isn't drilled out. This one is. It's not the same weapon as I saw yesterday." He concentrated on the players.

"Is there some problem, Chief Inspector?" Melanie asked.

"Yes, madam, there is. I asked you yesterday, how many prop guns are in your possession here?"

"Just the one. Why?"

"In a moment, madam. " Grant turned his attention to Carlin. "Mr Murray tells me that you hid the prop pistol in the grounds yesterday, sir."

"That's right," the actor admitted. He, too, had the worried look of someone who was afraid he had done wrong but could not work out what his offence was.

"Would you mind showing me where you hid it, sir?"

"But it's been found. You've just sent it away with your sergeant."

"That, Mr Carlin, was not the prop pistol you showed me yesterday morning," Grant admitted. "That is a live weapon, and if I'm right, it was used to murder Grimshaw."

The actors gaped as one.

"Now," Grant insisted, "would you show me where you hid

the pistol?"

Pulling himself together, putting on his overcoat and adjusting his battered trilby, Carlin led the way from the bar, through reception, Grant and Joe tagging along. Outside, the actor turned left along the front of the building and then left again, up the side, towards the redbrick extension.

"Hold on a minute," Joe said as Carlin stopped by a planter. "Kendrew's wife said they found the pistol on the other side of the hotel."

Carlin shook his head, lit a cigarette and gestured down into the planter at his feet. "This is where I hid it, and if you look, it's still there."

Putting on a pair of forensic gloves, Grant crouched down, reached in through the barren thorns, and retrieved the pistol. Taking a seal-easy bag from his pocket, he dropped it in. "I don't think there's a problem, Mr Carlin, but I need to get it checked." He passed the bag to Joe. "Look down the barrel."

Joe did so, and he could see that half an inch in, the barrel was almost totally blocked off by studs protruding from either side. He handed it back.

"So this is the movie gun, and the other is the real thing? Kendrew couldn't possibly hope to get away with it."

"You never know," Grant said. "The Markham Murder Mysteries players would have gone home tomorrow and probably never checked that gun until God knows when. Alternatively, this gun may have come to light when the gardeners turned up next spring. Aside from the barrel, the two pistols are practically identical."

Carlin drew heavily on his cigarette. "Listen, old lad," he said to Grant, "I know I'm not supposed to know what's going on here, but I can tell you that when I came out here to hide the pistol yesterday, young Kendrew was at the front door griping about everything, and he saw me wandering off to the other side of the hotel."

"I wondered about that," Joe said, "because when we got

off the bus from Lincoln, yesterday, I saw you coming back from this side."

"I was waiting for Kendrew to clear off," Carlin said through another cloud of cigarette smoke. "It was obvious I was up to something and he would have figured out what, so I went the other way just to trick him."

"You never said anything yesterday when his wife told you where they'd found it," Joe objected.

"Didn't twig, old son," Carlin replied. "Besides, she didn't actually say where they'd found it. She just pointed out of the dining room. It was only as we got here just now that I twigged. So what's going on? Kendrew shot his boss and tried to hide it behind the play?"

Grant and Joe both lit cigarettes.

"It's possible," the chief inspector said. "You don't say a word about this, Carlin, but the killings seem to be following your play. Now in the play, the Romanian countess has been strangled by a cord from the bedside lamp... at least that's what Joe tells me the fictitious doctor said. But Joe also says the guests are due to learn that she was actually murdered by a weapon more consistent with cheese wire. Do you have a cheese-cutter that you hide like you hid the gun?"

Carlin puffed agitatedly on his cigarette, and shifted his weight from one foot to the other and back again. "Look, I can't really say, Chief Inspector. Joe, here, is one of the punters."

"Stop being a berk," Joe grumbled. "Melanie's already told me most of it and I have an agreement with her that I won't reveal anything. Just answer Grant's question."

Carlin took a deep drag on his smoke again, and tossed it to the gravel, crushing it underfoot. He gazed across the hotel car park and out towards the city, his eyes distant and unseeing. Eventually, he focussed on the two men. "Yes. Yes, we do." Taking out another cigarette, lighting it with shaking hands, he said, "Apparently a cheese-cutter was a makeshift commando weapon in World War Two. Silent killer. Obviously, because of health and safety, ours isn't a real one. It's fine, metallic-finish thread. Snaps like that." He yanked his hands far apart and clicked his fingers.

"And where is it now, Mr Carlin?"

"In the prop room. I'm supposed to place it during lunch before Inspector O'Keefe gives his next summary." He beseeched Joe. "For God's sake, don't say anything. If Melanie finds out I've told you, she'll use real cheese wire to cut me off at the crown jewels."

"Don't worry about it," Joe assured him. "Where would you hide it?"

"Directly under Zara's window, which is…" Carlin looked up at the four-storey building. "Round the other side."

Joe followed his gaze. "Grant, where was Naomi's room in respect to us?"

The chief inspector also looked up. "Grimshaw's room was on other side, too, where they found the pistol, and she was opposite them, but one floor higher, so she'd be on this side, right about… there!"

He marched further along the hotel wall to the next trough of plants, where he crouched and, with his hands still encased in forensic gloves, began to part the twigs and thin foliage. Suddenly, he dug into his pocket, pulled out a second seal-easy bag, and reached down to retrieved the cheese-cutter.

It was a length of fine wire, with wooden handles at either end. When Grant stretched it out, there was a clear line of blood in the centre area.

"That's where it cut into Naomi Barton's throat," he said, dropping it into his second bag.

Carlin's face twisted in disgust. "Yuk."

"Is this your prop, Carlin?"

The actor shook his head. "No way. And if you don't believe me, I'll go to the prop room and get ours."

"We'll come with you," Grant agreed. "Joe, Carlin, not a

word about this to anyone until I've spoken to Kendrew."

***

The three men walked purposefully back into the hotel. Grant paused at reception to speak with Cliff Denshaw. They then took the lift to the first floor, and the prop room, where Carlin let them in.

Tossing the various costumes to one side, Carlin lifted a trunk onto the bed, unfastened the padlock, and threw the lid open. He began to remove items. A fake knife, magnifying glass, a metal tea tray, items of fake jewellery, until he finally found the cheese wire and passed it to Grant.

While Carlin replaced the other props in the trunk, Joe and Grant compared the fake one to the real thing. They were practically identical. The chief inspector ran his fingers along the thread of the fake, and invited Joe to do the same.

"Cotton," Joe said. "It wouldn't cut through cheese, never mind human skin."

"As I told you," Carlin said, locking up the trunk and dropping it back on the floor. "Any danger we can have that back, Chief Inspector? I don't know what Melanie's plans are, but I need to place it for the punters."

"I'll need to get it photographed first, but I'll make sure you get it back pronto."

"Listen, Phil, will you need to take statements from everyone? Again?" Joe asked.

"I don't think so. I won't know for sure until I've spoken to Kendrew... again."

***

They returned to the ground floor and the Gibson Room where Carlin took his seat with the rest of the Markham Murder Mysteries cast, and Joe joined his companions. After a

185

brief, whispered word with Idleman, Grant escorted Kendrew to the manager's office.

Following the chief inspector, with Idleman behind him, Kendrew kept up a constant stream of protest. Neither officer responded until they were in the privacy of Denshaw's office, but even then it was only to order Kendrew to sit.

It was a small room, hardly befitting the manager of a large hotel like the Twin Spires. Filing cabinets, against which Idleman leaned, took up one side; the desk filled the centre of the small floor area. Even to Grant, it felt claustrophobic, and Kendrew was obviously already feeling the pressure. That suited Grant.

Taking a seat opposite, the chief inspector took the prop gun and genuine cheese wire from his pockets and placed them on the desk.

"Now, Mr Kendrew, I'm going to ask you to explain certain inconsistencies."

"Am I under arrest?" Kendrew demanded. His knee bounced regularly as his feet worked on the floor.

"Not yet, sir, but pending the outcome of this interview, you may well be." The chief inspector looked up at his partner. "Sergeant Idleman, have you had the fingerprint report on the pistol I gave you earlier?"

"Preliminary report only, sir. There is one set of fingerprints on it. They're currently unidentified."

Grant's attention swung back to Kendrew. "I suspect, Mr Kendrew, those prints will be yours. You did, after all, pick the pistol up."

"And I suspect you're not telling me what this is about."

The chief inspector had been a policeman long enough to know that Kendrew's challenge was nothing more than bravado.

"Very well, sir. The pistol you found yesterday, was not the drama group's prop gun. It was a real revolver, capable of firing a live round, and although I haven't yet had it confirmed, I

186

suspect it was the weapon used in the murder of Reginald Grimshaw." He picked up the evidence bag. "This is the drama group's gun. It cannot be fired. What interests me is why you went to the Western wall of the hotel when Gerald Carlin, the gentleman playing the part of Inspector O'Keefe in the drama, planted his theatrical revolver on the other side of the hotel, by the eastern wall."

Kendrew's colour drained. "No. No, wait a minute, that's not right. I saw him walk to the area where I found that pistol."

"Mr Carlin admits that he did walk in that direction, but only to dupe you. He did not want you working out where he had planted the fake pistol. He retraced his steps after you had gone back into the hotel. But it's fascinating that although you went in the opposite direction, you still found a weapon, and not just any weapon, but the real thing."

"I, er, I'm telling you, listen to me, I'm telling you, that is exactly how it happened. My wife was with me. She'll verify it. In fact… in fact, it was Fliss who spotted it."

"I'm sure she will, Mr Kendrew. Just as I'm sure that you planted the gun there after you shot Grimshaw."

Sweat broke on Kendrew's forehead. "That's so much twaddle. How? When? I went to bed on Friday night. Fliss was with me all night."

"Your wife was not with you when you went out of the hotel at one in the morning, Mr Kendrew," Idleman pointed out. "Both you and she told us you were absent for about three-quarters of an hour.

"I told you about that. I had a smoke. That's all."

"And we have only your word for that, sir, and right now your word is not good enough," Grant warned him. "You were known to be concerned for your position within the company, you had an antipathy for Ms Barton because you were convinced your boss was sleeping with her and it would work in her favour. We know you have some financial difficulties.

You have the motive, Mr Kendrew, you have had the opportunity, and we have the means here." Grant spread his large hands above the evidence bags, then held up the bag containing the cheese wire. "And I'll tell you something else; it doesn't matter how much you've cleaned the revolver and this bloody ligature, when our scientific people get to work on it, we'll find traces of you on it."

Kendrew stared frantically around, and for a moment, Grant thought he was going to run for it. Sergeant Idleman must have had similar thoughts because she positioned herself between Kendrew and the door.

The young man turned his head back to face Grant. "This is ridiculous."

"You're the one who's ridiculous," the chief inspector countered. "Thinking you could get away with it."

"Listen to me, Chief Inspector. It... was... not... me." Kendrew punctuated each word by jabbing his fingers into the desk top.

More bravado, Grant diagnosed. He felt pleased with the way the interview was going. Robbie Kendrew may be a tough nut when it came to negotiating a signature on the bottom line of a kitchen contract, but Grant, and particularly Idleman, would make mincemeat of him.

"Let me ask you another question. When did you last see a production of Haliwell's Heroes?"

Kendrew frowned. "I've never seen it."

"No? When we interviewed Naomi Barton yesterday, she told us that you and she took it in turns to organise these company outings, and you organised this one. So if you've never seen it before, how did you come across it?"

"Wendy told me about it," Kendrew replied. "Wendy Grimshaw. She knew that Carlin guy years ago. When she was an actress."

"And did she tell you about the play? About the Markham Murder Mysteries method of hiding props around the venue so that guests could find them?"

Kendrew had the look of a man whose every word took him one step nearer the gallows. "Well, yes. She told me a little."

Sensing the time was right, Grant launched a direct attack. "And you used that knowledge, didn't you? Used it to murder your boss and your competitor in order to further your own career."

"No."

Kendrew was practically in tears. Grant nodded meaningfully to his sergeant.

"Robert Kendrew," she intoned, "I am arresting you on suspicion of the murders of Reginald Grimshaw and Naomi Barton. You do not have to say anything, but it may harm your defence if you fail to mention when questioned something which you intend to rely on in court. Anything you say may be given in evidence."

"This is ridiculous."

***

Joe, Sheila and Brenda joined a crowd of people gathered at the windows of the Scampton Room and watched as Robbie Kendrew was helped into a patrol car, while his wife, screamed and pleaded with the uniformed officers. A policewoman held her back. Fliss ducked and weaved in an effort to get past her, get to her husband. The car doors closed and it drove off.

Fliss turned back and, seeing the chief inspector and his sergeant making for their vehicles, ran for them pleading with them.

Sergeant Idleman took her off to one side and spoke to her. The words were inaudible, but there was sufficient pointing and shaking of a warning finger from Idleman for the onlookers to guess. In the meantime, Grant drove off.

Finished with Fliss, Sergeant Idleman followed, the

distraught woman hurried back towards the hotel and the crowd around the window broke up.

"That poor girl," Sheila commented as they took a vacant nearby table.

"Shocking start to the New Year for her," Brenda agreed.

"Whereas Reggie Grimshaw and his wife and Naomi Barton are having a beano," Joe grumbled.

"We don't know that Kendrew is guilty," Brenda reminded him, "but even if he is, it's not just his own life he's ruined, but the poor child's too. She's his wife, Joe. How would it feel to learn that your husband is a killer?"

Joe said nothing. There was little point arguing with either woman when they were in their sympathetic mode.

The door burst open and Fliss rushed. She was wet, and looked bedraggled. Her dark hair hung in straggles, her makeup had run, partly through the rain, mostly, Joe guessed, from tears.

"Help me, someone," she cried. "Please help me. They've taken Robbie away."

No one moved. People would not look at her. They did not speak, but they did not pay her any heed. They looked at each other, at the display behind the bar, at the pictures of World War Two fighters and bombers on the walls; anywhere but at Fliss Kendrew.

Joe noticed a glance pass between Sheila and Brenda. Before he could say anything, they stood and crossed the room. Sheila took Fliss' hand and spoke softly to her. Brenda made for the bar and could be heard arguing with the barman for a glass of brandy.

"I don't care about opening hours. The girl needs something to steady her."

The barman, Joe judged, was learning a lesson many a man and woman had learned over the years: never argue with Brenda Jump when she was on a mission.

Sheila gently encouraged Fliss towards their table and Joe

steeled himself. There would be harsh words before they could talk civilly.

The room remained silent. Crossing from the bar with the brandy, Brenda's angry stare took in everyone.

"What the hell is wrong with you lot?" she shouted. "You had plenty to talk about before they carted her husband off."

Joe almost laughed. When she was on this kind of form, Brenda could be cringeworthily embarrassing. Her shaft struck home, and many of the Sanford crowd were shamed into studying the room or their feet once more.

As she drew close to the table and her eyes fell upon him, Fliss let rip with unbridled malevolence.

"You. You horrible, vicious little man. This is all your fault. Are you satisfied now they've taken Robbie away? Happy now that he's locked up in a police cell?"

Like Brenda, Joe was not about to become spectator sport for the rest of the room. "I had to warn your husband —"

"Someone should have strangled you," Fliss cut him off. "You should be in that cell, you spiteful, odious little creep. You poisoned them against Robbie."

"If you say one more word, I won't be responsible," Joe warned her.

"What are you going to do?" she hissed. "Have me locked up? Get someone to press a gun against my head and blow my brains out?"

Joe felt his temper rising. Sheila could see it too, but she made faces urging him to ride out the storm. She gently eased Fliss into a chair, and Brenda dropped a glass of brandy in front of her.

"Calm down, chicken," Brenda advised, "and get that down you."

"Is there cyanide in it?" Fliss demanded. "If there is, I'll force it down his throat."

Sheila sat next to her and continued to pat her hand. "Try to calm down, Felicity. We know how upset you are. Just take a few, deep breaths, and drink the brandy. It will do you the power of good."

Joe took out his tobacco. "I'm going for a smoke."

"I hope it kills you."

His temper reached snapping point. "I didn't murder anyone, lady, and I didn't put the cops onto your husband. He did that himself by opening his big, bloody mouth."

He stormed out of the bar, through the lobby and out into the rainy morning. Pulling in a deep breath to calm his irritation, he quickly rolled a cigarette and as he lit it, Gerry Carlin joined him.

"Have to say, you took that well, old lad."

"I felt like ripping her head off," Joe confessed and drew in a lungful of smoke. Letting it out with a hiss, savouring the bite in his chest, he went on, "She's just letting it out. She'll be all right when Sheila and Brenda have calmed her down."

Carlin lit a cigarette and blew out a cloud of smoke. Joe watched it blend with the rainy air until it was impossible to say where the smoke began and the damp morning took over.

"Must be a bit of a bugger, though, realising your husband is a murderer. And on New Year's Day."

"She should look on the bright side. The year can only get better."

Carlin laughed until he realised Joe was not joking. Coughing to hide his amusement, he ventured, "Cops must have pinned him down fairly quickly, eh?"

"Unless he was being obstructive." Noticing the puzzlement on the other's face, Joe explained, "If a suspect can't adequately explain A, B or C, the cops will arrest them on suspicion, and take them to the station, where they're formally interviewed. They take prints and DNA swabs, take the clothing and have it examined by their scientific support team. That's probably what Grant is doing with Kendrew. It doesn't mean they have him banged to rights, just that they suspect him."

Carlin puffed on his cigarette. "Well, if you ask me, the law have it dead right. I was talking to Wendy... did I tell you I knew her years ago? Anyway, I was talking to her and she was telling me how much lip Kendrew was giving her about the direction the company should go and how he should be the one to run it when old Reggie retired. Seems to me that he chose to retire Reggie sooner than the old lad wanted to. Pity we don't still have the rope for buggers like that."

"Hmm. The only trouble is, when they get it wrong, it's difficult to compensate someone who's been hanged." Joe stubbed out his cigarette. "I'll go see if she's calmed down yet."

Chapter Thirteen

When Joe stepped back into the Scampton Room, it was to find the place its usual hive of chatter and clinking glasses. He checked his watch and was surprised to learn that it was after twelve noon.

By the window, Sheila and Brenda had secured drinks (a glass of lager stood in front of his vacant place) and were still trying to calm a tearful Fliss Kendrew.

He sidled between his two companions, and sat down, staring at the distressed woman.

She was pitiable, almost unrecognisable from the smartly dressed young woman who had danced with her husband on Friday night. Her clothing hung on her like a sack, her hair and makeup were a mess, and her eyes, which had sparkled as recently as yesterday when she collected the champagne, were empty and hollow. As she sat, she looked up and at him, but her eyes did not register his presence. It was as if she were looking through him.

"I'm sorry," he said, "but you can't escape the facts by blaming me."

She gave the tiniest shake of the head, and Joe thought for a moment that it was acceptance. He was wrong. "He didn't do it," she said in a voice so tiny and distant that he felt she was talking more to herself than him.

Joe took a sip of lager, and sat forward. "Listen, Felicity, I know how hard this must be, but you have to face it. I heard your husband arguing with Reggie on Friday night, you, yourself admitted he was missing for almost an hour, and he led you to find the real gun out there, not the prop gun the drama group are using." It was a half lie, he knew. He had not heard Robbie Kendrew answering Reggie, but there was no point nitpicking now.

Fliss shook her head again. "You didn't hear him arguing with Reggie because he never went near Reggie on Friday night."

Joe sighed in frustration. "I heard Reggie warn him off. About midnight. As I passed the Grimshaw's room."

Some of her fire returned. "You're so bloody sure of yourself aren't you? Well, if you heard Robbie arguing with Reggie at midnight, explain how he was smooching with me on the dance floor at exactly the same time."

The announcement pulled Joe up short as he was about to take another mouthful of lager. He noticed another glance pass between Sheila and Brenda, but it was surprise this time.

"Are you sure of the time, Fliss?" Brenda asked.

She nodded. "The DJ pointed up at the clock." She, too, pointed to the wall clock in the corner, depicting a Lancaster bomber flying over Lincoln Cathedral. "He said, 'there's only twenty-four hours of the year left, ladies and gentlemen'." She glowered at Joe. "Or are you going to tell me, Robbie altered the clocks, too?"

Rapidly evaluating this new evidence, Joe shook his head. "No. No, I'm not." He swallowed more lager. Those questions which had plagued him since Friday, and which he thought had been answered by Kendrew's arrest, suddenly returned.

"All right, so maybe it wasn't him I heard. But Reggie was killed later in the morning and, like I said, you admitted he was gone for almost an hour. If he didn't do it then, if he really did go outside for a smoke, he may well have sneaked out in the early hours. The same goes for the murder of Naomi, this morning, and the only way you can guarantee that Robbie never left your side on either night is if you didn't sleep. Well?"

"I slept for several hours on Friday night. Not so much last night because I was busy cleaning up after him. He spent most of the night throwing up." She did not look any the more interested, but her voice was stronger, more determined to prove her point. "I can tell you he was drunk on Friday night and again last night. In fact, he was even worse last night thanks to the tummy troubles."

"He didn't have far to point the gun, did he? So drink doesn't make a lot of difference. And so he was puking. I assume he took something for that. A seltzer or something. It wouldn't stop him sneaking out to murder Naomi."

Fliss made to get up. "There's obviously no point talking to you, Mr Murray. You and everyone else in this room have made your mind up that Robbie is guilty, and that's an end of it. If you'll excuse me, I'd better shower and change and then get down to the police station."

"Sit down," Joe barked.

"Joe," Sheila protested. "Don't be so rude."

"What? Her husband is arrested for two murders, she comes in here slagging me off, screaming at me, wishing me dead, but that's all right because she's upset. Me? I'm supposed to be polite." His fiery gaze pinned Fliss to her seat. "You sit where you are. If you go to the police station they won't let you see him or talk to him anyway. Not for hours, yet. You can do him more good here."

Joe took a moment to let his anger subside. Around the room, they were still the focus of attention, but it was passing instead of fixed. People engaged in conversation cast the occasional glance in their direction, those waiting for service at the crowded bar would look around and in doing so, just for a brief second, their eyes would light upon him, his two companions and the dishevelled woman sat in their company.

Calming down, he launched another, yet milder, attack upon her. "You sit there, the dutiful wife, swearing your sweet little husband would never do anything like that, and for all I know you're going to promise us that he supports homeless children and animals, but it's not knowledge. It's blind faith, based on love, and that isn't enough. There's more evidence to convict your other half than there is to free him. He had the motive. He had the means... or we think he had the means. You say he didn't have the opportunity, I say you only *believe* that, you don't know it. We know he had the opportunity."

As he continued speaking, Joe's finger wagged between Sheila and Brenda.

"I know these two. They've already fallen for you. They'd feel sorry for a mass murderer on his way to the electric chair. And I know what they'll do next. Bring pressure to bear on me so that I'll work to clear your husband's name. Well, fine. I don't mind. What the hell am I here for if not work?" The wagging finger stopped and homed in on Fliss. "But you give me something to work on, something more than faith, because right now, I'm sure he's as guilty as hell."

He fell silent and none of the three women responded. He had expected Sheila or Brenda to pick him up, but they did not, and for a few moments, the chatter and clatter of the room swamped them.

Eventually, it was Fliss who spoke. "Do you really mean that, Mr Murray?"

"What? About him being guilty? Yes, I do."

"No, not that. Did you mean it when you said you'd help to prove him innocent?"

He fumed. "What is it about dunderheaded women who can listen to the whole of Hamlet's soliloquy and only hear him say 'to be or not to be'?"

"You're overstepping the mark, Joe," Brenda warned. "We're not thick, and I don't think Felicity is, either. She's just very distressed."

"And I'm not? We came here for a New Year break and we're in the middle of a double murder... again."

"You fought tooth and nail for Brenda in Chester," Sheila pointed out in tones of attempted mediation. "You wouldn't let go in Filey because you insisted Nicola had been murdered, you harangued the police to death in Leeds to get George Robson off the hook."

"Because I know Brenda, and George, and I knew Nicola," Joe insisted. "I knew George was no killer, and neither was Brenda, and Nicola's death was just too suspicious. Well, this time, I know again, only I know Robbie Kendrew is guilty."

Fliss shook her head. "He's innocent."

"Tell me why," Joe demanded.

"I… I can't. I just know it."

Joe spread his hands. "End of argument. Anyone want another drink?"

"I'll ask a question," Brenda challenged brightly, "and if you can answer it, Joe, I'll stand the next round."

He groaned loudly. "Go on."

"How did Robbie know that Reggie was alone on Friday night? How could he possibly know that Wendy wasn't with him?"

Joe stood up. "I'll get the drink. You want another, young lady?"

She shook her head. "Thank you, but no."

Brenda's question was one of those he had purposely avoided and now here he was confronting it. The argument between Reggie and his unseen, unheard companion had answered it prior to Fliss' announcement of a few moments ago. But if Reggie's overheard warning were not directed at Kendrew, then who, and how *did* the killer know Reggie was alone later?

While waiting for his drinks, he tossed a number of alternatives round his head. There were possibilities but even he had to admit they were remote.

"So, Murray, you're changing sides?"

He found Les Tanner stood at his elbow. "Oh. Hi, Les. No. I'm still convinced it's Kendrew, but Sheila and Brenda are pushing me into proving myself wrong."

"Shouldn't be difficult given your track record as an administrator." Tanner grinned sadistically and Joe reminded himself just how much the old fool enjoyed winding him up.

"Tell me something, Les. Do the council run courses on how to be a total prat?" Before Tanner could rise to the bait, another question shot into Joe's mind. "No. Strike that, and tell me how easy it is to get hold of a British service revolver."

"The Webley Mark IV? Not easy, but not difficult either. You have to get round the firearms act, y'see." Tanner licked his lips in anticipation of delivering a long and solid lecture. "Webley stopped making them in the seventies, and most of those available would be considered antique or collector's items, and they'd be deactivated..."

Joe cut the history lesson short. "You mean they can't be fired?"

"Correct. They can be dry fired; letting the hammer fall on an empty chamber. Many of them have the firing pin filed down or removed altogether, but no matter what method of deactivation is used, the pistol needs a proof certificate."

Joe paid for his drinks. "All right. So how difficult would it be to get hold of a Webley thirty-eight that will fire live rounds."

Tanner smiled his superiority. "I think your niece would be the best person to ask about that."

Thanking Tanner and collecting his drinks, Joe made his way back to the table with the thought that the captain was right. His niece, Detective Sergeant Gemma Craddock of Sanford CID, would know, but she would also ask too many questions if he rang her.

He squeezed himself back into his seat, sipped his lager, and then called his small audience to attention.

"There are a number of ways he could have known Reggie was alone. Perhaps he called later than the argument I'd heard. Perhaps he spotted Wendy shacking up with Carlin."

Brenda laughed and gulped down a generous slug of

Campari. "Typical amateur."

Joe's natural irritation rose. "What? Who are you calling an amateur?"

"You. You're an amateur bed-hopper. Listen to me, Lothario, a woman like Wendy Grimshaw, married, staying here with her husband, isn't going to advertise the fact that she's screwing another man. For crying out loud, Joe, we didn't know you were jumping Melanie Markham, and when it comes to discretion, you're in the same league as a brass band marching down the High Street."

"I wish you'd shut up about me and Melanie."

Joe risked a furtive glance at Fliss to see if Brenda's announcement had had any effect upon her, but she had not changed. She was still and silent, staring emptily at the table, and he knew there was only one thing on her mind.

"How many guns does Robbie own?" he asked.

Realisation that he was speaking to her, spread slowly through Fliss' face and she stirred. "What? Oh. Sorry. Er, one. A twelve gauge shotgun." She smiled weakly, apologetically. "We live in a rural area and we have trouble with foxes now and then."

"So he's no stranger to weapons," Joe pointed out. "I just spoke to Captain Marvel…" He trailed off. Sheila and Brenda would understand immediately, but Fliss would not. "Captain Les Tanner. Territorial Army. He's one of our party and an old, er, friend for want of a better word."

"Only in the same way a lion befriends a zebra at lunchtime," Sheila joked.

Joe, too, smiled. "Les is a proper pain in the arse, but he knows his stuff. He's just told me that it wouldn't be too difficult to get hold of the revolver, but there might be a problem getting one that works; one that hasn't been deactivated."

"Robbie does not own a pistol, Mr Murray."

"Do you keep track of your husband's credit card

transactions, Felicity?" Sheila asked. For the benefit of Joe and Brenda, she explained, "He may have bought one using his plastic."

Joe clucked. "Saints preserve me from honest women." He eyed Brenda. "Even those with crooked haloes. Sheila, if he had a live firing pistol, he probably got it from some back street dealer, and they tend to deal in cash."

"Oh. I never thought of that."

Fliss dragged them back on topic. "I repeat, Robbie does not own a pistol."

"To your knowledge," Joe corrected. "Now listen, luv, if you want me to help, I will, but you have to be practical about it, and you have to answer my questions as honestly as you can." He allowed a short pause for the advice to sink in. "We know you have money problems and Robbie was desperate for promotion."

"And he's gone the best way about getting it, hasn't he?"

Fliss' sarcasm was not lost on Joe's companions, both of whom laughed and then apologised to the distraught younger woman.

"We do not have financial problems," Fliss went on. "Well, we do, but they're not as severe as you make them sound. We're struggling to meet the mortgage on the house. The property is too big for our budget, and I warned Robbie about that when we first took it on, but he insisted. He was so sure we could cover it. When we first began to struggle, he cracked the whip with his team and went out selling again to increase his income. But he always said that when Reggie retired this year, if he could secure the top job, Sales Director, we'd be all right."

"Yet he thought Naomi Barton was jumping Grimshaw to make sure she got the job."

"Yes. I don't know how true that is, but the rumour factory insists Naomi was sleeping with Reggie."

"She as good as told me so yesterday," Joe admitted, "but

she also said it would not get her the sales director's job. She said Grimshaw had a habit of promoting on merit, not upon who dropped her knickers."

"Robbie didn't believe that," Fliss insisted.

"Generally speaking, how did Robbie get on with Reggie?" Sheila asked.

"All right," Fliss replied. "They had their ups and downs, and lately, it was more down than up. Sales were, well, not poor, but not brilliant either. Reggie was always hassling Robbie and Naomi to get more out of their teams. And I know there was some problem last year which worried Robbie. Something to do with Midland Kitchens."

"Why would that worry Robbie?" Sheila asked.

"He was concerned that Midland Kitchens only wanted the factory. He and the rest of the sales force could be facing redundancy. That would aggravate our mortgage problems."

Joe had his next question ready, but when it came out, it was not in his voice. It was almost as if Brenda had read his mind.

"How did you feel about Reggie?"

Fliss' face distorted disdainfully. She checked over her shoulder, scanned the room and her eyes lighted momentarily on Wendy Grimshaw. Joe guessed she had been making sure the newly widowed woman was out of earshot.

"He was an appalling man. Noisy, brash, a terrible bully. Publicly, he was all, yes please and thank you, but in private he bullied everyone; his staff, his wife, even his customers. Arrogant and ignorant."

"Did he ever make a pass at you?" Joe asked.

"No. I'm not saying he would be beyond it, but he never hit on me personally. I think he knew I didn't like him."

"What about other wives, other saleswomen?"

Fliss had to think about it. "I don't know them well. The men and women in Robbie's team, yes. I had to arrange dinner parties for them and so on, but even so, I only got to know them superficially. There was Naomi, of course, but you've already mentioned her."

"And how did you feel about her?" Joe wanted to know.

"If you're looking to pin a motive on Robbie through me, you can forget it, Mr Murray. I didn't like Naomi. I don't like direct salespeople in general. I'd have preferred it if Robbie took another job, even if meant giving up the house and taking a cut in salary. Like all of them Naomi was too pushy. Simple as that. And I don't care what she told you, if she was sleeping with Reggie, it would have been as a means to an end."

"And to Reggie's end," Brenda quipped.

Joe frowned at her, then switched his attention back to Fliss. "But you didn't heap more slime on her when you were speaking to your husband? You know. Encouraging him to dislike her."

"I didn't have to. Robbie hated her." The wagging finger came back, directed at Joe. "However, he would not have killed her. He wasn't like that; there are others, you know, who may have had a motive."

"I was just going to come to that," Joe pleaded. "You must know something about the crew at Grimshaw's, even if it's only scuttlebutt from your husband. How many of them hated Reggie and Naomi enough to kill them?"

Fliss' pliable features went through another transformation this time edging frustration with irritation. "As far as I'm aware, none. We're from Sheffield, Mr Murray, not Chicago or Sicily. People in Sheffield don't murder their bosses just because they hate them."

Joe took a nonchalant sip of his ale. "I dunno about Chicago or Sicily, or even Sheffield. I think you're living on Fantasy Island. Don't you read the papers? There are murders in every big city, almost every day, and often, they're carried out for the most trivial of reasons."

Fliss looked as if she had been personally offended.

Joe put his glass down and leaned forward on his elbows. "Listen to me. You're asking me to help you prove your husband in innocent. You have to give me something to work with. All you've told me so far makes your husband odds on favourite."

"Because I don't know anything about the people he worked with or the company?" Fliss protested. "Does your wife know much about the people you work for?"

"Plenty," Joe retorted. "I work for myself, Sheila and Brenda work for me, and my wife did too, before I married her. And she cleared off because she got fed up of working for me, so let's leave my wife out of this."

Joe drummed his fingers on the table, wondering where to take the debate next. Sheila collected their glasses and made for the bar, Brenda excused herself and went to the ladies, and Joe contemplated whether or not the young woman was trying to take a rise out of him.

It was not without precedent. For all his tough, grumpy exterior Joe knew he was a soft touch for women who cried, and he had felt sorry for Fliss when her husband was carried off by Grant and his crew. Could it be, he asked himself, that she knew Robbie was guilty and she was simply using Joe to angle for his release?

He decided she was not. The police had it right as far as he was concerned, but even so, small inconsistencies were showing through the certainty, and they would need to be accounted for before Kendrew or anyone else could be charged with these crimes.

A thought occurred to him. "The murder mystery thing. Where did you and your husband last see it?"

Fliss, who had fallen into a morose silence (Joe presumed it was preferable to speaking to him without the support of his two companions) stirred. "Sorry? Haliwell's Heroes? We haven't seen it before. I've seen other murder mysteries, but Robbie never has. He never has the time."

"You've seen others put on by this group?"

"What is this?" she protested. "Shouldn't you be thinking of proving my husband innocent instead of prattling about the play? Or are you worried that the woman you're sleeping with might have had other men in other hotels?"

The acid comment irritated Joe again. "You're asking for my help, but you don't go out of your way to encourage me, do you? Just answer the bloody question. Have you seen murder mysteries from this group before?"

"No. Happy?"

"No. Far from it."

Joe played absently with his empty glass, his agile mind churning over the new information and filing it where it belonged. Unfortunately, it was in the area marked 'unanswered' and it had a lot of company.

"Do you have friends, family you can call on?"

Tears sparkled in her eyes at the mention of others within her personal circles. She fought a brief battle with them, gaining control over her fluctuation emotions, before she answered.

"They're all up in Sheffield. I don't want to leave Lincoln. Not while Robbie is still at the police station. And it's New Year's Day. I don't want to spoil their parties by letting them know he's been arrested."

"I take your point," Joe agreed. "Here's what I want you to do. When we go for lunch, and at dinner this evening, I want you to join Sheila, Brenda and me, at our table."

Fliss' response was scathing. "I don't want to intrude upon your little ménage a trois."

Joe would have laughed if it had not been for the dripping cynicism.

"Cut it out. Understand? Just knock it off. You want me to help, then you speak to me with a civil tongue." Once more he leaned into the table, stressing his anger. "You know, I deal with bolshie truckers every day of the week. They give me more earache in one day than the missus did in ten years of wedded hell. At the side of them, you're easy. I have to put up with them because it's my business and I need them. I don't have to put up with you."

She backed off. "I'm sorry. Like I said, I don't want to intrude upon your weekend anymore than I want to trouble my family."

"You won't be intruding on anything." Joe advised her. "But I don't want you sitting alone in the dining room like a bloody wallflower with everyone feeling sorry for you. I shouldn't think Wendy Grimshaw will welcome you with open arms, so stay with us. My two girls are the best in the world when it comes to looking after other people, and they won't mind. It also means you're close by when something, anything occurs to you." He spotted Sheila coming from the bar. "Now, if you'll excuse me, I'm going for another smoke. Think, Felicity. Think hard about who else might have been happy to see Reggie and Naomi dead."

***

Within a minute of Sheila settling back on her seat, Brenda returned. Grateful as she was for their company, Fliss' mind was obsessed with the thought of her husband in a police cell, and even when Sheila put another glass of brandy before her, she barely acknowledged the gesture.

"Has Joe been riling you?" Sheila asked.

Fliss barely registered the question. "What? Oh, no. I don't think he likes me very much."

Sheila giggled. "Nothing new there, then."

Fliss frowned. "I'm sorry?"

"Joe Murray doesn't like anyone," Brenda explained. "In fact, I'm convinced there are times when he doesn't even like himself. He's the original grumpy old man."

"But don't let that fool you," Sheila cautioned. "He misses

nothing. There are times when he sees things which may not mean much, but when they're tied up with something else, he eventually gets the meaning and it takes him one step further forward. Isn't that right, Brenda?"

Her best friend nodded. "He really is the best, Fliss."

Fliss tried to put a note of appeasement in her voice, and found it impossible. "He thinks Robbie is guilty."

"That's because everything is pointing at Robbie, right now," Sheila told her. "But if Robbie is innocent, and I'm sure he is, Joe will find something that proves it. Trust us."

Brenda took a swallow of Campari. "You'll forgive me, Fliss, but even without all this, you didn't appear to be having the best of weekends."

"No. We weren't." Fliss found herself better able to speak to these sympathetic women than she had Joe. "Are you married?"

"Widowed," Sheila replied. "Both of us."

"And within months of each other. That's why we're the best of friends."

"Mark you, we have been good friends since we were children, haven't we, Brenda?"

"We have."

"Robbie and I have been married nearly ten years," Fliss told them, "but this last two years, it's been hell. Money troubles, mainly." Her bitterness flooded out. "That bloody house. And it's all because of Naomi Barton."

She spotted a glance pass between Sheila and Brenda.

"I'm sorry," she said. "I know you shouldn't speak ill of the dead, but I'll make an exception where that woman is concerned. Everything in our lives has revolved around Naomi Barton. She was one of Robbie's salespeople, you know. Worked in his team, and he spoke very highly of her. Then she got promoted, and right away her team began to outdo Robbie's. He couldn't have that, so he really pushed his people to improve the team's performance. Then it got worse. She bought herself a flash car, he bought one that was flasher. She enjoyed a Shakespeare weekend in London, we had to go to Stratford-upon-Avon for the festival. All the time it was Naomi this, Naomi that, Naomi annoys me, I hate Naomi. Everything Naomi did, we had to do it better. She lived in a shabby little apartment in Sheffield, but she was house hunting. Then she spotted Parkfield – the house where we live – and put in an offer. When she told Robbie, he went to the agent and gazumped her." Fliss put on a poor impression of a man's voice. "Ah'm not having that Naomi bitch Barton put one over on me." She shook her head sadly and reverted to her normal speech. "He was obsessed with beating her at every turn. She began to dominate our lives without even knowing about it." Fliss looked up at the two women, her eyes appealing for their understanding. "I didn't care about her. All I wanted was Robbie. I would have been happier if we lived in a council house, happier if he left Grimshaw's and we never spoke about her again."

Brenda patted her hand in an effort to soothe her.

"Have you no children?" Sheila asked.

"We were trying, and then when the mortgage bill hit us, Robbie persuaded me that we couldn't afford them." Fliss sniffed disdainfully. "It's a pity Naomi Barton didn't have kids. Robbie would have wanted at least one more than her."

Chapter Fourteen

Joe was pacing back and forth across the front of the hotel, his mind churning over the events of the last 48 hours, the bits and pieces he had learned, the questions that still bothered him, when Wendy Grimshaw left the hotel, and walked out of the grounds towards the Minster.

He checked his watch. 12:30. Lunch was half an hour away, but Wendy was one of those people he needed to speak to and he had not yet had the opportunity.

Taking out his mobile phone and dialling, he hurried after her. "Sheila? It's Joe. There's something I have to take care of, so I may be late back for lunch. Ask them to put me something to one side, would you?"

"Carvery, Joe," Sheila reminded him. "Self service. How long will you be?"

"I dunno. An hour, maybe longer."

"You'll miss the next episode of Haliwell's Heroes," Sheila warned him.

"So I'll get it on video when I get back. Just take care of lunch, will you?"

"Is it to do with the murders?"

"Would I miss my food for anything else?"

She giggled. "No. I suppose not. Leave it with me."

Joe shut the phone down, dropped it in his pocket and hurried to keep Wendy in sight.

Crossing the road outside the hotel, she cut slightly left and then right, towards the city centre, along Priorygate, where, 50 yards further down, at the point where the peculiar cone of St

Andrew's Chapel blotted out the cathedral behind, she turned into the grounds, and made her way around the chapel, to the Minster.

Discreetly following her, Joe found the colossus overpowering. Lincoln Cathedral was not simply large, it was gargantuan, and he reminded himself of the lecture Sheila had given him on the bus from Sanford: at one time, it was the tallest building in the world. From Minster Yard, the twin towers, their upper reaches almost lost to the misty skies, dominated. He had to crane his neck backwards to look up at them. And what they had in height, the rest of the building possessed in breadth. Visible for miles around, at this close range, it was simply awe-inspiring.

Wendy made her way into the cathedral via a door in the South East walls, and when Joe entered, he saw her sat on a wooden pew, facing the Angel choir and its amazing stained windows, a series of eight, narrow glasses rising up, and topped off by two small and one large rose window above. The rising windows depicted various Biblical scenes, including (inevitably in Joe's opinion) Adam and Eve and the Serpent in the Garden of Eden, the arrival of the Shepherds and Magi in Bethlehem and the Crucifixion. The richness of the colours standing out against the low-level interior lighting struck a chord with him and once more he felt the overwhelming majesty of the place. Somewhere in this same area, he knew, sat the Lincoln Imp, one of the city's most famous legends, but although he looked for it, he could not see it.

A chubby man, clad in a surplice and cassock, passed Joe, and with a benign smile, pointed to his head. With an apologetic wince, Joe removed his cap, and stepped quietly across the memorial floor stones, to join Wendy.

"There was no need to be so furtive, Mr Murray," she said. "You could have walked with me. I would have appreciated the company."

Joe silently congratulated her on her powers of observation, and excused himself. "I didn't want to intrude upon your grief."

"Ah. Aren't we a polite lot?" Wendy smiled and stared at the windows. "The police had to interview me, but they were very soft, back-pedalling, and everyone knows I have to be questioned, but no one wishes to intrude upon my bereavement. I was watching you just now, you know, in the bar, talking to Felicity. Has she persuaded you that her darling, wonderful husband didn't do it?"

"No. Not yet," Joe admitted. "But she's raising issues that need to be addressed sooner rather than later."

"Questions such as who would want both Reggie and Naomi dead?"

"That's one of them, for sure," Joe agreed.

Wendy did not answer immediately. She was intent upon the images in the rising columns of stained glass.

"Do you believe in God, Mr Murray?"

"Tough question," Joe admitted. "Belief outweighs logic, but although I tend to run on reason, that doesn't mean to say I dismiss faith. Does it matter?"

"To you, probably not. To me, yes. There are times when I feel the need to commune with God. Whether you interpret that as being at one with some all-powerful being or with my inner-self, is irrelevant. I need answers to deeper questions; answers which can only be found through introspection. Reggie wasn't like that. He was like you; a practical man. To him, all the answers he needed were to be found in a toolbox or on a balance sheet. He was also an unfaithful bully, whose only interest was self-interest."

Her words made little sense to Joe. "And you need to ask God why he was like that?"

"No. I need to ask God why I created the monster that Reggie had become." A wan smile of reminiscence played on her lips. "When I met him, Reggie was a small businessman. He built and installed bespoke kitchens. He made a good living. He was an honest man and a craftsman. I suppose to you it's the same difference as taking the raw materials and baking your own steak and kidney pies or buying the frozen variety from your wholesaler. I persuaded Reggie that he should expand his business, set up the factory, cash in on the home improvement boom of the 1980s. He did, and it changed him. He became obsessed with profits, with money, to the exclusion of everything else. He employed pushy snots like Kendrew and the Barton woman to sell his high-priced rubbish. Because that's what it was, Mr Murray. Rubbish. The kitchens Grimshaw's sell are not a patch on the work Reggie Grimshaw carried out as a master tradesman. They're fibreboard garbage, mass produced, sold at prices which are at least three times what they're really worth." She sighed. "And I created that situation, Mr Murray."

Joe found it hard to accept what she was saying. "And now it's been resolved? Seems a pretty harsh way of dealing with a problem."

"And in that, you have my reason for talking to God. Yes, the situation is resolved. A year from now, Grimshaw Kitchens will be a subsidiary of Midland Kitchens. I will take the decision that Reggie wouldn't, and I will finally be absolved, but will that cancel out my original sin?"

Joe frowned. He badly needed a cigarette to help clear the fug in his brain. "So what role does the murderer play in this? God's avenging angel?"

Wendy laughed. "I fear not. Do you know the tale of the Lincoln Imp?"

"Some of it."

"There are many variations, Mr Murray. In my favourite version, there were two imps, both servants of Satan, and they went, first to Chesterfield, where they sat on the church spire and twisted it, which is why you will still see the crooked spire to this day. The two imps then came here, to Lincoln where, working on the devil's orders, they caused mayhem. They

212

smashed up tables and chairs, tripped up the Bishop and then they started destroying the Angel Choir." She gestured at the magnificent area around them. "An angel appeared and told them to stop. One of the imps was brave enough to throw rocks at the angel but the other imp cowered under the broken tables and chairs. The angel turned the first imp to stone and this gave the second imp a chance to escape. The stone imp still sits here where he was turned to stone."

She pointed up at a pillar behind them, and Joe craned his neck once more to see the carving of the imp, an evil grin on his face, one leg crossed over the other. He sat in the curved V where the pillar head spread out into the arched ceiling.

Taking a photograph with his mobile phone, still wondering what the woman was trying to say to him, Joe commented, "Very amusing."

"And apposite," Wendy assured him. "I can't decide if Reggie's killer was the imp that got away or the Lord's angel come to ensure that, once again, good triumphs over evil."

"But you don't know who the imp – or angel – is?"

Wendy smiled sweetly and gave the barest shake of her head. "I can tell you that you should widen the net. Look further than Kendrew. That trollop you're sleeping with, Melanie Markham. She and Grimshaw Kitchens go back a long way."

The news stunned Joe. "What?"

"If you'll excuse me, Mr Murray," Wendy said. "I need some time alone."

Joe stared at her, expecting more, hoping the pressure of his insistent gaze would prompt her, but she had returned to looking fixedly at the stained glass windows. Jumping to his feet, fishing into his pocket for some coins, pausing only to drop a few pounds into the fixed offertory, he marched out of the cathedral, and turned towards the hotel, hurrying along, almost breaking into a run, spurred by the nagging thought that once again some woman had been deceiving him, using him for her own nefarious ends.

A clock somewhere (he didn't know if it was the cathedral tower) chimed the hour as he passed through the hotel lobby. Most of the guests were shuffling from the Scampton Room to the Gibson Room. As he fought through them, into the bar, he met with Sheila and Brenda.

"You're going the wrong way, Joe," Brenda told him. "The food is in this direction." She pointed to the queue.

"Five minutes," he promised.

"And we have some news for you."

"I said, later." He carried on, battling his way into the bar.

He found the Markham Murder Mysteries crew in the far corner, discussing scene changes to accommodate the ever-changing circumstances of the police inquiry.

Hovering over them, he said, "Melanie. I need a word."

"Can it wait, Joe? We're a little tied up and we're due on anytime now."

"Now."

His demanding tone prompted Lee Sissons to jump up. "Who the hell…"

"Shut it, you dipstick," Joe interrupted. "This isn't one of your plays, and you're not a former Lieutenant in the Supply Corps. Melanie, I need to speak to you now."

With a sigh, she ordered Sissons to sit down and accompanied Joe across the room to a quieter corner, where he went straight on the attack.

"Why didn't you tell me you knew Reggie Grimshaw years ago?"

Melanie's face fell. "Because before he was killed, I didn't think it was any of your business, and after he was killed, I knew that you knew I couldn't have done it." She sighed. "I did, however, tell the police."

"And it never occurred to them that you could have been using me to give you cover while you had an accomplice bumping him off?"

214

"What?" Melanie gaped. "Is that what you believe?"

"It's a possibility," Joe replied angrily. "And you, yourself pointed me at your own party this morning."

"Yes, but I didn't mean me. You're being absurd, Joe. Listen to me; I had nothing to do with the murder of Reggie Grimshaw. And if you believe otherwise, then… then, just get the hell away from me."

Joe took a deep breath and forced himself to calm down. "Okay, okay. This is all going wrong. I didn't mean it to be like this. I'm sorry. Let's just rewind and start again, huh? Tell me how you knew Reggie."

"It goes back years," Melanie replied. "I was in art college. They'd just opened the factory and they needed a kitchen designer. Gerry knew Wendy. They'd met at the Central School of Speech and Drama in London, when I was on placement as a set designer at the Nottingham Playhouse."

"He told me about that. But he said you asked him about the murder mystery set up."

"That was later," Melanie admitted. "Anyway, he recommended me to the Grimshaws and I got the job. It didn't pay much, but it was work and it allowed me to develop my skills as a commercial artist. I was with them for two years. Then I was offered a permanent post in Nottingham as the assistant set designer. It was more in tune with what I wanted, so I took it. That's also where I took acting lessons, by the way. At the time, the rights to the Grimshaw Kitchens designs were mine, and I got a small commission on every sale they made."

"The same way you want to use the rights to my casebooks?"

"That's right. When I cut out, I sold them outright to the Grimshaws for a few thousand pounds. There's nothing underhanded about this, Joe. That deal put money in my bank account and helped me buy my first flat in Nottingham. Anyway, a few years later, Gerry was back in Nottingham, and we met up again, and that's when I came up with the idea of

Markham Murder Mysteries. We needed money to finance it. Actors had to be hired, and they had to be paid for rehearsals so we had to get out there and sell the idea to venues like this, and we needed the plots and the props. It wasn't cheap. So I went back to the Grimshaws and asked if they would pay me more for the designs. You must understand, Joe, that two thousand pounds, although it was a lot of money at the time, was nothing at the side of the money Grimshaw Kitchens made from those designs."

"And I'll bet Grimshaw told you where to go."

She nodded. "And how. Oh, I lost my rag, all right. Told him he hadn't heard the last of it, but of course, he had. He was within his rights and I couldn't do a thing about it."

"So how did you finance Markham Murder Mysteries?"

"The same as everyone financed everything back in the nineties, Joe. I borrowed against my flat. I'm still paying for it. Markham Murder Mysteries does well, but we don't make huge profits because the company, as a company, owes me so much." She smiled wanly. "I may break even by the time I retire."

Joe tossed the information around for several minutes. "If the Midland Kitchens deal had gone through, would it make any difference to you?"

"Yes and no. It would mean that I could approach them and pressure them into paying me for the designs. But that doesn't mean I would get any further with them than I did with the Grimshaws, and I certainly wouldn't murder Reggie to find out."

Feeling rather foolish, Joe took her hand. "I'm sorry, I only found out about twenty minutes ago, and I had the idea you had been using me."

"So you don't think I'm a suspect any longer?"

"The story as you tell it could make you a suspect in the murder of Reggie, but it wouldn't account for Naomi. I take it you didn't know her?"

Melanie shook her head. "Never met her until Reggie introduced us on Friday night."

Joe frowned. "She is the bugbear, you know. There are plenty of people here with a motive for getting rid of Reggie. He was, by all accounts, a complete dictator, and disliked by many people. But Naomi is different. The only one who admits to not liking her is Kendrew... well, Wendy didn't care for her, either, but she didn't care for salespeople as a breed."

"She's not alone, and you are absolutely right about Reggie. He was always more concerned with money than people, like so many big business concerns these days, and I'm not entirely happy it's the right approach." In an obvious attempt at amelioration, Melanie went on, "Brenda and Sheila appear to be very happy working for you, Joe."

"And they should be," he laughed. "They've got the easiest job in the world, working for the friendliest boss." He stood up. "I'd better get through for lunch. I'll catch you later."

Carrying the new information in his head, Joe made his way through the dining room, where he collected cold cuts and a few vegetables from the carvery, and joined his two companions.

"Where is Fliss?" he asked. "I told her she should sit with us for lunch and at dinner tonight."

"Gone to bed," Sheila told him. "Poor girl is under terrible stress."

"And it's just as well," Brenda said, chewing through a lettuce leaf. "We have news for you."

"News?"

"It may open your eyes a little," Brenda promised.

"You're going to tell me that Melanie knew Reggie years ago? Forget it, I already know."

Sheila was surprised. "Did she? We didn't know that. No, Joe, we have something much more devious to tell you."

While he ate, Joe listened to them. When they got to their conclusion, he gaped. Once the final message had firmly sunk in, he took out his mobile, dialled Chief Inspector Grant and made arrangements to go to the police station later in the afternoon.

At the front of the room, the Markham Murder Mysteries players were taking their places. Joe fished into his gilet for his notebook and pen and arranged them alongside his plate.

Almost on cue, Melanie appeared.

"Good afternoon, ladies and gentlemen. I'll not dwell on any of the terrible events taking place around us. Instead, I'll let Inspector O'Keefe and the cast of Haliwell's Heroes lead us straight into the next scene."

The lights at the front came up.

***

On the board at O'Keefe's shoulder, the tissue had been removed from the photographs, and they now showed Zara Lucescu's body, a fine weal around her neck, from several angles.

"Dr Wilson," O'Keefe began, "at my request, you examined the body of Countess Lucescu. Would you mind repeating your conclusions, for the benefit of everyone else?"

"Of course." Valerie Wilson left her seat and moved to the other side of the display board where she pointed to the weal around Zara's neck. "The ligature marks indicate that the countess was strangled by the cable on the bedside table lamp." She pointed to a second photograph which showed the lamp and its braided, rayon flex in close up. "Madame Lucescu's face was pale, her lips blue, a state known as cyanosis which is caused by lack of oxygen, while the rest of her body was livid. These are classic signs of manual strangulation. Rigor mortis had set in, so I conclude that the murder must have been carried out sometime during the night." She directed everyone's attention to photographs of the room in general. "Note the signs of a struggle. The lamp was found on the floor, quite close to the countess' body, and pieces of furniture have been overturned. One can only conclude that Madame Lucescu fought quite bravely against her attacker, but he was too powerful for her."

"And you therefore assume it is a man?" O'Keefe asked.

"I know I did not kill Zara, and I believe Miss Theresa and Mrs Sadie Haliwell would not have the physical strength to overcome the countess. I therefore conclude that it was either Mr Crenshaw or Mr McLintock."

Both men protested loudly, but O'Keefe silenced them with an upraised finger.

"I notice she's leaving her damned husband out of it," McLintock protested.

"That will do, Mr McLintock," O'Keefe replied. "I appreciate your concerns, but Dr Wilson has vouched for her husband, and I am in possession of other information which may have a bearing on the identity of Madame Lucescu's killer."

"Such as what?" Crenshaw demanded.

"I'm coming to that, sir." The inspector took out his pocketbook and thumbed through the pages. "Now, you will all recall that after the death of the colonel, the countess asked to speak to me in private. During that conversation, she imparted certain facts to me. Facts which I have subsequently ascertained to be true. She was not a Romanian countess. She was not even Romanian, but a British subject, and her real name was Sarah Lumley. She was, ladies and gentlemen, an agent of His Majesty's Treasury."

The announcement was greeted with gasps from the table.

"A treasury agent?" McLintock repeated. "But what the devil was she doing here?"

"She had been working undercover for some months, sir, and having tricked her way into the colonel's confidence, she was looking into his financial activities… and those of Mr Crenshaw and Captain Wilson, *and* you, Mr McLintock."

There was more bluster from those seated around the table.

O'Keefe allowed it to settle. "And now, Ms Haliwell, I must ask you, how did your husband finance his business affairs after the war?"

Sadie surged drunkenly. "I have absolutely no idea. He dabbled a little before the war, you know. Stocks, shares and so on. McLintock should know. His father dealt with all of Gregory's investments."

"I specifically asked about his investments after the war, madam."

"Sorry," Sadie replied. "Can't help you."

"Are you suggesting my father was a crook?" Theresa demanded.

"I'm suggesting nothing, miss," O'Keefe replied, "But the countess was investigating his business activities." O'Keefe cast his gaze on McLintock. "Sir?"

"I can't tell you much," the young stockbroker admitted, "because quite frankly, I don't know much, but the colonel approached me in 1946 with a large sum of money he wanted to spread over as many holdings as he could. He took some safe stock, some less safe, in an effort to balance his returns."

"How much is a large sum?" O'Keefe demanded.

"A hundred and twenty-five thousand pounds."

More gasps came from the table.

"Did he say where this money had come from, Mr McLintock?"

"America," McLintock replied promptly. "Apparently, while he was working with the Americans, on exercises in Devon, he received one or two excellent tips from the Yanks, and he dabbled with money over the course of the war from 1941 until early in '46, then materialised all his holdings so he could bring them back here to Great Britain." The stockbroker spread his hands almost apologetically. "All right, so maybe it wasn't quite above board. You could argue that it was his patriotic duty to put his money into war bonds, but let's face it, the colonel was already a hero. He'd done enough for this country, and he had a right to expect some return on it."

"Of course, sir," O'Keefe agreed. "Did you actually see the transfer of funds from the USA?"

"Yes, of course I did. Bearer bonds."

"Thank you, Mr McLintock. That is most enlightening."

Captain Wilson voiced his objections. "I don't like the way you said that, Inspector. Are you insinuating that the colonel wasn't telling the truth when he approached McLintock?"

"I'm not insinuating anything, Captain. I'm saying he didn't tell the truth. The truth, sir, lay under the rubble of Chateau Armand." The inspector smiled. "A fortune in gold bullion which the Nazis had to leave behind when Colonel Haliwell and his team launched their assault on the chateau."

"Not that old chestnut," Wilson snapped. "I warned Zara about that the other night. Take it from me, Inspector, there was no gold at Chateau Armand. I know."

"Zara, or Sarah, to call her by her correct name, knew otherwise, Captain. There was a considerable amount of gold at the chateau. Its value was estimated at £150,000. And that, ladies and gentlemen, leaves us with a problem. If Colonel Haliwell had £125,000 to play with, who got the other £25,000?"

**

The lights dimmed, applause broke out and Melanie took the front of the dining room again.

"There is one final scene, ladies and gentlemen, to be played this evening, before dinner. After that, it will be time for you to present your written solutions and the complete answer will be given to you at breakfast tomorrow morning. For now, Inspector O'Keefe and the cast will be around the hotel for the remainder of the day, and as an extra incentive, there is another murder weapon hidden somewhere in the hotel or its grounds. Study the photographs carefully and they will give you a clue as to where it is and *what* it is."

As the room dissolved into chatter, Melanie made her way across to Joe. "A word?"

"Yes. Of course." He pocketed his notebook and acknowledging Brenda's sly grin with a wince, followed Melanie to the front of the room.

"I spoke to Gerry earlier," she announced. "Normally, he delivers the solution. However, he's happy to stand to one side tomorrow morning, and we'd like you to deliver it."

"I, er, oh…" Joe felt his cheeks burning. "Come on, Melanie. I'm no performer."

She smiled coyly. "I wouldn't say that." More seriously she urged him, "You are so close to the solution that it's incredible, and we'll give you the full written solution to fill in any gaps. And you keep telling me you're the DJ for your club discos."

"I… Oh, all right then, but if I bugger it up, it's your fault."

She beamed. "That's great. I'll announce after breakfast tomorrow. Oh, did you, er, book the table for tonight."

Joe blushed again. "Hell. I'm sorry. With the two real murders and all the running around…" he trailed off lamely.

"It's no problem," Melanie let him off. "Why don't we just have dinner together here. In the restaurant next door?"

"Sounds like a plan. Now, if you'll excuse me, I have to get off down to the cop shop."

Chapter Fifteen

On the way there by taxi, Joe rehearsed his approach. Grant, he knew, would be amenable. Idleman would not. The new found knowledge he had gleaned from his best friends would persuade her.

To Joe's surprise, the taxi driver did not make for the city centre, but instead, turned north along the inner ring road.

"Too many bleed'n' blocked off streets, guv," said the driver. "Only about a mile, but you gotta give a bitta ground afore you can make any."

Driving through suburban Lincoln, it would take less than five minutes to get to the police station. January 1st. New Year's Day, and while the town might be busy with drinkers and diners, the side roads were devoid of traffic. Joe could imagine the scenes in the cottages, bungalows and rambling detached houses they passed along the way. Parties, get-togethers which would run on until late night/early morning as families reminisced about the year just past and prepared for the one to come. He and his friends would engage in the same way, but not until they returned to Sanford tomorrow.

When the driver turned south again, towards the city centre, Joe caught a fleeting glimpse of Lincoln Castle, its hilltop location overlooking its domain, and he remembered it had been one of the places on their itinerary, one of the places scratched thanks to the actions of a person or persons, as yet unknown, who had tried to solve problems the wrong way.

The police station, sited just outside the city centre, off the western ring road, had an air of function about it. A long, low rise building, sitting well with its surroundings, but with an air of austerity as if warning callers off.

Announcing himself in reception, he was shown to the open plan CID room, where only a few officers were on shift, and into Grant's small enclave, partitioned off in one corner, and there, as he had anticipated, Sergeant Idleman voiced her immediate objection.

"Sir, Kendrew is under caution, and we should not let members of the public see or speak to him. It may jeopardise our case against him."

Having listened to Joe, Grant disagreed. "Our job is as much to protect the innocent as it is to prosecute the guilty, Sergeant, and so far we haven't had any luck trying to draw Kendrew out." For Joe's benefit, he added, "He's said nothing to us other than he's innocent. That's all we get out of him. He won't even tell us why he went to Naomi's room this morning, and he hasn't even asked for a solicitor."

"I think he may be telling the truth, Phil, when he says he's innocent, and I know why he went to her room. It's the reason he's saying nothing," Joe pointed out, much to the dismay of the sergeant, "but I need to confront him with the things I think I know."

"You *think* you know?" Idleman protested. "You mean you're not certain?"

"That's right, Sergeant. I think I know. Ten minutes with Kendrew will prove it one way or the other. And you two will be sat in with us, so you know I won't be screwing around with your case."

At length, despite Idleman's continued reservations and Joe's refusal to divulge his information, Grant ruled that the meeting would be allowed, and the two police officers led Joe along the ground floor to a large interview room where Kendrew was already waiting with a uniformed constable in attendance.

The hours since his arrest had taken their toll. He looked as bedraggled and dishevelled as his wife had appeared to Joe. Handcuffed and clad in police holding overalls, a plain white jump suit, while his own clothing had been sent for analysis, he looked thoroughly wretched.

"Now, Mr Kendrew, Mr Murray would like a word with you," Sergeant Idleman announced. "I must advise you that he is not a police officer and you are under no obligation to speak to him, but he has said he may be able to help."

"I've nothing to say to him."

Joe recalled the time a salesman, similar to Kendrew, had arrived at the Lazy Luncheonette. Before he could say a word, Joe had said, 'I'm not interested,' to which the salesman responded, 'how do you know when you haven't heard what I have to offer?' Joe applied the same principle now.

"How do you know when you don't know what I have to say?"

Kendrew grunted. "It's your fault I'm here."

"No, Kendrew, it's your own fault. If you'd been a bit more honest, the chief inspector and the sergeant, here, may have thought twice. And right now, if you don't want to speak to me, I'm cool. I'll go back to the hotel and leave you to rot. I'll be able to read about your life sentence in the papers."

Some of Kendrew's arrogance returned. "I'm innocent."

"No you're not," Joe argued. "You're guilty as hell, and you know it. But you're not guilty of the murders. Now do you want me to leave, cos it's New Year's Day and there's a party on at the hotel. I'd much rather be there than here."

Kendrew remained silent for a long time. First he looked down at his cuffed wrists, then he stared up at the narrow windows running along near the ceiling pining, Joe surmised, for his freedom. His eyes, Joe noticed, were pale and bloodshot, his square features worked agitatedly as if he were carrying on some internal argument with himself.

In order to turn on the pressure, Joe scraped his chair back and stood. "All right. You can roast him for all I care, Phil.

Pity the real killer will get away, but what the hell, it'll look good on your returns. Help keep the Chief Constable off your back."

Some of the Kendrew's attention returned. The hollow eyes bored into Joe. "Just say your piece and get lost."

"Fine. I'll do that." Joe paused a moment and sat down again. "Tell me about you and Naomi Barton."

The agonised face twisted into a demonised mask. "I hated her. She was a…"

Joe held up a finger for silence. "The French have a thing about English food, you know. They say we Brits only know three vegetables, and two of those are cabbage. And I spend my working life cooking cabbage." He narrowed stern eyes on Kendrew. "But don't let that fool you into thinking I am a cabbage. I'm smarter, sharper than an idiot like you will ever be. When I ask you to tell me about you and Naomi, I don't mean the smokescreen you've been putting up for the last two years. I mean how long had you been having an affair with her, and what were your plans?"

The look of horror on Kendrew's face could have been mistaken for incredulity at the outrageousness of the accusation, but Joe was not fooled. It was the astonishment of one caught in the act despite the care he had taken to cover his tracks.

Kendrew dismissed the allegation. "You're out of your mind. I told you, I hated the cow."

Joe ignored the bluster. "You were good; the pair of you. I spoke to Naomi yesterday, and she had me convinced. Dropping oh so slight hints that she was sleeping with Reggie, the same way you had, only much subtler than you. She was actually, skilfully hiding the fact that she was sleeping with you."

"Look, I told you…"

"Shut your mouth and open your ears," Joe snapped. "Right now, you are looking at a life sentence. That can be anything from ten years to whole of life. The only thing that stands between you and that is me. The police are working through Naomi's room right now, and they will find traces of you on the bed, because that's where you were on Friday night, when your poor, gormless wife thought you'd got up to go for a smoke. Those traces, plus your prints on the pistol that killed Reggie will probably be enough to convict you. But I know you didn't do it. Now either answer me straight, or I walk out of here, go back to the Twin Spires, get drunk and hopefully attend another, er, business meeting with Melanie Markham before I go home to Sanford tomorrow morning."

Kendrew's shoulders slumped. "How did you guess?"

"I didn't. My friends, Sheila Riley and Brenda Jump did. Like I said, your missus is a poor, gormless child who's hopelessly in love with you, and love is a funny thing. I wouldn't know because I've never been in love... not properly anyway. But Sheila and Brenda have, and they know how it can blind people. Fliss' love for you, plus your little game of 'I hate Naomi Barton more than she hates me', has blinded your wife to the truth."

Kendrew swallowed hard. "Have you told Fliss?"

"No. I don't think it's my place to tell her anything. It's yours. And she's so distressed that Sheila and Brenda won't say a word, either, because they don't want to hurt her any more than today's events have already." Joe spread his hands in a casual gesture of superiority. "Quite frankly, people like you sicken me when you don't make me laugh. You think yourself so superior, so intelligent, and yet when someone looks closely enough at your actions, you're transparent."

Anger suffused the sallow cheeks. "What the hell are you talking about?"

"Would a supposedly intelligent man take on a huge house, drop himself in way over his head, just to spite a woman he dislikes? Would he hell as like. But he would take it on if he was planning to push his wife out and bring in his new girlfriend, who also happens to earn a huge salary, because between them, they could easily afford the place. When were you planning on dumping Fliss?"

Kendrew leaned forward. The anger was gone again, and he had the air of a man who was beaten, ready to throw himself upon the mercy of his enemies.

"When Reggie retired," he admitted.

"Because when Reggie retired one of you would step up to Sales Director, and let's be frank about this, Kendrew, it didn't matter which one, did it?"

Kendrew shook his head. "We couldn't do anything before, because it would be obvious to Reggie that we were creating a... I dunno... kingdom within a kingdom. Reggie was a control freak. He wouldn't have tolerated that, and instead he would have brought someone in from the outside. So we had to wait until he retired next year... pardon me, *this* year. Once one of us moved up, we would be earning well over a hundred thousand a year between us. The mortgage on Parkfield would be easy."

"And it would be too late for Reggie to do anything about it other than fire one or both of you, and if he did that without good reason, you'd nail him for a settlement that would practically bankrupt the company."

Kendrew nodded miserably, and the anger took over again. He glared at Joe. "Do you know what it's like to struggle? Never enough money, scraping and scratching your way to payday every month, waiting and waiting for that old fool to get out of the way and let someone take over who could do the job. Fifty bloody thousand a year?" he sneered. "It's nothing. Nothing at all."

"Yes I know what it's like to struggle," Joe hissed, "because right now I'm struggling to keep my hands off you. I employ two women who don't earn a third of that, but I don't see them plotting behind someone else's back. I don't see them ready to drop me at a minute's notice once I've put my nephew in charge. You're scum, you. D'you know? You're not fit to work as a doormat."

"Take it easy, Joe," Grant advised. "And what of your wife, Mr Kendrew?"

The younger man shrugged. "Fliss is a good woman, but Naomi was just... I dunno... better."

Still struggling to keep his temper under control, Joe hammered at him. "The worst thing that could have happened was Reggie dying," Joe said. "Naomi was telling the truth about that, wasn't she?"

Again there was the slightest incline of Kendrew's head in agreement. "We'd managed to persuade Reggie that selling out to Midland Kitchens was the wrong move, but Wendy has never had any serious interest in the business, and she'll probably sell up, and Naomi and I will probably both get the boot. Either that or we'll be demoted. Our plans are in ruins."

"Naomi would have got the boot," Joe corrected. "She's dead, too. And do you know why she's dead?" He leaned angrily forward and only just stopped himself from reaching across the table and yanking Kendrew's head upright to a position where he could look him in the eye. "Because someone believed the claptrap you put out about her screwing Reggie. Someone believed that because she was his mistress, she might know why Reggie was killed, and in turn she might know who killed him. So she had to be silenced."

The young man broke down, his shoulders heaving, his body racked with sobs.

Joe sat back and poured forth his disdain. "You disgust me, Kendrew. You and all those like you. All you ever stop to think about is yourself. You have a good looking wife who adores you, yet all you ever did for that poor kid was use her. She doesn't matter to you. All you care about is your bit on the side and the ruin of your plans. I ought to walk out of here and let you stew in the mess you've made."

"Hear, hear," said Sergeant Idleman.

After fuming for a moment, Joe homed in on Kendrew again. "You were arguing with Reggie in his room on Friday night. What about?"

Pulling himself together Kendrew shook his head. "It wasn't me. I'm not saying you didn't hear Reggie shooting his mouth off, but it was me. At midnight, I was with Fliss. Half an hour later, I was with Naomi. Half an hour after that, your friends saw me in reception. I didn't see Reggie all night. Not after he left the bar at half past ten."

"And last night?"

Kendrew shuddered. "I was unwell. I don't know whether it was the vol-au-vents, the chicken, or maybe bad beer, but I kept throwing up. I didn't leave our room until after eight this morning when I went to Naomi. And that's when I found her."

Still angry, more at his own misinterpretation of events, Joe stood up. "Do what you want with him, Phil. I don't care."

"Wait there a minute, Joe," Grant insisted. He addressed the uniformed constable. "Take him back to the cells. I'll want to talk to him again." He concentrated on his suspect. "I'll need to formally interview you, sir, and this time, if you want to get out of here, I'll need some answers."

While Kendrew was led from the interview room, Joe rolled a cigarette. Holding it up, he asked, "Smoking area?"

"Outside," Grant said, and he and Idleman led the way.

"I must say, I was wrong about you," Idleman commented as they ambled along the dimly lit corridor towards the rear car park.

"Most people are. They just think I'm a grumbling old nosy parker."

"And you are," said Idleman as they stepped out into the gloomy day, "but I would never have guessed about him and Naomi Barton."

"It wasn't my doing," Joe confessed. "It really was Sheila and Brenda who rumbled it."

The car park was half full of patrol cars and private saloons. The far side had no walls, but all Joe could see were the terraced houses opposite, hiding the city of Lincoln beyond them. A pair of uniformed officers were busy checking their vehicle before setting out on their patrol, but other than them, there was no sign of life.

"New Year's Day, huh?"

"Quiet," Grant commented. "It'll liven up when the pubs open tonight." He lit a cigarette. "All right, Joe, where does all this leave us?"

"Up a gum tree," Joe admitted. "I'm certain Kendrew didn't kill either of them. I think he should be hung, drawn and quartered for the way he's treated his wife."

"Hear, hear," Sergeant Idleman repeated much to the amusement of the two men.

Joe chuckled. "But he's not our killer. Y'see, and this never occurred to me before, but if he was, he did too much."

"How so?" Grant asked.

"Take the pistol, for example. All right, so he hid it in the shrubbery, but why not leave it there? When we found the movie gun, you said it could have stayed there for months without being discovered. The same applies to the real gun, so why did he lead his wife right to it, then pick it up to get his dabs all over it?"

"Double bluff," Idleman suggested. "We nick him then let him go after all this comes out."

"Possible," Joe admitted, "but then why kill Naomi?"

"Because their plans were screwed up after Reggie was killed."

"Which only prompts me to ask, why kill Reggie in the first place? You heard him say that he and Naomi had persuaded Reggie not to sell, but Naomi told me, and he's just confirmed that where Wendy is concerned, it's no contest."

Idleman pondered the question. "We could be looking for two killers."

231

The chief inspector shook his head. "I don't believe that."

"Me neither," Joe said. "And then there's the problem of the killings matching the murder mystery play. Both he and his wife swear they've never seen the thing before. No; I think someone has used him as a patsy."

"If that is the case, it's possible that Naomi was murdered purely to point the finger at him," Grant said.

Idleman shuddered. "That's appalling, sir. I mean, there's never a good excuse for murder, but to kill someone so callously, simply to get another man jailed for it, is shocking."

Joe puffed on his reluctant cigarette. "I sometimes wonder what they teach you people about motives." He noticed her scowl, signalling a return to her earlier animosity. "It's all right, Sergeant, I'm not having a go at you, but at the system. What you have to bear in mind is that the motive always makes sense to the killer."

"True enough," Grant agreed. "It doesn't matter how crazy he seems to the rest of us, he does what he does because it makes absolute sense to him." Dragging deeply on his smoke, he asked, "Anything else springing to mind from the Twin Spires, Joe?"

"Suspect-wise? No. We're swimming in them."

"The Grimshaw Kitchens lot are favourite, surely?" Idleman commented.

"You'd think so," Joe agreed, "but don't knock the crowd from Markham Murder Mysteries. Melanie knew Grimshaw years ago, and Gerry Carlin was humping Wendy on Friday night."

Idleman almost choked. "I must say, Mr Murray, I don't care for your terminology."

"I am what I am, Sergeant. I speak as I was brought up to speak. Making love is not an option in Sanford... usually because love is the last thing on most men's minds." Joe crushed out his cigarette. "Right, I'll grab a cab back up the hill and do some more nosying."

"Sergeant, run Mr Murray back to the Twin Spires." Joe was about to protest, but Grant got there first. "Least we can do, Joe."

"Good of you," Joe thanked him. "What will you do about Kendrew?"

"I'll interview him again, right now. As long as he gives me some answers, I'll let him go" He frowned. "I think you're right. I don't think he killed either of them. But that still leaves us with the question of who did."

"Well, while you're talking to him, see if you can persuade him to go down on bended knees to beg his wife's forgiveness. If I had someone like her for a missus, I maybe wouldn't be so grouchy."

***

As it turned out, Kendrew arrived back at the Twin Spires less than fifteen minutes after Joe, to be greeted effusively by his wife, who smothered him in hugs and kisses.

And when she was through with her husband, she hugged and kissed Joe, too.

"Thank you, Mr Murray. Your friends said you'd do it and you have."

"Yes, well, I think your husband needs to clean himself up, Fliss. Police cells aren't the most hygienic of places."

Kendrew swallowed hard, stared malevolently at Joe, and then down at his wife. When he looked at Joe again, his glower had subsided. Slowly, he offered his hand. "Thank you, Murray."

Joe shook hands. "No problem, son. Now take your missus somewhere private and expensive. You owe her big time. If she hadn't hassled me, you'd be rotting in that cell forever." Joe delivered a meaningful glance. "Remember. You owe her."

Joe watched them amble towards the lift, then sensed a presence at his side. "Hello, Brenda."

"Did you tell her?" his companion asked.

Joe shook his head. "I'm more discreet than that, and you know it. It's not my place to tell her anything, but I made it clear he should. Especially if he wants her back."

"He doesn't deserve her, and if she's only second best, she shouldn't take him back."

Joe led the way towards the bar. "I agree, but it's not our decision to make, is it?"

Brenda tugged at his sleeve. "Come on, Joe. Sheila and I have been doing some detecting and you need to see what we've noticed."

He followed her through Reception and into the dining room where Sheila stood at the information board, looking over the photographs. Running an eye over the table, Joe noticed instantly that the fake cheese wire had turned up.

"Who found that?" he asked.

"Oh, Julia Staines," Sheila replied. "Apparently they win a bottle of champagne for it, and Inspector O'Keefe will announce its importance before dinner. Joe, look at this, will you?"

Moving to join her at the board, Joe said, "That reminds me, I won't be with you for dinner this evening."

Brenda's eyes opened wide. "Oh yes? And who's the lucky woman?"

"Melanie. Who else?"

"Joe, I need you to look at this and confirm what I'm saying."

He ignored Sheila."I promised her on Friday if I got the solution early, I'd stand her dinner tonight. Then I forgot to book the restaurant."

"Please, Joe," Sheila begged. "Our solutions have to be in tonight."

Brenda was more interested in the growing bond between Joe and Melanie. "You're not going Dutch are you?"

"Of course not. I'm paying."

"Joe." Sheila began to sound frustrated, but still Brenda would not let go.

"Well don't pull the old stunt of forgetting your wallet. There's nothing worse for killing the mood."

"I bow to your superior experience, Brenda."

"For God's sake, Joe, will you look at this bloody picture?"

Sheila's raised voice caused several heads to turn.

In deference to her irritation, Joe followed her pointing finger.

The image was of Zara Lucescu's room and the toppled bedside lamp.

"So what's wrong with it?" Joe asked.

The lamp was on the floor, but the flex ran up behind the bedside cabinet. Tracing its line with her finger, Sheila explained, "Look at the way the cord rises behind the cabinet. We think it's still plugged into the wall."

"Yes. And?"

Sheila kept her voice low so that no one could overhear. "How could she have been strangled with the bedside lamp if it's still plugged into a wall socket?"

"And you need to speculate to work that out?" Joe demanded. He moved across and indicated the photograph of the strangled countess.

At once, he wished he had not. Expertly applied makeup gave Zara the appearance of having been strangled right down to the narrow weal around her slender neck, and it reminded him instantly of Naomi Barton the way he had seen her after breakfast. The disarray, the smell of cold, damp and death assaulted his memory.

He reminded himself that Zara, or rather actress Emma Pemberley, was playing a part. Naomi Barton was for real; a woman who, less than twenty-four hours previously had been living and breathing and now lay naked on a mortuary slab, and so far he had made zero progress in finding her killer.

He pulled himself together and pointed to the weal around

Zara's neck. "Look at it, study it, then look at the electrical flex, and when you've done that, look on the table."

With that, he turned on his heels and marched out of the dining room.

Chapter Sixteen

Returning to his room, Joe flopped on the bed, intent on catching an hour's sleep.

With the clock reading almost 4 p.m. the sky had darkened, night was approaching and without the lights on, the room was comfortably warm enough to induce sleep, but it would not come. Instead, as he stared into the gathering darkness, images flashed through his mind like a video movie on fast-forward. Meeting Reggie, sneaking to Melanie's room, Reggie arguing with his unseen visitor, Reggie dead, Naomi dead, Naomi turning her venom on him, Kendrew grabbing him, Wendy staring at the stained glass windows of the Angel Choir, the blood spattered over Reggie's bedside cabinet, Naomi's bedside cabinet in a state of disarray.

Somewhere in amongst it all, he was missing something. As usual it was tiny, it was trivial, insignificant, but it was the lack of significance that paradoxically made it of such importance.

The events of the whole weekend eventually conspired to send him into a disturbed sleep, but he was wide awake again just after five, the problem still nagging at him.

I need to ask God why I created the monster that Reggie had become. If I slept with Reggie, and I stress, 'if', it was because I saw it as expedient, and not because he brought any undue pressure to bear. Wendy has never had any serious interest in the business, and she'll probably sell up, and Naomi and I will probably both get the boot.

Reggie's face swam up through the darkness and laughed at him. "The answer's obvious, me ducks."

But it wasn't obvious. Not to Joe. From every angle he arrived at the same conclusion and it was the wrong one; the one that he had *proved* to be wrong.

He took out his netbook, set it up on the escritoire, and stared gloomily out at the illuminated towers of Lincoln Cathedral while he waited for it to boot up. When it was running, he opened a spreadsheet and filled its cells with every name he could think of that was connected to the case. Then he began to shuffle them around, mixing and matching known pairs, unlikely pairs, desperately seeking that elusive connection, and still it would not come to him. At five thirty, angry, frustrated, he took a hot shower and shaved.

In dressing for dinner, he opted not to wear a tie. "Don't see why I should change the habits of a lifetime," he muttered to the mirror. Instead he put on a pair of dark grey, casual trousers, a fresh, short-sleeved shirt, and his ubiquitous gilet, then, locking the door behind him, made his way along the landing to wait for the lift.

He met Sheila and Brenda in the lobby, where they were studying leaflets on the attractions of Lincoln and the surrounding countryside. Brenda complimented him on his attire, Sheila added her approval, criticising him only for not putting on a tie, and they moved to the dining room for the final act of Haliwell's Heroes.

Taking their seats, they found summary sheets in front of them. When Joe studied the single sheet of A4 paper, he found it laid out quite simply. There were slots for his name and room number at the top, the heading *Haliwell's Heroes* beneath them, and under that, three widely spaced headings; *Murderer(s); Motive; Clues.*

"Ignoring the play, have you made any progress with the murders of Reggie Grimshaw and Naomi Barton?" Sheila asked.

"I've cleared young Kendrew," he said, "and I notice their table is empty." He jerked his head backwards at the vacant table behind them. "I've no doubt they're having a good old heart to heart."

"It should be knife to heart," Brenda grumbled. "When I think of his contempt for that poor girl, it makes my blood boil."

"I agree," Joe said, "but at least they're not murderers. Neither of them."

Sheila fussed, setting out her notebook and pen. "That's looking on the bright side. I'm afraid that whatever marriage they have left will crumble. As for the murders, I think we'll find they really were *crimes passionnel*."

Her opinion set Joe's mind thinking once more, and it continued to grind on the various possibilities until Melanie appeared at the front of the room.

"Good evening, ladies and gentlemen. It's time for the penultimate act of Haliwell's Heroes, the final scene before Inspector O'Keefe makes his arrest tomorrow morning. You all have summary sheets in front of you. If you want to take part in our competition, all you have to do is complete the summary sheet, and hand it to me or one of my cast before midnight tonight. The lucky winner will be announced after Inspector O'Keefe makes his arrest tomorrow morning. And now, without further ado, let me hand you over to Inspector O'Keefe for his summary of the events."

Melanie backed off and the lights at the front of the dining room came up.

***

Standing to one side of the remaining dinner guests, O'Keefe held up a polythene bag containing the cheese wire.

"Captain Wilson, may I ask about your role on D-Day?"

Wilson fingered his bowtie. "I told you, I was with the 50th Infantry Division at Bayeux."

"Indeed, sir, but you were not a member of the 50th, were

239

you? And you didn't come ashore on either Gold or Sword, did you? In fact you were with the Royal Marine Commandos, and you actually parachuted into Normandy on the night of June 5th, didn't you, in order to make contact with the French Resistance."

Wilson made visible effort to control himself. "I'm sorry, Inspector, but our work is still classified under the Official Secret Act."

"I'm investigating three nasty murders, sir, and nothing is secret from me. Not even your war record. May I ask, do you know what this is?"

O'Keefe passed the bag to Wilson who studied it.

"It's a cheese-cutter."

"Precisely, sir," the inspector agreed. "A cheese-cutter. And the cheese-cutter was one of the commando's preferred weapons during World War Two, was it not? A silent killer."

Wilson looked uncomfortable again. "We used them, yes. They were efficient and silent. Now, look here, O'Keefe, are you insinuating that I had something to do with these murders? Because if you are, may I remind you that my wife examined the countess and reported that she was strangled with the electricity flex of the bedside lamp."

"I'm aware of that, sir." O'Keefe held up the cheese-cutter again. "But this weapon was found in the grounds by one of my officers earlier today."

Putting down the weapon, O'Keefe made a show of checking his pocketbook before concentrating on Wilson again.

"At Chateau Armand it's reported that a British officer, Lieutenant Creasey, was killed in a friendly fire incident. Can you tell me anything about that, Captain?"

"Simple case of mistaken identity, Inspector. Colonel Haliwell lost most of his officers during the assault. With the chateau secured, there was always the threat of a German counterattack, so we had the place heavily guarded. Creasey was challenged by sentries, but didn't give the correct response and he was shot. I doubt that it was the only such incident during the D-Day offensive."

"Of course not, but this officer had already been in touch with the division HQ expressing his concern over certain, er, matters, let's say, at Chateau Armand. The War Office had no details of the substance of his complaints. Could you throw any light on that?"

Wilson shrugged. "I have no knowledge of it whatsoever. I can speculate, I suppose. The colonel was known to be a hard taskmaster. Perhaps some of the enlisted men had complained about his treatment of them and perhaps Creasey felt it his duty to make the complaints known to HQ."

"Thank you, sir," O'Keefe said. "Now, Captain, may I ask about your business activities since the war?"

"I became a venture capitalist," Wilson replied. "The country needed investment, and like my friend, the colonel, I saw it as my patriotic duty to invest the little savings that I had in projects which would help get the country moving again."

"And how much did you invest in the country, sir?"

Wilson was deliberately vague. "Well, not as much as Colonel Haliwell, of course, but I'd says, roughly twenty thousand pounds."

O'Keefe had another surprise for them. "My inquiries lead me to believe it was much more than that, sir. In fact it was thirty thousand pounds. Not all the money was yours. About one fifth of it was your lady wife's."

The accusing tone sparked Valerie Wilson to protest. "This is the 1950s, you know, Inspector. We women are not simply expected to sit at home cooking dinner and looking after the children. I have my own money and I was entitled to invest it as I saw fit."

"Of course, madam." Apparently put out by her complaint, O'Keefe shifted his attention to Crenshaw. "Let's look at your activities since the war, shall we, sir?"

The younger man did not appear concerned. "I have nothing to hide, Inspector."

"Of course not. In that case, sir, may I ask how you managed to persuade Colonel Haliwell to insist upon his daughter's engagement to you?"

Crenshaw opened his mouth to protest, but O'Keefe pressed on before he could say anything.

"You see, sir, we know quite a bit about your war record, as I indicated before, and although no charges were ever laid against you, I have to wonder just how much the influence of your father, Jeremy Crenshaw, 13th Earl of Eppingham, might have to do with that."

"I resent that," Crenshaw bit back. "My record, as you will know if you checked with the War Office, was exemplary."

"The official record, yes," O'Keefe agreed, "but we checked with battalion HQ and off the record, they tell us a different tale. I just wonder, sir, whether those two missing trucks were, in fact, diverted to Chateau Armand, in order to assist with the removal of £150,000 worth of gold bullion."

"I knew nothing about the whereabouts of those trucks," Crenshaw argued.

"No, sir. But many months later, after the advance into Germany, two similar lorries were found in Marseilles. Quite convenient for offloading illicit cargo onto a ship for onward transportation to, say, North Africa. I wonder, Mr Crenshaw, how much you *really* knew about them, and whether that influenced the colonel in a choice of suitor for his only daughter." O'Keefe's pinpoint stare rested on McLintock. "Much more persuasive than the arguments of a stockbroker questioning the source of a post war fortune."

His accusations were greeted with howls of protest, not least from Theresa.

"I resent that, Inspector," she cried "Michael and I are very much in love."

"That's what you said to me before Crenshaw showed up,"

242

McLintock complained.

"You mean before I pointed out what a crooked coward you are," Crenshaw growled.

McLintock got to his feet, stripping off his dinner jacket. "I'll show you who's a coward."

Crenshaw, too, rose. Wilson began to bark orders at them, Theresa flapped.

"All right, gentlemen. That will do." O'Keefe's voice boomed around the room, drowning out everyone else.

Order was restored, the two combatants returned to their seats, glowering at each other, and O'Keefe took control again.

"Your efforts, gentlemen, during World War Two do not interest me. Whatever crimes you may or may not have committed during the Normandy offensive are no concern of mine. The murders of Colonel Gregory Haliwell, Miss Kerry Dolman and Miss Sarah Lumley are. I shall return tomorrow morning, and at that time, I expect to be making an arrest."

***

The lights dimmed and applause broke out around the dining room.

"Crenshaw," Brenda said.

"I think McLintock," Sheila declared."I think he's very angry with Haliwell for handing his daughter over to Crenshaw."

"Why did he kill Kerry and Zara?" Brenda wanted to know.

"Kerry because she probably rejected his advances, and Zara because he knew she was a Treasury Agent and she was investigating some of his iffy transactions as a stockbroker."

"Ooh, I never thought of that." Brenda scribbled out her ideas and penned in fresh ones. "What about you, Joe?"

"I knew on Friday night, and I've seen nothing to make me change my mind." Joe folded away his notebook and dropped it in his pocket as Melanie appeared up front.

"There you have it, ladies and gentlemen. The identity of the killer should be apparent to you by now, but you will need to use some logical deduction to arrive at a motive. Don't forget, summary sheets in by midnight tonight to be included in our competition, and the arrest will be made at breakfast tomorrow morning."

Julia Staines was called out and awarded a bottle of champagne for finding the cheese-cutter, after which Melanie bowed out to a round of applause and the room settled down to wait for dinner.

Joe got to his feet. "Right, girls. I'll catch you later, at the disco. I have a lady to woo."

"Be gentle with her, Joe," Brenda advised.

***

The 617 catered for the Twin Spires' non-resident patrons. Set aside from the main hotel, on the ground floor of the redbrick annexe, the subdued lighting, smaller windows, and candlelit tables set into booths, was less cramped and more intimate than the hotel dining room.

At least that was the impression Joe had when the maître d showed them to their table overlooking the car park.

Joe had booked the table after explaining to Melanie that he had forgotten to book her original choice. They arrived to find the place three-quarters full, but in contrast to the hotel, the low-level chatter of other diners did not impinge upon the cosiness of their booth.

Joe ordered drinks, a glass of lager for himself, a Bacardi and coke for Melanie, while they studied the menu. Eventually, Joe decided on lamb cutlets for himself while Melanie chose veal medallions in a white wine butter sauce, and he added a bottle of house red to the order.

"Did the Lazy Luncheonette never aspire to such grandeur, Joe?" Melanie asked with a gesture at the room.

He gave a grunting little laugh of real pleasure. "Hell, no. The Lazy Luncheonette started out as Alf's Caff on Doncaster Road, just after the war. Alf was my old dad. He knew what he was doing. Post war rebuilding, the pits and the foundries were going hell for leather and there were lorries trundling up and down that road day and night." He toyed with his glass, and nodded at the convivial comfort around them. "A place like this, believe it or not, won't make as much as the Lazy Luncheonette on a meal by meal basis. They employ high-class chefs, waiters, bar people, a manager. It all creams off the top, you know. My joint… well, we have eighty covers, and there are only four of us running it. Me, Sheila, Brenda, and my nephew Lee. Don't make no mistake. The meals these people turn out, Lee and I can do. We both went to catering college. But we don't get much call for veal in white wine and butter sauce."

A waiter arrived and laid out their cutlery.

"It's been a bizarre weekend," Melanie commented, when the young man left them.

"Par for the course for a Sanford 3rd Age Club outing, I'm afraid," Joe replied. "It's like every nutter in the country waits for us to arrive before carrying out his killings."

Melanie reached across the table and played with his gnarled fingers. "I haven't yet seen the great Joe Murray crack the case, either."

He frowned and smiled at the same time, twisting his face into a crooked mask of cheerful defeat. "You're not likely to, either. It has me beat." He sighed. "Too many people with too many motives."

"You saved that young man from a false arrest," Melanie reminded him.

"The only trouble being, he deserved it."

She laughed. "You're quite strait-laced about such matters, aren't you, Joe?"

He took back his hand and swallowed some lager. "I'm no

prude… as you've guessed. But I believe in monogamous relationships. You shouldn't be fooling around with someone else when you're, er, with a person. My marriage broke down, true enough, but there was no third party involved. That young fella has treated his wife disgracefully and he should be made to pay for it." He sighed again. "But he isn't a killer."

Their meals arrived. While they ate, Melanie asked, "The techniques you used to solve Haliwell's Heroes, could you not apply them to the real murders?"

"I did," Joe replied, "but real life is a lot more complicated. You planted your little clues which led me to the solution. In real life, killers often leave little clues about, but they're mainly scientific, and the police are the ones who dig them up, not me. What I look for are small inconsistencies. You need a good memory to be a good liar, and most people will slip up somewhere along the line. Your case was a lot easier than the real thing."

Melanie swallowed a piece of veal and, washing it down with a small swallow of wine, smiled. "That is exactly the opposite of what you told me on Friday morning."

"Yes I know. Funny how these things come back to haunt you, isn't it?"

She put down her knife and fork while chewing on another piece of meat. Swallowing it, she asked, "Does it annoy you?"

"Glass, bottle, bottle, glass."

The poor impression of Tommy Cooper drew Joe's attention. "Not half as much as Gerry's impressions."

Melanie turned her head, following Joe's finger pointing two booths further down where Gerry Carlin sat with Wendy Grimshaw.

"He's trying to get his feet under the table," Melanie announced, returning to her meal. "I don't think it will do him much good. With Reggie dead, Wendy is in a position where she can pick and choose, and I wouldn't think she'd pick a ham like him."

"Ham?" Joe was surprised. "I thought he was a good actor."

"He is," Melanie replied. "But he's a shocking impressionist." She took another mouthful of wine. "I was asking if it annoyed you. Not solving the murders?"

"I wouldn't say annoyed, it's not like I'll lose sleep over it or anything." He chuckled "I've lost enough already. But it will irritate me for a while. There's something, you see, Melanie, something I'm missing. It happens all the time in these affairs. It's something so tiny that most people would miss it. This time, I'm missing it. It nags and niggles and nibbles at me, but whatever the connection, I can't get the little bugger." He shook his head sadly. "I'll go home tomorrow morning, Phil Grant and his people will carry on working, and I'm sure they'll get there, and when they do, I'll read it in the papers and think, 'Yeah. That was it'."

Melanie put down her cutlery and pushed her plate away. Joe followed suit. "Dessert?"

She shook her head and patted her tummy. "Not bothered. You?"

"I'll pass, then."

Melanie took her time over the wine, allowing Joe to top up her glass before adding to his own.

"You'll go home tomorrow, I'll go to Mansfield tomorrow and that's us, too, isn't it? Ships passing in the night."

Anxious not to upset her, Joe chose his words carefully. "I'm not good with women, Melanie. I'm clumsy, awkward, and too easily embarrassed. In any other walk of life, I'm the bee's knees, but not where women are concerned. Too afraid of rejection, I suppose. Especially after the way Alison and I fell apart. What happens after this weekend is up to you, not me. I'm my own boss, remember. Master of all I survey, even if it is only eighty covers at the Lazy Luncheonette."

She smiled easily, and Joe felt comfortable in her company. "We'll see, shall we?"

***

They left the restaurant just after nine and ambled back to the hotel, Melanie's arm linked in his, but they did not go into the disco. Instead, they went back to Melanie's room where they took to the bed for what Joe imagined would be the last time.

Afterwards, they returned to the disco, Melanie joining her party, Joe sitting with Brenda and Sheila. The main topic of conversation was the murders; three fictitious and two real. Joe divorced himself from it as much as he could, and sat drinking, occasionally stepping out for a cigarette, trying instead to evaluate his life.

He had spent the years since Alison's departure in a sexual void, throwing himself into his work, disseminating his needs in irritability. Having begun again with Melanie this weekend, he was reluctant to return to his celibacy, but like the problem of the real murders, he could see no way through. Candidates of Melanie's calibre were thin on the ground in his Sanford circles, and the only two realistic contenders also happened to be his best friends. No way would he threaten his lifelong friendship with them simply to satisfy other urges.

And through it all, the problems of the Twin Spires' murders reared their ugly heads. The who, the how, the why… particularly the why. The suspects paraded through his thinking to the point where he felt his brain would burst.

And his companions noticed. Even Les Tanner, never slow to pick at Joe for one reason or another, backed off when given short shrift. Sheila and Brenda, his two most trusted lieutenants, gave up on him, and Brenda, who could not get a response to her constant innuendo, took herself to the dance floor with George Robson, while Sheila chatted with Sylvia and Julia Staines, comparing their experiences of the weekend and their various solutions to Haliwell's Heroes.

Reminded by Melanie of the need to prepare his address to

the guests, tomorrow morning, Joe took himself to his room just after eleven, and spent an hour or so putting a crib sheet together, but even then, the various machinations of the weekend invaded and distracted his concentration.

Nottingham was hardly within commuting distance of Sanford, but he could make it in less than two hours. Who killed the mysterious, unidentified officer in the friendly fire incident at Chateau Armand? Who was Reggie arguing with on Friday night, if not Kendrew? Perhaps he could register with a dating agency. Why did the real killings match the drama so closely? What really happened to Lydia Beauchamp?

Frustration fuelling his anger, he completed the crib sheet, saved it to a memory stick, threw off his clothing and climbed into bed, but even then, sleep eluded him as his mind whirled and twirled on the confusion in his brain.

It was going to be a long night.

Chapter Seventeen

"You could have put a tie on," Sheila complained over breakfast.

"It wouldn't have gone well with my jeans and trainers," Joe complained.

"He does have a point, Sheila." Brenda sliced the top off her boiled egg. "He won't wear a tie in his own café, will he?"

"It's the Lazy Luncheonette not Ritzy Joe's. If I listened to you two, I'd be serving the truckers dressed in a tuxedo. Besides, posh dress like that would put the draymen off their breakfast." He sliced through a sausage. "Like you're trying to put me off mine, now."

Helping herself to toast and spooning into the egg, Brenda asked, "You're not going to tell us whodunit?"

"You wait until after breakfast, same as everyone else."

Sheila's face puckered at the tang of grapefruit on her tongue. "It would have been much better if we could have found out who did the real murders."

"Appalling," Joe said.

"What? The murders or the fact that the murderer beat you?" Brenda grinned to demonstrate she was winding him up again.

Joe refused the bait. "Not just me he beat. It's the cops as well."

"You don't appear too worried, Joe," Sheila observed.

Swallowing a mouthful of fried bread and washing it down with tea, Joe said, "I'm not... well, I am, but it's only personal pride. I meanersay, I'm an amateur, aren't I? It's not like I do it professionally, and this isn't the first case to stump me, is it? Remember that professional gang of shoplifters in Leeds a few years ago. We knew damn well who was doing it, but we had no proof and, try as I could, I couldn't pin them all down." Pushing his plate away, he, too, helped himself from the toast rack. "The problem with this case is identifying the common motive. The idea that Naomi and Reggie were having an affair is likeliest, but we know that it was a fairy tale."

"That doesn't eliminate the idea, though," Sheila pointed out.

"True, but it doesn't point the finger, either, except maybe at Wendy Grimshaw, but even if we can't eliminate her from Naomi's killing, we know exactly where she was when Reggie was killed. And come to think, we can't really eliminate anyone from Naomi's murder."

Done with her grapefruit, Sheila took a slice of toast, spread it with a thin coating of butter and poured herself more tea. Clicking a single saccharin tablet into it, she added milk. "Let's assume the motive was, oh, I don't know, jealousy. Someone who, say, wanted Naomi and, as you've suggested, believed she was having an affair with her boss. First he killed Reggie to get him out of the way, then approached Naomi, she said no, and he killed her. Does that sound reasonable?"

Joe chewed his toast. "Yeah. Go on. I'll buy it for now. But it doesn't have to be a man. In this day and age, women are allowed to pursue women."

Sheila ignored the comment. "Who is the most likely suspect?"

"Robbie Kendrew," Brenda declared. "But we already know he didn't do it because he *knew* Naomi wasn't having it off with Reggie."

"And there's no one else?" Sheila asked.

"We'd need to know a lot more about them to find out," Joe said. Finishing his tea and toast, he took out his tobacco. "And we're all off home in a few hours, so let's leave it to Phil

Grant and Hayley Idleman, huh?" He set about rolling a cigarette.

Brenda leaned into Sheila and grinned. "Have you noticed how he's on first name terms with so many women? Fliss Kendrew, Hayley Idleman and not forgetting Melanie Markham."

"He's on more than first name terms with Melanie," Sheila chuckled.

"Wham, bang, thank you ma'am terms."

The women dissolved into girlish laughter.

Joe rose above it. Completing his cigarette, he tucked it in his shirt pocket, drank the last few dregs of his tea and stood up.

"Envy," he announced, "does not become either of you. I'm off for a smoke before my big moment."

Leaving them giggling after him, he made his way to the front entrance where he sat out and lit his cigarette.

The day promised brighter things. Although the city lay under a film of grey cloud, he could see patches of morning blue far away to the east, and it was chillier than it had been over the last few days. He sensed a familiar, January high-pressure zone making its way across the country and he knew that it would bring plenty of sunshine, if freezing cold nights.

Contrary to their good-natured ribbing, he was happy to leave the investigation to the police. It had been a good weekend, marred only by the two murders and he would prefer to take the happier memories with him; the memories of Melanie, memories of the drama she and her friends had put on. He was happy to live without the memories of being first on the scene after Reggie's death and Naomi's.

He sensed a presence alongside him. "Morning, Gerry," he said without looking round.

"Clever bit of deduction, Joe," Carlin said and sat next to him.

"Not deduction. Knowledge. Aside from me and you, and

Billy now and then, I don't think anyone else has used this bench over the weekend."

Carlin lit a cigarette. "On your way home today?"

"Bus is due after one," Joe confirmed. "How about you?"

"Hotel in Mansfield tonight until Friday, then it's over to Skegness for the weekend."

"Varied life."

Carlin snorted. "Not so's you'd notice. No roots, old lad. I have a flat in Nottingham. Haven't been there since Boxing Day and I won't be back until the end of the month." He puffed vigorously on his cigarette. "No complaints, I suppose, I knew what I was getting into, but we're not all Hollywood stars cracking out five million a movie. And I enjoy acting. I like being the centre of the audience's attention." Blowing out another lungful of smoke, he sighed. "There are times, though, when I envy people like you. Settled in one place, know what time you start work, what time you'll finish."

"Grass is always greener," Joe said. "You envy me, I think my life is fine, but boring, and I envy you. I'd like a taste of your life."

Carlin checked his watch. "Well, you'll be getting a taste any time now, old son. I usually deliver the summary as Inspector O'Keefe." Carlin doffed his trilby, revealing the bruise on his forehead. "We're letting you do it for a change."

Joe's cigarette had gone out. He took out his brass Zippo and made a show of relighting it. Happily puffing away on it, he said, "Yeah. I was gonna talk to you about that."

"Not chickening out, are you?"

For all the humour of Carlin's question, Joe got the impression of a schoolyard challenge.

"No, it's not that. It's you. I don't like stealing your big moment."

Carlin laughed. It was the short, sharp cackle of the disdainful. "Don't even think about it, old lad. Didn't I just say that life is a boring round of shows, travelling, shows, travelling, and although you might not spot it, the process does eventually become automatic and tedious. I've delivered O'Keefe's closing speech so many times, I know it backwards. I'm quite happy to hand it over to someone else just for a change."

Joe stubbed out his smoke, and got to his feet. "As long as you're sure."

"Never been surer, old son. Looking forward to listening to you."

***

Joe got back to the dining room to find one lot of staff clearing the tables, a second lot sliding back the partition to open out into the Scampton Room, and as they did so, some people migrated to the bar. Melanie and her team were deep in discussion at their table, Billy Norman poring over a road map.

"Nearly time for you big moment, Joe," Sheila said as he rejoined his colleagues. "Are you nervous?"

"Trembling," he lied.

"Have a word with Melanie," Brenda suggested. "I'll bet she knows a cure for the trembles."

"New item on the Lazy Luncheonette menu tomorrow, Sheila," Joe announced. "Brenda Jump pie. Limited edition, only available until the body is fully disposed of."

In Joe's estimation, Brenda was still trying to come up with a catty rejoinder, when Melanie stood front and centre.

"Good morning, ladies and gentlemen." Her bright, breezy voice boomed through the two rooms. "Well, it's been a startling weekend here at the Twin Spires, with a real life mystery mixing with our drama. Our condolences go to those who are suffering, and we truly hope that the terrible crimes are quickly cleared up by the police. However, it's time for us to bring our fictitious crimes to a conclusion. Normally, our very own Inspector O'Keefe would deliver his summary and arrest the mystery killer, but we've decided to do things slightly different this time. Instead of Inspector O'Keefe, we're going to ask Mr Joe Murray of the Sanford 3rd Age Club to tell you how the murders of Haliwell's Heroes were committed."

She paused to lead a small round of applause for Joe.

"I'm sure you're all aware that Mr Murray has a reputation as a private investigator, and we know he has been of immense assistance to the police this weekend. What you may not know is that Joe solved the mystery of Haliwell's Heroes on Friday night, and showed me his written solution before graciously agreeing not to say anything to anyone. So I'm going to call on Joe right now to tell us whodunit, how they dunit, and how he arrived at the solution."

Standing back, Melanie led the applause for him. Taking out the crib sheet he had prepared in his room, Joe moved to the front of the room, standing by the display board and waited for the audience to settle.

"Thanks, Melanie, and thank you all. For those of you who don't know me, I'm not an ex-cop or anything, just a caterer, and if you're ever in Sanford, drop in at the Lazy Luncheonette. The food's good, the prices are cheap, and you're sure of a warm welcome."

"But not from you, Joe," Alec Staines called out and most people laughed.

"Thanks, Alec. Remind me to call you next time I'm planning a publicity campaign." Joe paused again to let more laughter die down. "To be honest, I'm not even a private investigator, just an inveterate puzzler with keen powers of observation, and I know a bit about murders. The real crimes at this hotel have eluded me as well as the police, but Haliwell's Heroes, as well as it was put together, did not, so let's look at it, eh?"

He checked his crib sheet again.

"Right, so, most of the clues came in the very first scene, and you should have been taking extensive notes. Let's see what they are." Joe reached to the table and picked up the newspaper. "In the opening moments, Colonel Haliwell was commenting on a story he had read in *The Times* about an unsolved murder, and he mentioned a World War Two secret agent, Lydia Beauchamp, a lady who worked with the French Resistance in the lead up to D-Day, and who was notoriously skilled with the garrotte. I want you to bear that in mind for later. You were given other background information on the various characters after that, but the most interesting snippets came from Captain Wilson. First he said he was never with the colonel at Chateau Armand. Instead, he was much further *north*, at Bayeux with the 50th Infantry Division."

Joe moved to his right and pointed to the map. "Look closely at it, ladies and gentlemen. Bayeux is *west* of Caen and Chateau Armand, not north. A simple mistake or a deliberate attempt to fudge matters? At that point we didn't know, but the captain also said something else of interest. He described Lydia Beauchamp as a dark-haired siren, with the look of a gypsy girl." He held up the newspaper again. "Then how come the newspaper article describes her as a blonde?"

A mutter ran round the crowded room.

"At this point, it's obvious that the captain is not telling it straight, but we don't know why. We're not yet finished with him, either. A short while later, Countess Lucescu hints that there was Nazi gold at Chateau Armand. The colonel shuts her up quite rudely, and Wilson says 'There never was any gold at Chateau Armand. You have my word upon that'. Let me ask you all a simple question. How does Captain Wilson know there was no Nazi gold if he was never at Chateau Armand?"

The rhubarb murmur of realisation was stronger this time, and Joe noted Sheila and Brenda talking with occasional gestures in his direction.

As quiet fell again, Joe took up his narrative. "We're still not through with that first evening. There's obviously something suspicious about Zara Lucescu herself. She claims to be Romanian, but insists her home town was Varna, which is actually in Bulgaria, and she didn't know that Romania was actually more sympathetic to the Axis powers in the early years of World War Two. She was no more Romanian than I am, but of course, by yesterday, Inspector O'Keefe had confirmed that for us all. We'll come back to Zara later, but there was some scuttlebutt about her swapping glasses with Captain Wilson. There was no great mystery. Wilson had dropped cigarette ash into her drink, and she took the opportunity to swap them in the confusion."

Putting down the newspaper, Joe picked up the encyclopaedia. "For those of you who want to complain that you knew nothing about World War Two, let me tell you, it was before my time, too…"

"We'll take your word on that, Joe," Brenda called and Joe gave her a sickly grin while waiting for the laughter to subside.

"All the information you needed was in this book. If you looked at it, several of the pages were dog-eared, and it was on those pages that you would find the scientific and historical information you needed."

He put the book down again.

"Most of the rest of the information you got from that first evening was smoke designed to create red herrings, but there was one other piece of evidence you should have questioned. Inspector O'Keefe rightly pointed out that anyone could have dropped the cyanide in the colonel's glass, and some people were obviously too far from the glass to do it. But what of the woman who pronounced it as cyanide? Dr Valerie Wilson." He gestured at the actress, Tanya Richmond. "If she's a doctor, I'll start putting soya in my meat pies."

Once more he waited for the laughter to settle.

"Dr Wilson sniffed the colonel's glass and declared it to contain potassium cyanide. The reason? It smelled of sweet

257

almonds. Now I didn't need to look it up because I knew, but if you didn't know about cyanide, the information was in the encyclopaedia. Potassium cyanide, prussic acid, call it what you will, smells of *burnt* almonds, not sweet. Dr Wilson was faking it, and yet, at a later stage, O'Keefe confirmed that the colonel had been poisoned with cyanide. So why didn't Dr Wilson describe it accurately? If she'd smelled burnt almonds, surely she would have described it that way? So could it be that our doctor is not a doctor and could it be that she has no sense of smell?"

More murmurs went round the room. Joe waited for them to settle.

"The encyclopaedia also raised other questions if you stopped to think about it. The article on Chateau Armand was particularly interesting. Why did the British insist that Haliwell take it intact? It had little or no strategic importance, it had no history. It was listed as a listening station, that's all. What was so important about it that they needed the building whole? Also, who shot Lieutenant Cresey, the British officer killed by friendly fire? Why did Haliwell and Wilson tell a different tale to the German soldier who had been stationed there and the British NCO who had been a part of Haliwell's assault force? These are matters you should have been bearing in mind."

"That just about sums up the first evening, but already the finger of suspicion is pointing at Captain Wilson and his wife. If you spoke to the actors during the evening, they would answer your questions, but most of their answers were, again, smoke, designed to lead you to the wrong conclusion." He cast a quick, disparaging glance at Tanya Richmond. "When they would speak to you at all, that is."

Joe checked his crib sheet. "So did our suspicions on day one lead you anywhere? If not, they should have done. They point clearly to Captain Wilson and his wife. The one is telling inconsistent stories and the other clearly doesn't know her poisons, and while there are any number of possibilities for others to be lying, this pair stand out. By Friday evening, I'd already concluded that Wilson was the murderer, and his wife – if indeed she is his wife – was covering for him. I wasn't sure why, but I felt it had something to do with the legendary Nazi gold. I'd also concluded that the gold was the reason the British wanted Chateau Armand intact."

At the back of the Scampton Room, Les Tanner stood up. "Where do you get that conclusion from, Murray? There was nothing at all on day one to indicate that the British were cashing Nazi gold."

"Ladies and gentlemen, allow me to introduce an old friend, mortal enemy, and fellow member of the Sanford 3rd Age Club, Captain Les Tanner. To answer your question Les, it was a process of deduction. The chateau had no strategic importance, and the only reason the British could want it would be for the gold – if it existed. At that time we were not given the value of the gold, but the British would have taken anything to help offset the cost of the war."

Les sat down again, and Joe continued with his analysis.

"The suspicion again was highlighted further on day two when we learned that Kerry Dolman was shot in the head with a thirty-eight calibre pistol and Wilson admitted to not only owning one, but having brought it with him. The whole of day two, however, contained little to take the case further forward. It had more to do with placing the pistol outside and encouraging you, the guests, to look for it."

"Day three, yesterday, was far more interesting, and you could draw many conclusions from it. First we had the murder of Zara Lucescu, and here again, Dr Valerie Wilson demonstrated a complete lack of medical knowledge when she described Zara's face as cyanotic, or blue in colour. In manual strangulation, the face is livid. It is the rest of the body that becomes cyanotic, and there was an excellent article in the encyclopaedia which would have told you that. Dr Wilson also claimed that the ligature used to strangle Zara was the cable on the bedside lamp." Joe moved once again to the information board and pointed to the close-up of the lamp. "First, look at the electrical cord. It's braided and covered with rayon. This was quite common back in the first half of the 20th century. Now look at the marks on Zara's neck." He pointed to the appropriate image. "In order to strangle someone, a great deal of strength is needed and the ligature will always leave a weal, but the marks on Zara's neck are from a fine wire, more consistent with cheese wire than the bedside lamp's flex. Conclusion; Dr Wilson doesn't know what she's talking about, and that logically leads us to conclude that she has had little or no medical training."

Leaving the display, Joe drank from a bottle of water.

"Inspector O'Keefe then told us that Zara was not a Romanian countess, but an agent of HM Treasury, and she had reason to investigate every man at the table. McLintock for his dodgy share dealing, Crenshaw for some rum goings on in Normandy during the aftermath of D-Day, the colonel and Wilson for the source of their funds. It's at this point where we can begin to draw some major conclusions, but you have to make some assumptions and apply a little logic to get there."

He flipped over his crib sheet to the next page.

"McLintock, we know, was exempted from military service on the grounds of a heart murmur which didn't exist. He also handled a large sum of money for the colonel in 1946. He says the colonel told him it was from American investments and he accepted that. Rubbish, is my view. I checked up on the internet, and in today's money that £125,000 would be worth about four and a half million. And the colonel made that from investments during a time of war? My eye. The money was stolen loot, and that leads us to conclude that the Nazi gold was real. The British wanted it, Haliwell and his people took it. They probably agreed to divide it up between themselves. According to the encyclopaedia, there were six officers in that division, but only two survived; Haliwell and Wilson. Three were killed during the battle and the fourth was shot in a friendly fire incident. Again, I ask, who shot him? Captain Wilson? Very likely. Why? Was Creasey losing his nerve and getting ready to tell the authorities what they really found before Haliwell ordered the chateau to be demolished? Again highly likely. So Wilson shot him. Haliwell considered it murder but reached an agreement with Wilson. He would take £125,000 and Wilson would be left with £25,000. Wilson had no choice. The alternative was to report the colonel to the British High Command in return for which, Haliwell would report him and he would be hanged for murdering a brother officer."

Again Joe checked his notes.

"Why was Crenshaw being investigated? Two trucks went missing. But Crenshaw was probably in the clear because Haliwell would have commandeered them. However, Crenshaw found out about it and the price of his silence was Theresa's hand in marriage, and a cut of the family fortunes when the colonel died and Theresa inherited."

Joe paused to take another mouthful of water and read through to the end of his notes. Melanie gave him an encouraging smile.

Turning to face his audience again, he went on:

"There was something the colonel didn't reckon on, and it takes us right back to the beginning. Lydia Beauchamp. Remember she was found dead in the Thames, but she was never properly identified because her face, according to the press report, was beaten to a pulp. It was not Lydia Beauchamp. It was Valerie Wilson."

A buzz of excited chatter ran round the room. George Robson summed it up.

"How can you be sure, Joe?"

Joe smiled easily. "Another of my members, ladies and gentlemen, Mr George Robson, possessed of a lethal charm with the ladies, but doubting the lethal deductive skills of his Chairman."

A ragged laugh rippled through the audience.

"It's obvious that Valerie Wilson is not a doctor, but the real Valerie Wilson was. O'Keefe told us as much when he said she'd been suspended for misdiagnosing a heart attack. The real Valerie Wilson would not have made such elementary mistakes about the poison or the ligature that killed Zara. So we know she is not who she claims to be, but how does that make her Lydia Beauchamp? We're told that Lydia was lethal with the garrotte and the cheese wire, as used by commandos in World War Two, and found by Julia Staines, was a garrotte. In addition, for Valerie to have mistaken the smell of cyanide, she can't have had a sense of smell, and again, we're told that Lydia Beauchamp had no sense of smell. Logical deduction, George."

Joe took in the whole audience again. "The way I see it, Wilson was determined to make Haliwell pay for the way he cheated him after the war, and he found the perfect alibi in Lydia Beauchamp, a woman who was a natural killer and skilled at posing as other people. Wilson dropped the cyanide in the colonel's glass. He shot Kerry Dolman because he didn't know what the colonel may have told her. When O'Keefe said that Zara was not a suspect, they guessed she was some kind of special investigator, and Lydia murdered her. My guess is they would then have begun to rip off or blackmail Sadie, Theresa and Crenshaw for the money they felt should rightfully be theirs."

Joe folded his notes away.

"And that, ladies and gentlemen is the solution to Haliwell's Heroes. But you don't have to take my word for it." He turned to the table. "I'm going to ask the real culprits to stand up and hand themselves over to Inspector O'Keefe so that justice can be done."

There was brief pause. The members of the cast looked at

each other as if daring one another to move. At length, Billy Norman and Tanya Richmond, as Captain and Mrs Wilson, stood up and Inspector O'Keefe slapped the handcuffs on them.

Chapter Eighteen

Joe stood back to a round of generous applause from his audience, and from the Markham Murder Mysteries crew. Melanie took centre stage while she waited for it to die down.

"Ladies and gentlemen, I'd like to thank Mr Murray for his presentation, and ask him formally, please don't attend anymore of our weekends. He's far too good for us." She smiled and the audience laughed along. "I'd also like to thank you for being such a wonderful audience and for putting up with some of our makeshift work. And now it's time to announce the winners of our competition for who presented the solution closest to the real one, and they are ..." she checked the name on her clipboard. "Mr and Mrs Gresty of Washington, Tyne and Wear."

Melanie led the applause as the middle-aged couple came forward to receive their prizes.

"Mr and Mrs Gresty got eighty percent of the solution correct," Melanie went on. "They win vouchers entitling them to free accommodation for one weekend at any of Accomplus nationwide chain of hotels, and also a bottle of champagne."

Melanie handed over the prizes with a theatrical air kiss, and led more applause for the winners.

"It only remains for me to thank you once again for being such a smashing audience, and wish you all a safe journey home. Ladies and gentlemen, one last time, please show your appreciation for the cast of... Haliwell's Heroes."

The players stood forward and took a bow. Joe joined in the applause and as it died down, asked Melanie, "They got to within eighty percent of the solution. Which bits did they get wrong?"

"The identity of Valerie Wilson stroke Lydia Beauchamp," Melanie replied. Turning to her crew she ordered, "We'd better start getting the van loaded." She faced Joe again. "Sorry, Joe, but we're in a bit of a rush. We have to be set up in Mansfield for this evening. Yes, they assumed that Mrs Wilson really was Mrs Wilson and that she'd never taken a medical degree. It led them off the beaten track somewhat."

Joe grunted. "And how. Right, well, I'd better get to my room and get my gear together."

Melanie looked downcast. "Will I see you again?"

He shrugged. "I don't know. Nottingham is about eighty miles from Sanford, so I could drive down, and if you're ever in the area, you could always drop by the Lazy Luncheonette, but give me a bell first. I'll do you a special meat and tater pie."

***

Dragging his small suitcase behind him, Joe handed his keys to Denshaw.

"I trust you enjoyed your stay, Mr Murray… circumstances excepted."

"Very pleasant," Joe replied, "but also disappointing."

The manager raised his head. "I'm sorry, sir?"

"I usually solve the murders. This one goes down as the one that snookered Joe Murray. Where do we wait for our bus?"

"The Gibson room is open for you, sir." Denshaw printed out Joe's bill and passed it over. "Your bar tab, Mr Murray."

Joe looked it over and blanched. "Who'd have thought we could go through so much booze in a weekend." He dug out his wallet and handed over his credit card.

"It's quite reasonable at the side of some of these we see, sir."

A chambermaid came hurrying up to the counter. "Stock cupboard key, please Mr Denshaw."

The manager frowned at her. "What is it now?"

"This lot are dragging their backsides getting out," the woman replied, "and if we don't get a move on, the next mob will be here before the rooms are ready."

Denshaw handed Joe the PIN reader, and Joe punched in his numbers. From the corner of his eye he watched the manager take down a key and hand it to the chambermaid.

Coming back to attend to Joe, Denshaw tore off the receipt and handed it over along with the credit card.

"I'm sorry about that, Mr Murray."

Joe grinned. "Don't worry about it. I have the same problem when I can't get shut of fed customers to let the unfed sit down. Thanks again for everything. You'll call us when our coach arrives."

"Of course, sir."

Joe wandered away from reception and into the Scampton Room where most of the Sanford 3rd Age Club crew were already gathered. In one corner Wendy Grimshaw and the rest of her party sat in silence, and on the opposite side of the room, most of Markham Murder Mysteries' crew were checking over their props and personal effects, while Carlin and Billy Norman were dismantling the large screen TVs.

"I've ordered tea for us all, Joe," Sheila told him when he joined his companions. "Is there a problem? Only you're looking very pensive."

The question snapped Joe out of it. "What? Oh, no. Just mulling over a few things, that's all."

Brenda nudged Sheila. "He's probably annoyed because he didn't nick the killer."

"You can't win them all, Joe."

"Huh?" Joe came alive again. "It's not that. It's something I've just heard and I can't think what it means." He shrugged it off and changed the subject. "Whisper is Wendy will definitely

266

sell out to Midland Kitchens."

"Probably wise," Sheila commented. "She must feel awful."

Brenda guffawed. "Yeah, awfully rich."

"I was thinking guilt after she got caught *in flagrante delicto*," Sheila grinned.

Two words rang through Joe's head; guilt, caught, guilt, caught.

A barmaid arrived with a tray of tea things. She bent between Sheila and Brenda, and began to unload her tray; cups and saucers, spoons, milk and sugar in a small, metal container, and a large, metal teapot. Joe watched as if hypnotised, his mind flashing back to Reggie Grimshaw's bedside. A cup and saucer, a teapot, a metal container with individual portions of milk and sachets of sugar... Denshaw's voice rang in his head. *I'll check the bathroom, see if he left the rest of the tea things in there.* Wendy Grimshaw dragging her heels. *This lot are dragging their backsides getting out.* A wave? Or a signal?

Images and impressions poured in on his brain. He looked around the room. There was Wendy, sat in her favourite corner, with the remnants of her party, Fliss Kendrew talking sternly to her husband. Nearby, at the bar, was George Robson, joking with Owen Frickley and Cyril Peck.

The busy dining room. *They assumed that Mrs Wilson really was Mrs Wilson.* The quiet corridor by the lifts. *Cracking barney on the first floor.* A convivial restaurant on New Year's Day. *He's trying to get his feet under the table.* The muted aura of the cathedral. *I created that situation, Mr Murray.* The silent padding across soft carpets to Melanie's room. *You'd do well to mind your own business, old lad.* A look in the mirror. *Don't see why I should change the habits of a lifetime... habits of a lifetime... habits of a lifetime...*

Joe stared frantically round the room. "Oh my god. How could I have been so stupid?"

"I'd say you've had plenty of practice, Joe," Brenda ribbed

him.

He ignored her, yanked out his mobile and quickly dialled Grant's number. "Get yourself out here, Phil, and bring a team with you. I know who did it, but they'll have to search for the evidence. And you need to hurry up before anyone drives off with the evidence."

"Joe, if you're wrong, this could cost me a fortune. Not to mention my next promotion and my pension."

"Just get yourself up here. We'll need to speak to Melanie Markham, Gerry Carlin and Wendy Grimshaw in particular."

"On my way."

Joe cut off the phone and stared across at Wendy. She was watching him. Joe's face split into a broad grin. *Gotcha!*

***

Sergeant Idleman was already sat with the trio when Joe and Grant entered Cliff Denshaw's office, and took their seats. Melanie appeared quite relaxed, Carlin less so, and Wendy clearly irritated. Outside, uniformed officers, having been briefed by Joe and Grant, were already searching the Markham Murder Mysteries props, despite protests from Melanie and her team.

Carlin went straight on the attack. "Can someone tell us what's going on here, Chief Inspector? Melanie and I should be helping the others load the van. We're supposed to be on our way to Mansfield."

"And I have to be on my way home, too," Wendy protested. "I have urgent matters to deal with, not least my poor husband's funeral."

The chief inspector was not persuaded. "I think we all need to hear what Mr Murray has to say. Joe?"

Joe noticed Carlin relax and he mirrored the movement, letting his shoulders drop a little, allowing his hands to idle with a paperclip on the desk top. But he fixed the actor with his eyes.

"I have to hand it to you. You were good. Your performance was worthy of an Oscar, but…" Joe paused for effect. "Unlike your partner, you weren't perfect. You made two mistakes. You didn't listen to the way Reggie spoke and you moved the tray."

Carlin laughed. Nervously? Cynically? Scathingly? Joe could not make up his mind.

"I don't know what you're talking about, Joe, but it's not funny."

Then why are you laughing? The thought flashed across Joe's mind, but he did not voice it.

Instead, he said, "Your impression of Tommy Cooper isn't funny, either, but at least it's accurate, which is more than can be said for your impersonation of Reggie Grimshaw."

"Now look, old lad –"

Joe cut Carlin off. "Did you hear that, Phil?" he asked. "'Old lad'. It's a common expression up our way." His eyes pinned Carlin back. "But Reggie wasn't a Yorkshireman. He was from Nottingham. He always said, 'me ducks' not 'old lad'."

The two police officers were puzzled, Melanie looked alarmed, Wendy displayed no emotion, but for a brief moment, Carlin's eyes let it slip. It was so fleeting most people would have missed it, but Joe had been expecting it.

"Y'see, the bugger factor in this case has always been the time of death. We *knew* Reggie was alive at midnight because I heard him tearing into someone when I was on my way to Melanie's room. As witnesses go, they don't come any better than me, and I distinctly heard him say, 'You'd do well to mind your own business, old lad'. But I didn't hear Reggie. I heard you, Carlin, impersonating him. And that means Reggie was already dead at that time, and in turn it means that all bets – and alibis – are off."

"What a lot of bull," Carlin chuckled. "I was in the

Grimshaw's room earlier in the day, true. Wendy and I met there. But I never went anywhere near the room that night."

"Oh yes, you did, and in a minute I'll prove it." Joe went on to the police. "As long as we believed that Reggie was still alive at midnight, we would never consider Carlin and Wendy, because we *knew* where they were. Hard at it in Carlin's room. Billy Norman could vouch for that. He listened at the door, not long after I joined Melanie, and he heard them. He had to sleep in the prop room. But it's Carlin's second mistake that lets them down. He removed the tea tray."

Sergeant Idleman frowned. "I'm sorry, Mr Murray, I don't understand. What tea tray?"

"I saw Wendy and Reggie leave the bar about half past ten and Reggie was carrying a tray of tea things, like the one the barmaid delivered to me and my friends half an hour ago. Now remember, I was first into Reggie's room the following morning. I saw only the one cup, the milk, sugar, the teapot, but there was no tray. Cliff Denshaw commented on it. He was gonna look for it until I stopped him." He pointed at the suspects. "The cup was in Carlin's room and they got rid of the tray."

Now Grant was puzzled. "Why?"

Joe pointed at the healing bruise just under Carlin's hairline. "Because Reggie hit him with it and caused that bruise, which meant there would be traces of his blood on the tray. Now think about it, Phil. If you found traces of Carlin on the carpet, the furniture, even the bed, it would mean nothing. He could claim to have been in the room earlier in the day, as he just did. Everyone knew he was shagging Wendy, anyway, so you wouldn't have suspected him of anything else. But to find traces of him on the tea tray would mean he was in the room after Reggie went back on Friday night. And they both knew that no matter how much they cleaned the tray, they couldn't guarantee getting all the traces out and your forensic people would find them, so they thought it was better to lose the tray altogether. And do you know what's really daft, Phil? We saw it. You and me. When Carlin was digging in the Markham Murder Mysteries prop trunk for the fake cheese wire."

Some of Carlin's confidence was waning. Boosted by it, Joe launched his next attack.

"Let me tell you what really happened. A friend of mine, George Robson, met Sheila, Brenda and me in the lobby at about half eleven on Friday night, and he told us he'd just heard a barney in room 104. Someone got battered with a tin tray. That is when Reggie was killed, and I can see it all now. I saw Wendy and Reggie leave the bar. I waved to them and I thought she was waving back at me, but she wasn't. She was signalling Carlin that the job was on. I was sat with Melanie, and a little while later, he came over to say goodnight. But he didn't go his own room. He went to the Grimshaws' where he pulled the gun and threatened Reggie, who lashed out with the first thing he laid hands on; the tray. It caught Carlin on the forehead. Carlin lost his rag, pressed Reggie to the mattress, put a pillow over his head and blew him away. Then they set about creating their alibi. Get rid of the tray, leave the room door ajar so that anyone coming from the lift would hear Reggie mouthing off, then back to Carlin's room for a bit of how's your father…that was for Billy Norman's benefit. And the following morning, he covered the bruise with Inspector O'Keefe's trilby. He even kept the bloody hat on when he dumped the overcoat on Saturday, just to keep the bruise hidden. And they were quite safe. They knew that it's impossible to fix a time of death accurately. Reggie could have died anywhere between eleven p.m. and, say, three or four in the morning. It was my evidence fixed the time of death after midnight, and that left them clean and green."

As Joe fell silent, Wendy maintained her poise, but Carlin applauded. "Author, author."

"So you still deny it?"

271

"It's a complete lot of nonsense... *old lad*," Carlin sneered.

This time Joe maintained his silence.

"You're asking the plod to take a lot on trust here, Murray," Carlin argued. "Like Wendy turning up at the Twin Spires just as I happen to be appearing here. Explain that."

"It's no coincidence," Joe replied. "I spoke to Kendrew, remember, and so did Chief Inspector Grant and Sergeant Idleman. It was his turn to organise the Grimshaw Kitchens outing, and he told all three of us that Wendy suggested this venue. Be honest about it, Carlin, you haven't just renewed your old friendship with Wendy. You've been in touch for years. I meanersay, if you'd really only just met up again, would she jump into bed with you?"

"Melanie did with you."

"Because Melanie wanted something from me, and it wasn't just a good rogering," Joe retorted. "No, Carlin, you admit you and Wendy go back a long way, and the truth is you've kept in touch over the years. Haven't you? You've probably talked about her leaving Reggie for years, too, and the final straw for her was the collapse of the Midland Kitchens deal."

"I don't understand the relevance, Joe," Grant said.

"As a company, Grimshaw Kitchens was in poor health," Joe explained. "Another friend of mine, Alec Staines, told me he'd seen examples of their work and it was crap. Wendy admitted to me that the product was rubbish. The company was struggling. Then along came Midland Kitchens with an offer. It wasn't big. Three or four million and not the ten Alec told me about, but it would give Reggie and Wendy a nice little personal nest egg. Something she could take half of when she demanded a divorce. But that idiot, Reggie refused to sell, and as far as Wendy was concerned, that was the end. She didn't want to wait any longer, so she took the dirty route out of it. If Reggie wouldn't shift, shine him on."

"This man is talking utter nonsense," Wendy insisted.

"Am I?" Joe challenged.

"Of course you are. I don't deny Gerry and I have been in contact, but it's been over the last few years, not twenty, and on Friday night, Mr Murray, although I left the bar with Reggie, I stayed only a short while in our room before joining Gerry in his. He had to go out for a few minutes at about a quarter past eleven. He had only one cup in his room, so he had to go to the bar for a second. But he wasn't gone long, and as we all know, Reggie was still alive at the time, so I knew Gerry couldn't have killed him."

"Except that I just proved that Reggie wasn't alive at midnight," Joe objected.

"No. You have demonstrated that he may have been killed earlier, that is all," Wendy objected. "Regardless of that, I was nowhere near our room all Friday night."

"And Gerry didn't leave you again, Wendy?"

"I don't think so," she said. "I fell asleep about a quarter to midnight and I didn't wake until gone eight the following morning."

"Because Gerry made sure you wouldn't. Y'see, as I said, the tray wasn't the only thing missing from Reggie's room. There was a cup missing, too. I know for a fact that Reggie had two cups on the tray when he went upstairs, but when Denshaw and I entered the room the following morning, there was only one. He didn't go to the bar for it. He took it from the Grimshaw's room." Joe smiled. "He probably gave you a sleeping pill, Wendy, and that proves you're innocent."

***

The admission brought howls of protest from everyone. Grant called for order, and then turned on Joe.

"What the hell is going on here? You told me you had it all cracked."

"And I do," Joe told him. "I've had days agonising about this, knowing that something was wrong, but unable to put my finger on it. Then, when I realised what had happened with the tray, I saw through Gerry and Wendy's plan right away. But I realised if it was Wendy, she'd done far too much. By killing Naomi, who was suspected of having an affair with Reggie, she actually drew attention to herself. Particularly when Kendrew was cleared. And then I finally twigged what I'd been missing all along." Joe grinned broadly. "We're dealing with a bunch of actors." He turned his head slowly to the left. "Aren't we, Melanie?"

She was convincingly surprised by the question. "What? I'm sorry, Joe?"

Joe grinned at Idleman. "Tell me something, Sergeant, would you consider me a babe magnet?"

She snorted, and quickly suppressed the response. "Well, er, Mr Murray, you're not exactly my cup of tea."

"Thank you for your honesty." He waved a hand at Melanie. "Ms Markham, here, fell for me on Friday night, and it took me until half an hour ago to work out why."

"Joe," she complained. "We had something special."

"Yes, we did, didn't we?" His mock-sweet smile faded. "They're actors, Phil, and what kind of skills do you need as an actor? Not just the ability to play a part. You have to understand timing, too. At eleven fifteen on Friday night, Gerry Carlin left Wendy in his room, went to Reggie's drum and killed him as I've described, but he and Melanie needed to make it look as if it happened later. But I didn't just *happen* to be passing the Grimshaw's room at midnight. I was meant to pass it because that's the time I was supposed to meet Melanie in her room further along the corridor. And as I passed, he delivered his impersonation. The timing was perfect. Billy was due back in Gerry's room within fifteen minutes, but all he needed was to let me hear Reggie's voice, and as I disappeared into Melanie's room, he went back to his own. It established a time at which Reggie was still alive and it gave Melanie a cast iron alibi. She could not possibly be involved because she was with me all night. Wendy, too, was innocent because she was with Gerry all night. They needed her to be cleared of any involvement, because once a decent enough interval had passed after Reggie's death, Gerry would become a permanent fixture in her life, and after another decent enough interval, Wendy would die. An accident, poisoning, maybe even Fliss Kendrew taking revenge after the false imprisonment of her husband. Gerry would naturally inherit Wendy's estate, which, after the sale of Grimshaw Kitchens, would run into a couple of million, and after yet another decent enough interval, his real love would move in to share his fortune... Melanie Markham."

Grant's eyes shifted constantly from Carlin to Melanie and back to Joe. "Then why murder Naomi Barton?"

"Because they're actors," Joe insisted. "There were three big threats to their plans. Me, Kendrew and Naomi. Melanie's free-fall knickers took care of me and, as well trained thespians, they'd already seen through the ham act Robbie Kendrew and Naomi were putting on. Kendrew was the sacrificial lamb. He would be blamed and jailed for Reggie's killing. Naomi could get him off. All she had to do was tell the truth, and at some stage, she would have done, so they murdered her, too. While Kendrew was giving out his, 'I hate Naomi' act, he would naturally be suspected of the crime. After killing Naomi, all Melanie had to do was keep me occupied for another forty-eight hours, and they were home free." He laughed. "But they didn't bank on my two girls. Sheila and Brenda may not be able to spot an act, but they've lived long lives and if there's one thing they can see, it's love. When Fliss told them the tale of Robbie's obsession for beating Naomi, my friends realised what was going on and it got Robbie off the hook. And that screwed up the grand plan."

"But it was too late to change things," Idleman said, the light dawning in her words.

"Far too late. The best they could do was keep their eye on

me, and Melanie did that really well, right down to asking me if I'd take Gerry's place by explaining the solution to Haliwell's Heroes this morning." Joe chewed spit. "And like a bloody fool, I fell for it."

Silence fell again, interrupted by a knock at the door. On Grant's prompt a uniformed constable stepped in, bent low and whispered to the chief inspector.

Grant thanked the officer and watched him leave, before addressing the two suspects. "Mr Carlin, can you explain how my uniformed crew have just found the missing tray amongst the props belonging to Markham Murder Mysteries?"

Carlin's face fell, but to her credit, Melanie held her features steady.

"The hotel should be able to identify it as their property," Grant went on, "and it's with my scientific support team right now. If they find one trace of you on that tray, Mr Carlin, you are in serious trouble, so my recommendation to you is, tell us it all, right now."

Carlin maintained his silence, and when Grant concentrated upon her, Melanie, too, refused to speak.

"Motive?" The chief inspector demanded.

"The rights to kitchen designs which Melanie had sold to Grimshaw Kitchens," Joe declared. "She'd been back and asked for more money, but the Grimshaws turned her down."

"Of course we did," Wendy declared. "The original sale of two thousand pounds was what we all agreed and she had no right to any more. I was always surprised when she came back anyway."

"You robbed me, you old cow," Melanie snapped, coming suddenly to life. "You and your overbearing, philandering, thieving husband took advantage of me."

"You didn't have to sell," Wendy told her. "You could have carried on taking royalties every time we used one of your designs. You asked us to buy them from you."

"Because I needed the money and you knew it." She

rounded angrily on Joe. "And you… You think sleeping with you was a pleasure? It was a necessary sacrifice. You're too smart for your own bloody good. We should have killed you, too, like I suggested to Gerry when we learned you were due here…"

"You bloody fool." Carlin's voice was a hiss and aimed at Melanie. "You stupid, bloody fool."

"Gerry, I…"

"They had nothing." He waved a frantic arm at Joe and the two police officers. "So they found the tray. So they may have found traces of me on it. What of it? The worst they could do me for was stealing the bloody tray. I could have cut my bloody finger on it for all they knew. It didn't prove I killed Reggie. Why didn't you just keep your mouth shut?"

"That's not strictly accurate, Mr Carlin," Idleman told him. "Thanks to Mr Murray, we would have looked more closely at the cheese wire used to murder Ms Barton, and no matter how well you cleaned it, we would have found traces to link it to you."

Joe smiled triumphantly at Melanie. "Now who's having the last laugh?" Before she could respond, he turned on Carlin. "What did you put in Sheila's drink, and Kendrew's, to make them so sick?"

"A few drops of gun oil. Not enough to notice, but enough to make them puke." Carlin smiled viciously. "I'm the responsible person under the Health and Safety at Work Act. I have to ensure our prop guns are in good working order, so I always carry oil with me."

"To what purpose?" Grant asked.

"Murray and his harem," Melanie said. "It's not just his reputation which goes before him, but theirs too. I could take care of him, but Gerry was busy with Wendy, so he couldn't work on those two bags. We just gave them something else to think about. And when it came to Kendrew, we were disorientating him, nothing more. And it worked. By Sunday morning, he didn't know his arse from his elbow. But we'd always intended to nail him. Wendy had been complaining to Gerry about him for long enough."

"I'll tell what I don't understand," Sergeant Idleman said. "How could you be so sure that Kendrew would find the gun?"

"We weren't." Carlin admitted. "But I made sure Kendrew saw me wander off to the right of the hotel, and I was outside later, earwigging when Kendrew was there with his wife. If Kendrew hadn't rumbled what I was up to, I would have tipped them the wink on how they could win a bottle of champagne. Course, I'd have been doing it because I felt sorry for them." He laughed.

Her anger increasing, the sergeant looked to her boss and he nodded.

"Gerald Carlin, Melanie Markham, I am arresting you both on suspicion of murder, conspiracy to commit murder and conspiracy to pervert the course of justice. You do not have to say anything, but it may harm your defence if you fail to mention when questioned something which you intend to rely on in court. Anything you say may be given in evidence."

Chapter Nineteen

With the time approaching noon, and transport for all the guests now parked outside the Twin Spires, Melanie Markham and Gerry Carlin had been taken off to the police station, and Grant and Idleman joined Joe, Sheila and Brenda in the Scampton Room, where they reported that both suspects had made full confessions.

"In many ways, Kendrew is as big a victim as Reggie and Naomi, but he was the architect of his own downfall," Grant said. "If he hadn't gone out of his way to persuade everyone that he hated Naomi, we may have cornered the other two that much quicker."

Joe shook his head sadly. "What a berk. I don't know how his life will turn out, but it should be hell all the way. He deserves it."

"What a pair of swine," Sheila cursed. "Carlin and Melanie, I mean, not Kendrew and Naomi. Fancy spiking my drink like that."

"It says something for the amount of booze these two had gone through that she never noticed," Joe said.

"We didn't have that much," Brenda denied.

"No? I just settled our bar bill. It reminded me of the national debt."

The police officers made ready to leave. Grant offered his hand, Joe shook it.

"Thanks for everything, Joe."

"No problem. Next time you're in Sanford, call into my place and you can enjoy one of my legendary steak and kidney pies." He looked Idleman up and down. "You too, Sergeant. You look like you need feeding up."

She patted her flat tummy. "Thank you, Mr Murray, but I'll work out my own diet if you don't mind."

***

A watery sun showed through thin cloud when Joe stood by the Sanford 3rd Age Club coach checking the members and the luggage aboard. The patch of blue sky Joe had seen earlier was gradually drawing nearer. Nearby, the Markham Murder Mysteries cast were reloading their van, and further over, the Grimshaw Kitchens party was boarding the minibus.

Checking Les Tanner and Sylvia Goodson aboard, Joe was distracted by Billy Norman. He passed his clipboard to Sheila.

"It's been an, er, interesting weekend, Joe," Billy said.

"Extenuating circumstances aside, it's been a fun weekend," he agreed.

"But we're without a producer, director and leading man, now. You were pretty good delivering the summary."

"I'm sure you'll find suitable replacements." Joe grinned savagely. "But don't look at me. Racking up the pies is my thing, not acting the fool in hotels."

Billy offered his hand and as he shook it, he said, "Our lawyers will be in touch about the rights to your cases, and I'm sure our paths will cross again someday."

"Let's hope it's in more pleasant circumstances." Joe released the hand, and with a final wave, Billy moved off to join his colleagues.

"Ships that pass in the night, eh, Joe?" Sheila commented.

"More like a tramp steamer, that Melanie," Brenda noted.

Joe grunted. "One of these days, Brenda, I'll take you up on your offer and give you a night to remember. A night with a *real* man."

"Ooh. You're going to fix me up with Daniel Craig?"

"Here's another pair of ships," Sheila said. "A pair adrift, this time."

Joe followed her gaze to the entrance where Fliss and Robbie Kendrew had just emerged.

He gazed sourly at Joe, then reluctantly offered his hand. "Thanks, Murray."

Joe kept his voice equally ambivalent. "You're welcome."

"You'd better get on the bus, Robbie," Fliss insisted, and Joe noted her more commanding tones.

They both watched him wander off to join his colleagues.

"He's told me everything," Fliss said.

"And you're kicking him out?" Joe asked. "Because that's what he deserves."

She sighed. "I know. But I love him, Mr Murray. I can't help that. However, I've laid the law down. I haven't decided whether we're going on or not, but I will be the one making that decision, and if he wants me, he's going to have to work bloody hard to get me. If he doesn't, if he's still pining after his tart, Naomi, then he can pack his bags and get out."

Joe gave her a lopsided smile. "You stick to your guns, lass. If I'd had a wife like you, I might still be married to her."

She stretched up and kissed him on the cheek. "Thanks for everything."

"You take care now."

With a final wave, Fliss strode across to the Grimshaw Kitchens minibus and then Wendy approached.

She, too, shook hands. "Thank you, Mr Murray."

"No problem, Wendy. And my condolences on your loss."

"No need," she told him. "I'm under no illusions about Reggie, so let's not kid ourselves. Whatever spark there was to our marriage died out years ago, and I'm well rid of him. I feel sorry for Ms Barton, but she, too, deserved what she got. I'm sorry if that sounds harsh. You, however, ensured that justice will be done." She kissed him on the cheek, and wandered away to join her party.

281

"You're scoring with 'em all this weekend, Joe," Brenda said.

"Yeah, well, some of us have it."

"In that case, make sure you don't give it to anyone else." Brenda said.

Sheila handed him the clipboard, and mock saluted. "All aboard, Cap'n, and we're ready to rock and roll."

His companions boarded the bus, and with a final glance at the twin towers of Lincoln Minster, Joe, too, climbed on.

"I wonder if this city sees me as the Lord's avenging angel?" he asked as he took the jump seat alongside Keith.

Sheila smiled mischievously. "Given your lack of height, Joe, I'd say you were more like the Lincoln Imp."

Brenda laughed. "You certainly put a twist in Melanie Markham's spire."

THE END

Fantastic Books
Great Authors

Meet our authors and discover our exciting range:

- Gripping Thrillers
- Cosy Mysteries
- Romantic Chick-Lit
- Fascinating Historicals
- Exciting Fantasy
- Young Adult and Children's Adventures

Visit us at:
www.crookedcatpublishing.com

Join us on facebook:
www.facebook.com/crookedcatpublishing

9791396R00170

Printed in Great Britain
by Amazon.co.uk, Ltd.,
Marston Gate.